belonging

Robin Lee HATCHER

WHERE THE HEART LIVES

ZONDERVAN®

ZONDERVAN.com/
AUTHORTRACKER
follow your favorite authors

ZONDERVAN

Belonging
Copyright © 2011 by RobinSong, Inc.

This title is also available as a Zondervan ebook.
Visit www.zondervan.com/ebooks.

This title is also available in a Zondervan audio edition.
Visit www.zondervan.fm.

Requests for information should be addressed to:
Zondervan, *Grand Rapids, Michigan 49530*

Library of Congress Cataloging-in-Publication Data

Hatcher, Robin Lee.
    Belonging / Robin Lee Hatcher.
        p.   cm. — (Where the heart lives)
    ISBN 978-0-310-25808-7 (softcover)
        1. Women teacher — Fiction. 2. Idaho — Fiction. I. Title.
PS3558.A73574B45 — 2011
813'.54 — dc22   2011009308

Most Scripture quotations are taken from the King James Version of the Bible.

Any Internet addresses (websites, blogs, etc.) and telephone numbers in this book are offered as a resource. They are not intended in any way to be or imply an endorsement by Zondervan, nor does Zondervan vouch for the content of these sites and numbers for the life of this book.

Cover design: Michelle Lenger
Cover illustration: Aleta Rafton
Interior design: Michelle Espinoza

Printed in the United States of America

11 12 13 14 15 16 /DCI/ 22 21 20 19 18 17 16 15 14 13 12 11 10 9 8 7 6 5 4 3 2 1

And we know that God causes all things to work together
for good to those who love God, to those who
are called according to His purpose.

Romans 8:28 NASB

belonging

PROLOGUE

CHICAGO, ILLINOIS, JANUARY 1881

Icy tentacles reached through the thin walls of the tenement building where Elethea Brennan lay dying, her three children standing at her bedside. There was Hugh, thirteen and the only boy, as handsome as his father ever was, with his dark hair and eyes. Next to him was ten-year-old Felicia, the quiet, bookish Brennan, her blue eyes seeming to understand far too much. And next to her was Diana, at six the youngest, and the only one to inherit her mother's red hair and green eyes.

Oh, how she loved them, these three. Loved them more than she'd ever thought possible when she married Sweeney Brennan and came with him to Chicago to build a new life. How she hated to leave them. She was ready for heaven, but it broke her heart all the same to say goodbye to the ones who'd made life worth living.

It took enormous effort, but somehow she managed to lift her left arm and take hold of her son's hand. "Promise ... me."

Hugh, still a boy but with the suggestion of manhood on his beloved face, leaned close. "Promise what, Mum?"

"See ... Dr. Cray ... Leave ... Chicago."

"Where should we go?"

"Away."

"What about Dad?"

She closed her eyes but didn't release his hand. How did a mother tell a boy of thirteen that his father would never return to them, that his father loved his whiskey more than his wife or his son and daughters? But she didn't have to tell him. Hugh was a bright boy. He knew the truth, even if he didn't want to accept it.

Elethea wanted a better life for her children. Perhaps her death could give them one. Dr. Cray had explained to her how poor and orphaned children of Chicago were being placed with families in the West, families who promised to care for them and love them and even to see that they were educated. There was little hope for the likes of Sweeney Brennan's offspring in Chicago. Here, they were just three more street urchins who would soon be completely alone in the world.

"Promise . . . me . . . Hugh," she whispered.

"I promise, Mum. I promise I'll go to Dr. Cray."

Drawing a deep breath, she forced her eyes open one last time and drank in the beauty of her children. It mattered not that they were dressed in tattered, worn clothes or that their faces could use a good washing. They were beautiful and perfect to their mother.

The darkness that had lingered around the edges of the room began to close in.

"Don't ever . . . be forgettin' . . . that I . . . love you . . . me dear ones."

ONE

The journey by train from eastern Wyoming to western Idaho hadn't been a long one. Only a single night and a part of two days. Nonetheless, Felicia Brennan Kristoffersen felt bone weary by the time she stepped from the passenger car onto the platform, where a hot August breeze tugged at the skirt of her black dress. She longed for a cool drink of water. But first she had to find Mr. Swanson, the president of the Frenchman's Bluff school board. He'd stated in his letter that he would be at the depot to meet her.

Whatever would she do if she couldn't find him, if he hadn't come for her after all? Her heart fluttered at the thought, but she quickly pushed the rising fear away. She wouldn't give in to it. Not even for a moment. She'd allowed too much fear into her heart through the years. Never more so than in recent months. But no more. God had not given her a spirit of fear.

Tightening her grip on the valise, she walked toward the doors leading into the station. Just as her hand reached to open it, she heard someone speak her name.

"Miss Kristoffersen?"

Relieved, she turned to face a short, squat man with generous white muttonchops and a friendly smile. "Yes, that's me. Are you Mr. Swanson?"

"Indeed I am. Have you been waiting long?"

"No. I disembarked only a few moments ago."

"Good. Good. And your luggage? I assume there's more than what you carry."

"Yes. I have a trunk." One trunk that held everything she owned in this world, although there was no need to tell him that.

"Why don't I take you to the wagon, and then I'll get it for you."

She nodded. "That's very kind."

Wordlessly, he held out his hand for her valise. She gave it to him and then followed him to the end of the platform, down a few steps, and around the side of the depot, where a buckboard pulled by two black horses awaited. Once there, Mr. Swanson dropped her valise into the wagon bed before helping her up to the seat.

"Be back directly, miss."

After Mr. Swanson disappeared inside the station, Felicia felt herself relax. Her journey was almost at an end. No catastrophe had befallen her. Soon she would be settled in a home of her own and could begin making a new life for herself. All would be well.

She sat a little straighter on the wagon seat and looked about. The terrain was similar to the area in Wyoming where she'd spent the past sixteen years—sagebrush and sand-colored earth in abundance—except Boise City had come to life along a river at the base of a pine-topped mountain range. That river now watered farms throughout the valley via a system of canals and creeks, bringing a lush green to land that was otherwise baked brown by the late summer sun.

"Right over there."

She turned to see Mr. Swanson walking toward the buckboard. Behind him was a porter pushing a cart that held her trunk. Thank goodness, for the heat was becoming unbearable, especially in her black gown and bonnet. She prayed it wasn't a long journey to Frenchman's Bluff.

Within minutes, Mr. Swanson had joined her on the wagon seat and the horses were turned away from the depot. They traveled east, leaving the city of Boise behind them. The road they followed was filled with ruts, and more than once Felicia wondered if her bones would be jarred from their sockets before they reached their destination.

"Folks are mighty excited that we'll have ourselves a school-teacher again," Mr. Swanson said after a long period of silence.

Not for the first time, Felicia wondered how many other teachers had applied for the position before it was awarded to her. The salary was small, to be sure. It couldn't possibly support a man with a family. Which meant most, if not all, applicants would have been unmarried women like herself. Why the school board had chosen Felicia was nothing short of a miracle. An answer to prayer, surely.

But what did it matter why they'd offered her the position? She had employment, and she was out on her own. She'd even been promised a house to live in rather than having to board with a different family each month. Such a luxury. She would no longer be dependent on the whims of others. She wouldn't be responsible to anyone but herself and her God. And more important, she wouldn't have to deal with another member of the Kristoffersen family ever again.

"Like I told you in my letter," Mr. Swanson continued, drawing her thoughts back to the present, "we've been without a teacher since Miss Lucas moved away. Some of our womenfolk took over the instruction of the children as best they could to finish out the session, but the school needs a trained teacher. Right glad we found you when we did."

She offered the man a smile and a nod, but inside, turmoil erupted, as it often had since receiving the letter from Mr. Swanson offering her the position. What if she failed as a teacher? It had been years since she'd completed her training. How would she support herself if she didn't succeed? For years she'd longed to leave the Kristoffersen homestead on the eastern plains of Wyoming, to experience a little bit of the world, but obligation had held her there. Now she had what she'd wanted, and she found herself scared half to death.

But could anything be worse than what I left behind?

She pictured Gunnar Kristoffersen, his face flushed. She heard his angry accusations and harsh demands. A shudder raced through her. No, it couldn't be worse. Whatever lay ahead of her had to be better than what she'd left behind.

From the doorway of the small cottage, Colin Murphy watched as his daughter, Charity, placed the vase of roses in the center of the kitchen table. She turned it this way and that, her mouth pursed and her eyes squinting, then adjusted it again and again.

Just like her mother used to do.

His heart pinched at the memory. And it hurt even more knowing that Charity hadn't learned it from her mother. His daughter had been only three when Margaret Murphy passed away. There'd been no time for her to learn the fine art of floral displays or her mother's mannerisms.

"Do you think the teacher'll like them, Papa?"

"Of course she will," he answered, moving a few steps into the kitchen. "All women seem to like roses."

His daughter turned her large brown eyes on him. "I hope she'll want to stay. Do you think Miss Kristoffersen will like it here? Enough to stay and keep teaching?"

He recognized her questions. It seemed his little girl had been eavesdropping on adult conversations again, something she'd been scolded for in the past. But Colin decided to let it go this time. He didn't want to spoil her excitement. He just wished he felt a degree of the same enthusiasm.

Colin checked his pocket watch. If the train had arrived on time, Walter Swanson should show up with the new schoolmarm any moment now. "Come on, Charity. I need to get back to the store."

His daughter was quick to obey, rushing on ahead of him while he closed the door of the cottage. Before she disappeared around the corner of the mercantile, she called back to him, "I'm gonna wait on the porch."

Colin shook his head. Charity never did anything by halves. She was prepared to love Miss Kristoffersen, sight unseen, and she would be devastated if the teacher didn't return those feelings.

He'd been against hiring another single female, especially one without actual teaching experience. Yes, she'd completed her teacher preparedness education at the State Normal School in Laramie, Wyoming, almost a decade earlier. Yes, she had all the appropriate credentials. But she'd never been employed as a teacher.

What if she wasn't capable? What if the children suffered because of her inabilities? What if *Charity* suffered because of her inabilities? And more important, what if she didn't last any longer than Miss Lucas or her predecessor? Just because Felicia Kristoffersen was willing to teach for the smaller fixed salary they'd offered didn't mean they should have given her the position.

Hadn't the board learned anything from their last two choices? As far as Colin could tell, all female teachers were more interested in gaining husbands than they were in the welfare of the children. A schoolmaster might have cost the town two or three hundred dollars more per year, but it would have saved them a world of grief in the end.

Now he could only hope the parents of Frenchman's Bluff wouldn't come to regret the board's choice once again. With luck, Miss Kristoffersen would surprise him for the better. He would welcome a pleasant surprise.

He gave his head another slow shake as he walked through the storeroom of the mercantile, his gaze taking in the shelves on both sides of him, noting which ones were full and which ones needed to be restocked.

It had been a good year for Murphy's Mercantile. The previous winter had been mild, and the weather this summer had been perfect. Just enough rain, just enough sun. Barring any natural disasters — God forbid — the ranchers and farmers in the area surrounding Frenchman's Bluff would enjoy good profits. And when the ranchers and farmers did well, Colin's business did well too.

When he entered the store a few moments later, Jimmy Bryant, his clerk, was adding the cost of several purchases for Kathleen Summerville. The young man glanced up, nodded, then went right back to his calculations. Kathleen, on the other hand, turned her full attention in Colin's direction.

"Good day, Mr. Murphy."

"Mrs. Summerville. How are you?"

"Very well, thank you. But my girls are anxious to meet their new teacher. They're on your home's front porch, watching for Mr. Swanson's wagon to appear around the bend. I saw Charity join them a few moments ago."

With a nod, Colin moved toward the large window at the front of the mercantile.

Kathleen came to stand beside him, holding her basket of supplies against her chest. "Things will be different this time. I just know they will."

Colin decided to keep his reservations to himself. Kathleen Summerville must have heard what they were anyway.

"You know,"—her right hand alighted on the back of his wrist—"I'll miss helping with the children's instruction."

He kept his eyes focused on the view outside the window, knowing full well Kathleen wanted him to look at her, wanted him to acknowledge her as something more than a customer in his store. He couldn't do it. While there was much to admire about this widowed mother of two daughters, that didn't make him want to marry again.

Thankfully, Walter Swanson drove his buckboard into view just then, giving Colin an excuse to step away, out from under her touch. "Here they are." He opened the front door, then waited for Kathleen to move outside before him.

"Hellooo!" Walter reined in the team of horses in front of the mercantile. "I said I would bring her back safely, and so I did."

"So you did." Colin shaded his eyes against the sun that rode low in the western sky, trying to see the new schoolmarm's face. He couldn't. Not yet.

Walter hopped down from the seat and hurried around to the other side, where he offered a hand to his passenger. Dressed all in black, from her hat to her shoes and stockings—which Colin glimpsed as she stepped onto the hub of the wheel—she was slender but with pleasing feminine curves.

He blinked and drew in a quick breath, annoyed at the direction his thoughts had taken.

"Thank you, Mr. Swanson," the teacher said as one foot alighted on the ground.

Walter drew her toward the boardwalk. "This here's Mr. Murphy. Owns the little house you'll be livin' in. It's right behind the mercantile. Looks out on First Street. And this here's Mrs. Summerville."

Felicia Kristoffersen's gaze turned to Colin. And a lovely gaze it was. He could see that now, the sun no longer intruding on his view. She had large eyes, the color of the bluebells that grew wild in the high country of Idaho. And she was attractive—one might even say striking—though not in the conventional way; her face had too many sharp angles for that. Her complexion was pale, as if she'd been shut up in a dark room for quite some time, a look exacerbated by the uninterrupted black of her attire.

There'd been a death in her family. Colin remembered something about it in her application. Her parents? That's what he seemed to recall.

It was Kathleen who broke the momentary silence. "Welcome to Frenchman's Bluff, Miss Kristoffersen. We're so glad you've come to teach the children."

"Mrs. Summerville. Mr. Murphy." Felicia Kristoffersen had a soft, melodic voice. It fit her somehow. "The pleasure is mine. I'm glad to be here at last."

Having left the front porch, the three girls arrived on the boardwalk in front of the mercantile, giggling and smiling, eager and shy at the same time. Charity joined Colin, slipping her small hand into his, tugging on him.

"Miss Kristoffersen, this is my daughter, Charity. One of your students."

"How do you do, Charity?" Felicia smiled, and the weariness he'd seen earlier vanished.

"Good, thanks."

Kathleen drew her own daughters forward. "These are my girls, Suzanne and Phoebe."

Felicia nodded, still smiling. "Are you looking forward to the start of school?"

"Yes, ma'am," Suzanne answered with enthusiasm.

"I am too." Felicia's gaze returned to Colin, and the smile faded, replaced once again by an expression of fatigue. "If you might be so kind as to show me to my living quarters."

"Of course." He glanced at Walter.

"You go on ahead," the man said. "I'll bring her trunk around in the wagon."

Colin nodded, then motioned with his head. "Just follow me, miss."

"Thank you."

Charity released his hand and fell back to walk beside the new schoolmistress while he led the way around the east side of the mercantile. "We got new readers for the school," his daughter said. "They came this summer. Did Mr. Swanson tell you that?"

"No, he didn't mention it."

"Well, we did. A big box of new McGuffey's. We didn't use to have enough for everybody, but now we do."

"How wonderful. Every student should have their own reader."

"I like the stories in 'em, but I think reading's hard."

Colin tensed. His daughter's struggle with reading was a sore point—perhaps because he was unable to help her as he wished he could—but also because of Miss Lucas's harsh assessment of Charity's learning abilities.

"It can be," Felicia answered. "But we can find ways to make it easier for you."

He released a breath he hadn't known he held, and the tension eased from his shoulders.

"I like history best," Charity continued.

"Do you? That's good. It's very important to know history. It helps us understand the present better if we know and understand the past."

"Ask me something, Miss Kristoffersen. See if I know it. Go on, ask me."

"Charity," Colin warned softly.

He heard his daughter sigh.

They arrived at the cottage, and he opened the door, then stepped back to allow the schoolteacher and his daughter to enter first. But it wasn't merely because he was acting the gentleman, doing the polite thing. The truth was, he always needed an extra moment to steel himself before he passed through this doorway. The small house held bittersweet memories for him.

He'd built the home for Margaret. His wife hadn't wanted to continue residing in the other half of the mercantile building. So he'd built this cottage for her, exactly as she'd wanted, with the parlor and the larger bedroom facing First Street, giving a view of the mountains to the north, and a porch that wrapped around from the front to one side where another door opened into the kitchen. He'd hoped it would bring her some happiness, hoped it would bring them closer together. Only she'd died before they could move into it.

"This is where I'm to live?"

Felicia's question pulled Colin's attention to the present.

"I hadn't anticipated anything so lovely as this," she said, looking at him.

The new schoolteacher was past the age at which most members of the fair sex married. In fact, his late wife had given birth once and miscarried three times before she was as old as Miss Kristoffersen. Colin had buried Margaret on her twenty-sixth birthday, which, according to the information the school board received, was the present age of the new teacher. Some would call Miss Kristoffersen an old maid, but that would be an unjust description of someone with such a smile. A smile that would draw single men to her as surely as bees are drawn to honey.

The school board would rue the day they hired her. Colin thought it as certain as the rising of the sun on the morrow.

TWO

Kathleen's daughters skipped along the sidewalk ahead of her as the threesome made their way home. Neither of the girls seemed to have been disappointed by their brief introduction to the new schoolteacher. Kathleen should have known it would be that way. Between the heat and the trip in Walter Swanson's buckboard from Boise City, she wouldn't have wanted to spend any length of time with strangers either.

Still, she dreaded going home with so little to report to Mother Summerville. Her mother-in-law would have many questions, and Kathleen would have few answers.

Suzanne stopped in front of the post office and turned around. "May I get the mail, Mama?"

Kathleen nodded.

Suzanne went into the building, Phoebe on her heels. A few seconds later, the door opened again and two men stepped outside. When they saw Kathleen, they both bent their hat brims in greeting.

She recognized them, of course. They were cowhands who worked for Glen Gilchrist on the Double G, a ranch about fifteen miles east of Frenchman's Bluff. The younger of the two, Oscar Jacobson, remained on the boardwalk while the other, Nate Evans, walked on across the street to the livery and blacksmith.

"Afternoon, Miz Summerville," Oscar said with his familiar crooked grin.

There was something about Oscar Jacobson that always made her feel happy and lighthearted. He was a tall drink of water — thin as a rail, with cheeks as smooth as a young boy's and a smile that never seemed far from his lips.

"Good afternoon, Mr. Jacobson."

"Another hot day." He bumped his hat back on his forehead.

"Yes."

"I hear tell the new schoolmarm came in today."

"Yes. Just a short while ago."

"Miz Carpenter said there's gonna be a potluck after church this Sunday in order for folks to meet her."

Kathleen imagined that all the single men in the area would be eager to make Miss Kristoffersen's acquaintance as soon as they heard how lovely she was. But perhaps the new schoolteacher wouldn't welcome their attentions since she was in mourning.

Her chest tightened, remembering her own loss. It had been more than two years since her husband passed, but the ache in her heart hadn't gone away the instant custom said it was permissible to stop wearing black. And there were times when Harold's mother made her feel guilty that she wasn't still draped in heavy crape with a veil over her face. A confusing circumstance since Mother Summerville also seemed eager for her to marry again.

"You all right, ma'am?" Oscar asked, his grin slipping a little.

How long had she been standing there, her thoughts wandering? How much had the young cowboy seen written on her face? Before she could answer him, Suzanne and Phoebe spilled out of the post office. Relieved, she turned her full attention upon her daughters.

"Mr. Reynolds had *four* letters for us," Suzanne said.

"Four of them." Phoebe held up her right hand, her fingers splayed.

"They're all for Grandmother," Suzanne added.

"Then we had better take them home." Kathleen looked at Oscar again. "Please excuse us, Mr. Jacobson."

"Of course, ma'am." He bent his hat brim a second time. "You take care now."

She hurried after her daughters, turning the corner onto Shoshone Street and following the sidewalk the rest of the way home, entering the house through the kitchen door in the back.

Victoria Hasting, the Summerville cook, glanced up from the vegetables she was chopping on the large table in the center of the room, gave an abrupt nod, and went straight back to work. After setting down her shopping basket, Kathleen continued through the kitchen, across the hall, and into the private sitting room where her mother-in-law spent most of her time when she wasn't entertaining guests or out on social calls.

"We brought the mail," Kathleen heard Suzanne announce.

"Ah. At last." Seated at her writing desk, Helen Summerville looked at Kathleen, who had stopped just inside the doorway. "I wondered what was keeping you."

Phoebe said, "We got to meet the new teacher. She's real pretty."

"Is she now?" Mother Summerville motioned for Kathleen to sit on the nearby sofa. Then she looked at her granddaughters. "You two go on up to your room and play. Your mother and I wish to have a talk." She leaned forward and turned her cheek for the expected kisses. Once the children had gone, she addressed Kathleen once again. "So tell me about her." Displeasure laced her words.

Kathleen knew why she sounded that way, of course. Helen Summerville had voted with Colin Murphy, the two negative votes against offering the position to Miss Kristoffersen. Kathleen suspected Helen had voted with Colin because she wanted the town's leading merchant to be obliged to her in the future; she liked people to be obliged to do her bidding. She especially seemed to enjoy that her daughter-in-law was obliged to her. Without the generosity of the Summervilles, Kathleen wouldn't be able to provide for her daughters. She had no money of her own, no home of her own. So she obediently followed along, doing as she was told, performing as she was expected.

Perhaps that was the reason she'd taken perverse pleasure when the other members of the school board didn't blindly follow Helen's example and vote against Miss Kristoffersen's hiring. Her mother-in-law was not used to being on the losing side of anything and had been infuriated from that day to this. She expected to lead the way and have others follow, and most often that was the way it worked. But not this time. Mother Summerville and Colin had been overruled.

"Kathleen, didn't you hear me? Tell me about Miss Kristoffersen."

"I liked her."

Helen's nostrils flared, and a shiver of dread went down Kathleen's spine. Mother Summerville had a notorious temper and could slay a lesser being with her icy gaze. Or at least it felt that way.

Kathleen hurried to add a few details. "She was polite and very warm with the children. Naturally, she was tired from her journey, so Mr. Murphy showed her to the cottage soon after she arrived. We had little time to visit."

"And *is* she pretty?"

"Yes. I think so."

"Hmm."

"Did you know she's in mourning?"

Mother Summerville held her head a little higher. "Of course I knew. That information was in her letter of introduction." She shook her head slowly. "I suppose if I want to know anything of value, I shall have to make a point of meeting her myself."

Kathleen felt the sting of rebuke in her words, but for a change, she didn't attempt to redeem herself in her mother-in-law's eyes. Instead, she pressed her lips together and said nothing.

After a few moments of silence, Helen flicked her fingers in the general direction of the door, her way of saying their talk was over. Kathleen rose and left the room.

A moonless sky glittered with stars, and soft, cool air caressed Felicia's face as she stepped to the edge of the porch and wrapped her right arm around an awning post outside the kitchen of her cottage. Most of the citizens of Frenchman's Bluff had retired long before now, evidenced by the silence that surrounded her and by the dark homes and buildings that dotted the streets of the small town. But lamplight still shone from a downstairs window in the living quarters of the Murphy home.

Felicia wasn't sure what to think of her landlord. Colin Murphy was polite, to be sure, but he also seemed cool and reserved. Felicia felt a rush of sympathy for his daughter. She knew all too well what it was like to live in a home where laughter and love were in short supply, where emotions were expected to be kept to oneself and never expressed to others.

She drew in a deep breath as she looked upward, her gaze sweeping the heavens until she located the Big Dipper. Seeing the familiar constellation, she recalled, as she always did, the last time she'd been with her older brother and younger sister.

"As long as you can see those stars," Hugh had said, pointing toward the night sky, "you'll know we're not far apart. Don't you worry. I'll find you again, Felicia. I'll find you both." She'd believed his promise for a long time.

She no longer believed it. How could she after so many years? Hugh had been a boy of thirteen. He'd made his promise never knowing how far Felicia would go on that train before someone wanted her.

Years ago, once before she'd gone to normal school, once after she'd returned to the Kristoffersen farm, she'd written to Dr. Cray's Asylum for Little Wanderers, hoping to locate her siblings. She hadn't received an answer either time.

A lump formed in her throat, and the diamond-studded sky blurred. She blinked back the unwelcome tears. "I should be ashamed," she whispered. "I was clothed and fed and educated. I never went without anything I truly needed."

Except love.

In her mind, she pictured the couple who'd raised her—Britta and Lars Kristoffersen. In their late sixties and childless, they'd come to the grange hall to see the last of the children from the asylum, the few who hadn't been taken at the other train stops between Chicago and Laramie. Boys who were strong enough to work on farms had been chosen at the earliest stops. And after those boys, the youngest children had gone next. A girl of ten, like Felicia, had been betwixt and between. But the Kristoffersens had wanted a girl, someone old enough to help Britta with the housework, someone young enough to still be with them as a comfort in their old age. Felicia had been the only girl of the right age remaining. They'd taken her with scarcely a glance.

She drew in a breath and let it out on a sigh. There was no point dwelling on the past. It was behind her now. The future would be what she made of it. She was young, strong, educated, capable. She would make a new life for herself in Frenchman's Bluff, Idaho. And if she didn't like it here, she could go elsewhere. There was no one to tell her she couldn't. She was free to do as she pleased.

For the first time in her life.

THREE

On the following afternoon, Colin and three other men sat on the benches outside the Benoit Feed Store, keeping to the shade while the sun beat down on the dusty main street of town. Across from the feed store, two of Quincy Daughtry's black Labradors lay flat on their sides underneath a wagon—looking more dead than alive—while horses in the livery stable's corral swatted at flies with their tails.

"Now that Cleveland's out of office, it'll happen," Arnold Hanson said with conviction. "The country's got too much invested in Cuba. You'll see. It's gonna mean war with Spain."

Noel Bryant looked at Colin. "What do you think, Murphy?"

"Sorry. I never can guess what those fellows in Washington will do."

Noel shifted his eyes to Gary Peters, who was busy whittling something with a knife. "What about you, Peters?"

"I agree with Arnold. There'll be another war." Gary curled off a thin slice of wood with the sharp blade. "Maybe not this year. Maybe not next year. But there'll be one."

"I suppose you're right." Noel rose from the bench, stretched, then looked up and down Main Street. "Sure is hot. Hottest August I can remember in these parts."

There was a general murmur of agreement from the others.

After a lengthy silence, Arnold looked at Colin. "I hear tell our new schoolteacher arrived yesterday."

"Yep."

"What's she like?" Noel asked.

Colin shrugged. "Like a schoolteacher, I guess. We didn't talk much. She was tired from her trip."

"She as pretty as Miss Lucas was?" Arnold persisted.

Colin stared out at the street, squinting at the bright light that bounced off the dirt. "Guess so. Maybe."

"He guesses." Arnold chuckled. "Maybe. Murphy, you're the limit. You've got another young single gal livin' in the house right behind yours, and all you can do is *guess* if she's pretty. No wonder you haven't married again if you can't even take notice of a gal's appearance."

Colin clenched his jaw. He didn't much care for Arnold Hanson. The man didn't know when to keep his mouth shut. And now would have been a good time for him to do so.

"Well," Noel interjected, "I reckon he's trying to be polite. I heard the schoolmarm's kinda dowdy."

Colin could have set Noel straight. Wearing mourning clothes didn't make a woman like Felicia Kristoffersen dowdy. But he didn't say so out loud. It would just lead to more jesting, and he wasn't in the mood for that. He stood, setting his hat on his head. "I'd better get back to the store." He stepped off the boardwalk and strode across the street.

"Tell my boy to go straight on home when he's done working," Noel called after him. "His ma's got some chores that need doing."

Maybe you should go straight on home and help your wife instead of sitting there like a bump on a log. It was an uncharitable thought, given that Colin had been idling away the last half hour, maybe longer, right along with Noel and the other men.

When he entered the mercantile, he found it empty, save for his daughter and Jimmy Bryant. Charity sat cross-legged on the counter, and she and his young store clerk were playing a game of cards. Jimmy straightened when he saw Colin, and a guilty flush reddened his face. As well it should. Colin didn't pay the boy to amuse his daughter with a deck of cards.

"Your dad said to get home to help your ma with some chores."

"Yessir." Jimmy removed his apron and took it into the storeroom. "I finished all the things you told me to do, Mr. Murphy." He appeared in the doorway again. "Hasn't been any customers since you left."

"Not surprised. Too hot to do much more than sit in the shade if you can help it." He jerked his head toward the door. "Get on with you."

"See you tomorrow, sir."

Colin turned toward the counter just as Charity's stockinged feet touched the floor. "What have I told you about that?" he asked, frowning.

"There wasn't anybody else in the store. Nobody saw me up there but you and Jimmy."

Colin cocked an eyebrow.

His daughter hung her head, eyes downcast. "I'm sorry, Papa. I won't do it again."

"See that you don't."

Margaret's voice whispered in his memory. *God Almighty, help me to be a good mother.* Colin could recall the scene as clearly now as if he'd heard her praying beside their daughter's bed the previous night. *"Help me to bring her up to be a lady in every respect. I'm so afraid I'll fail."*

What sort of God took a wife and mother from the family who needed her? And for all the things that hadn't been right in their little family, they *had* needed one another. Given more time, Margaret would have become a good mother, and Colin would have become a better husband. He was sure of it.

Charity came to stand next to him. "Want me to scramble eggs for supper?"

"Sure. Eggs would be good." He resisted the urge to ruffle her hair, not wanting to relent just yet. Charity needed to know she couldn't talk her way out of trouble as easily as an "I'm sorry."

The bell above the entrance jingled, and he turned to see who'd entered the store. Even before he saw her face, Felicia's black gown gave her identity away.

"Miss Kristoffersen. How are you today?"

"I'm well, thank you, Mr. Murphy."

"Is there something you need?"

"Yes." She held a slip of paper toward him. "I've written down everything that I require."

He shook his head, not taking the paper from her. "Just tell me what you're after, and I'll get it for you." He moved toward the wall and took up a large basket. "It's faster that way."

"All right," she answered, a note of surprise in her voice. "I need a scrub brush ... a house broom ... some China laundry soap ..."

Colin moved around the store, finding the requested items quickly. The smaller items went into the basket, the broom he leaned against the counter.

"Some English breakfast tea ... a pair of reading spectacles, number thirty ... and fishing tackle."

"Fishing tackle?" He stopped and turned to face her, certain he'd misunderstood.

"Are there no streams or rivers to fish in hereabouts?"

"Well, yes. But—"

"Then I shall require fishing tackle. I enjoy the exercise it provides as well as being outdoors, and I like nothing so much as fresh trout for dinner."

He wouldn't have pegged her as the outdoors type, but he wasn't one to argue with a customer. Her money was as good as anyone's. "What precisely do you need?"

"I was unable to bring any gear with me." A pink flush colored her pale cheeks. "I shall require all of the basics. Pole, reel, line, hooks, basket, landing net. That should suffice for now. But I—," the blush deepened, "I must be careful how much I spend. Until I draw my first pay."

"Of course. I understand. Give me a few minutes, and I'll put everything together for you."

Felicia relaxed a little after Colin Murphy turned away. It was galling to have to admit her funds were in such short supply. It shouldn't be embarrassing, of course. That was her pride. And as everyone knew, pride went before a fall.

"Miss Kristoffersen?"

She turned to find the Murphy girl standing nearby. Charity wore a simple gingham dress of green and white with stockings on her feet but no shoes. Her dark hair was caught back at the nape with a wrinkled white ribbon, the bow uneven.

"Have you been over to see the schoolhouse yet?" the child asked.

Felicia nodded. "Yes, I went this morning. The classroom needs a good scrubbing before school starts. I thought I would take care of that tomorrow morning when it isn't quite so hot."

"Can I help you?"

"*May* you help me." She smiled to soften the correction. "Are you sure you wouldn't rather play with your friends than help me clean?"

"Nah. I can play with Suzanne and Phoebe anytime, and I like to help. Honest."

"Well, I suppose the answer is yes, then, as long your father doesn't mind."

"Can I—I mean, *may* I, Papa?"

Colin reached to take a fishing rod from a display on the far wall. "May you what?"

"Help Miss Kristoffersen clean the schoolhouse."

That brought him around. "If you want to clean, you could start with your room."

"*Papa.*" Charity rolled her eyes.

Felicia stifled a laugh.

Colin looked at her. "She might be more hindrance than help. She can be a chatterbox."

Felicia smiled. "I believe I should like her company anyway."

"Then I suppose it's okay by me." He turned back to the display of fishing tackle, this time selecting a reel.

As she watched him, Felicia found herself wondering about his wife. She had yet to meet Mrs. Murphy. Hadn't caught so much as a glimpse of the woman yesterday or today. She hoped they would meet soon. She would like to thank her for the use of the lovely cottage. Surely a woman had a hand in making it so warm and welcoming.

Perhaps we'll become friends.

She would like to have a friend, someone with whom she could share her thoughts, her hopes and dreams. She'd enjoyed some casual friendships while in normal school, but she hadn't had a close, tell-me-your-secrets, share-with-me-your-dreams kind of friendship since she left the city of Chicago at the age of ten. Back then it had been with a girl named Jana Lynch, who'd lived in the same tenement building, one flight up. The two of them, who'd shared not only their deepest secrets but also the same birthday, had been thick as thieves. But after leaving Chicago, Felicia had lost touch with Jana, just as she had with her brother and sister.

It would be nice to have someone like Jana in her life again. Felicia didn't mind being alone. Solitude was not a thing to be dreaded. But it would be nice to have a friend, all the same.

"Miss Kristoffersen?"

Lost in thought, she hadn't realized Colin Murphy had turned to look at her once again. "Yes?"

"I'll have to place an order for a trout basket and the reading spectacles. I'll have them in by next week."

"That will be fine." She followed him to the counter, where he quickly totaled her purchases.

"Three dollars and eighteen cents," he said as he looked up.

Oh dear. Her small savings would surely not last her for the next five weeks at this rate.

"If you'd like, I can put it on account."

Felicia shook her head. "No, I prefer to pay for it now. But thank you."

If the frugal Kristoffersens had drummed anything into her head over the years she was with them, it was that she should never live beyond her means. The Frenchman's Bluff school board had provided her not only with housing but with a well-stocked larder. Her needs should be few in the weeks to come. Surely she could manage until she received her pay, even with the cost of cleaning supplies and fishing gear.

She opened her purse and counted out the coins until they equaled the amount due. "I believe that's accurate." She slid the money across the counter.

"Do you need help carrying everything?"

"No, I—"

"I'll help her, Papa!" Charity hurried to stand beside Felicia, her eyes bright with excitement, as if carrying a customer's purchases was the highlight of her day. "Can I help, Miss Kristoffersen?"

"May I," Felicia corrected again. "May I help. And yes, you may." She looked down at Charity's stockinged feet. "But I think you'd better put some shoes on first."

"Oh! Right! I'll get 'em." In an instant, Charity disappeared into the adjoining living quarters.

A short while later, Felicia and the girl entered the cottage behind the mercantile. Felicia set the items in her arms on the kitchen table, and Charity followed suit.

"Do you often help your father in the store?"

"Sure. Lots." Charity leaned over and sniffed the roses that were still in the center of the table. "He likes me to be there with him most of the time."

"And what of your mother?"

Charity glanced up. "I don't have a mother. She died when I was little."

"Oh. I'm sorry. I didn't know."

The girl shrugged. "I don't remember her."

"I was ten when my mother passed away." Felicia sank onto a chair. "I still miss her."

"I'm eight."

"Are you? I thought you were at least nine."

"I am, almost. My birthday's comin' up in September. September fifth. Ten more days." She took a quick breath. "Papa says I look like my mama."

Felicia smiled at the girl. "Then your mother must have been very pretty."

"Papa says so."

She felt a tug of empathy for her landlord. He too knew about the loss of a loved one. Perhaps that explained his reserve. Perhaps he wasn't as emotionally withdrawn from his daughter as she'd first thought him.

"Are you gonna go fishing today?" Charity asked.

"No. Not today. And tomorrow I'm going to be busy at the school. But perhaps on Friday, if someone will be kind enough to show me the way."

"I can show you. Papa and I go fishing on the river lots in the summer. I know the way to our favorite spot. I could take you there."

Felicia felt a rush of affection for the girl. "That's very kind, Charity, but maybe your father doesn't want anyone else to know the location of your favorite place to fish."

"He won't care if *you* know."

"Well, we'll see. Don't tell me anything until you ask him."

FOUR

The schoolhouse was a single-story, rectangular building with white clapboard siding and a gabled roof. It was set on a stone foundation that rose several feet above the ground, giving it a somewhat imposing air. Rather than being hung in a steeple, a cast-iron bell had been attached to the wall on the right side of the entry.

On her second morning in Frenchman's Bluff, Felicia stood in the opening that separated the cloakroom from the classroom, a sense of satisfaction and expectation rising in her chest. How she'd longed for this opportunity. The years of frustration were behind her now. Very soon she would stand before her students and begin teaching them. She would be able to open their eyes to a world beyond this land of sagebrush and rabbits, cattle and sheep. She wanted that for all of her students, of course, but especially for the girls. She wanted them to understand that they weren't inferior to men, only different from them. That they could reach higher than they thought possible. That God had ever so much more in store for them than they could even dream.

She set aside the water pail and wooden crate that held her cleaning supplies and walked about the classroom. A teacher's desk sat on a raised platform at the front. Behind it, blackboards and chalk trays ran the full length of the room and continued halfway down the left wall as well. Eight windows, the lower halves covered with gingham curtains to discourage daydreaming, let in plenty of light for studying.

Twenty-one student desks were arranged in three rows of seven, and as she walked down one of the aisles, her fingers trailing over the desktops, Felicia pictured each seat filled with a pupil, younger students in the front, older students in the back. Here, as elsewhere in the country, children often left school too soon, some of them by age thirteen or even younger. She wanted to change those dismal statistics in this community, in this school. She hoped she would one day see many of her students go on to study at universities.

First, however, she must make a good impression on the parents and the members of the school board so they would want her to stay on as the teacher, year after year.

"So I'd best get busy," she said to herself as she began pushing desks toward the walls.

"I'm here, Miss Kristoffersen!"

Felicia turned in time to see Charity Murphy dash into the classroom.

"Did you start without me?"

"No." Felicia laughed softly. "I haven't begun anything except to move the desks."

"What can I do?"

"We'll need some water. Can you take the pail and fill it from the pump?"

"Sure."

Bucket in hand, the girl disappeared as quickly as she'd arrived.

Rolling up her sleeves, Felicia walked to the small storage closet in the back corner of the room. From it, she withdrew the sturdy broom she'd found there the previous day, along with a second water pail, and began sweeping the wooden tongue-and-groove floor, starting at the front and working her way toward the doorway. A few minutes later, she heard Charity's voice outside. Again she smiled. Mr. Murphy was right. His daughter was a chatterbox, talking even when there was no one near.

But she was mistaken about that. Charity wasn't alone when she reentered the classroom. A woman was with her.

"Mrs. Summerville," Felicia said aloud, thankful she'd remembered her name. "Good morning."

"Good morning, Miss Kristoffersen. I heard you were giving our schoolhouse a good cleaning and hoped I could be of help to you."

"That's very kind, but I wouldn't want to impose."

Kathleen Summerville tied around her waist the apron she'd brought with her. "Don't be silly. It's no imposition. Where would you like me to start?"

"And me," Charity chimed in. "What d'ya want me to do? I got the water."

Felicia drew in a quick breath. "I'll have you" — she looked at Charity — "wash the blackboards." Her gaze shifted to Kathleen. "And you and I can scrub and oil the floor, if you don't mind."

"It's why I'm here. Let's get started."

Charity must have had the opportunity to clean the blackboards before, for she knew exactly what to do. With a rag and the bucket of water in hand, she went to the far end of the blackboard. She needed a stool to reach the top part of the blackboard, but she didn't seem to mind climbing on and off the stool again and again as she inched her way across the front of the room.

The two women quickly set to work as well. Sharing a bucket of wash water between them, they got down on their hands and knees and began scrubbing the floor.

"Where's Suzanne and Phoebe?" Charity asked after a lengthy period of silence.

"At home," Kathleen answered. "They're baking cookies with Mrs. Hasting. Maybe you'd like to go help them when you're finished here."

"Oh, boy! Would I!"

Felicia laughed along with Kathleen when both women noticed Charity moving the wet cloth in bigger and faster circles.

"Your daughters and Charity must be good friends," Felicia said as she applied more elbow grease to her own task.

"Yes, they are. They've known one another since they were toddlers."

"And your husband? Is he in business here in Frenchman's Bluff?"

"My husband passed away two years ago this past spring."

"I'm sorry."

Kathleen sat back on her heels. "Harold managed the bank for his father before he took ill."

"I'm sorry," Felicia said again. "He must have been young when he died."

A bittersweet smile touched Kathleen's lips. "Yes. Too young. After he died, the girls and I moved in with Harold's parents. I don't know what I would have done without them." She shook her head, then said, "But you've lost someone too." She motioned with the scrub brush toward Felicia's black attire.

Felicia answered the unspoken question. "The couple who raised me. They died last March."

For most of her life, she'd thought the Kristoffersens had adopted her. They'd introduced her to others as their daughter. She bore their surname. Not until they were dead had she learned the truth. There'd been no legal adoption. Perhaps they'd meant to, but they never had. And while the Kristoffersens hadn't bothered to tell her she wasn't legally their daughter, her "cousin" had been quick to set her straight.

"Is that why you left Wyoming?" Kathleen asked, bringing Felicia's thoughts to the present.

"Yes." It was easier to answer that way than to say she'd had only two choices: marry one of Lars Kristoffersen's grandnephews or strike out on her own.

The choice had been an easy one to make.

Joe Reynolds, postmaster of Frenchman's Bluff, placed a catalog and an envelope on the mail counter and slid them toward Colin. "See you've got another letter from Margaret's mother."

Colin grunted an acknowledgment.

"That woman's more dependable than the turning of the seasons. Come rain or come shine, she writes to you and your girl every month."

"That she does." Colin took the mail from the counter, the letter from his mother-in-law resting on top of the catalog. He didn't have to wait to get home to know what the letter said. Olive Day would ask when Colin and Charity were coming for a visit. She would inquire about his daughter's schooling and bemoan the absence of culture to be found in a small town. Then she would offer some sort of incentive to lure him back to Ohio.

Why did the woman refuse to believe him when he told her that he and Charity planned to remain in Idaho, that they were content here, that this was their home? Yes, she was faithful in her correspondence, as Joe had said, but she was also obtuse. Or perhaps she was merely stubborn — not unlike Margaret had been at times.

"Hey, I've got something here for the new schoolmarm." Joe held up another envelope. "Mind takin' it with you?"

"Don't mind at all."

Colin bid the postmaster a good day and exited the post office, pausing for a moment on the boardwalk. The day was shaping up to be another scorcher. It wasn't yet noon, and already the heat was intense. But clouds were riding the western horizon. With any luck, they would sweep across the valley and bring rain, and cooler temperatures, with them.

Colin tugged on the brim of his hat to better shade his eyes. He'd intended to return straightway to the mercantile, but instead, he set off in the direction of the schoolhouse. After all, he had a letter for Felicia Kristoffersen to deliver. He glanced at the envelope. An initial and last name were written in the upper left corner. A name that matched the one in the center. A relative, no doubt, but who? Miss Kristoffersen hadn't mentioned remaining family in her application. He'd gotten the impression she was alone in the world, but it didn't seem so now. Who could it be?

His curiosity surprised him. What did it matter who wrote to her or what the relationship was? She wouldn't be in Frenchman's Bluff for long. These single female teachers never were. And it would be the children who suffered because of the board's tight fist with a dollar.

He scowled. If he felt so sure that would happen, that Felicia Kristoffersen had come to their town only to find a husband, why was he allowing Charity to spend so much time with her? Wouldn't it be better to limit their interactions as much as possible? He could have told Charity she had her own chores to do rather than let her join her teacher at the school.

A few minutes later, as he climbed the steps of the building, he heard laughter coming from inside. When he stopped in the doorway to the classroom, he observed two women — Felicia Kristoffersen and Kathleen Summerville — on their knees, the fabric of their skirts dampened by wash water as they scrubbed the floor, and his daughter seated on a stool, watching them, a dirty rag in her hand.

"Papa!" Charity slid off the stool and darted over to him. "You should hear Miss Kristoffersen's story about when she learned to ride a pony. It's funny."

Colin glanced in Felicia's direction. Her cheeks were flushed. From the laughter or from embarrassment?

Kathleen rose from the floor. "Have you come to help, Mr. Murphy?"

"Actually, I wondered if Miss Kristoffersen might need me to take Charity back to the store."

"Oh, no, Papa. I wanted to go bake cookies with Phoebe and Suzanne. Can I? I mean, may I? Mrs. Summerville said I could when I was done cleaning the blackboards, and I'm done. Aren't I, Miss Kristoffersen?"

Felicia swept a few strands of honey-brown hair off her forehead with the back of her hand. "Yes. You're finished, Charity. Thank you for doing such a good job."

"Can I . . . I mean, *may* I"—she looked toward her teacher and received a nod of approval—"go over to Phoebe's and Suzanne's, Papa?"

"It's close to lunch time," he answered. "You don't need to be filling up on sweets before you've had a decent meal."

Kathleen moved toward him, a soft smile curving the corners of her mouth. "The girls would be delighted to have Charity join them for lunch. And you needn't worry about her eating too many cookies and spoiling her appetite. Mother Summerville will see to that." She placed her hand atop Charity's dark hair. "You would be sure to eat your lunch first, wouldn't you?"

"Yes, ma'am," his daughter answered, eyes sparkling.

"Then you'll let her?" Kathleen finished.

Colin realized he'd been outmaneuvered. Done in by a woman's pretty smile and a child's pair of pleading brown eyes. "I suppose you can go for a couple of hours. But then it's straight home. You've got chores still to do."

"May I go now?" Charity started for the exit without waiting for his reply.

"Yes," he called after her.

"Thank you." Kathleen touched his forearm, as she was prone to do whenever they stood near each other. "My girls so enjoy Charity's company. It's good for them to play together."

He nodded before turning his eyes toward Felicia. "Is there anything you need me to do, Miss Kristoffersen?"

"No, thank you, Mr. Murphy. We're almost finished here. Charity and Mrs. Summerville made the morning's work much lighter."

"Well then." He took a step backward. "Guess I'd best return to the mercantile. Good day, ladies."

"Good day, Mr. Murphy," they replied together.

He started to turn, then stopped. "Mr. Reynolds over at the post office gave me a letter for you." He moved to where Felicia knelt on the floor and put the envelope in her outstretched hand.

He would have been hard-pressed to describe the expression that crossed her face. Displeasure? Fear? Revulsion? It was there and then gone, so fast that he wondered if he'd seen her expression change at all.

"Thank you, Mr. Murphy." She stuffed the letter into the pocket of her skirt.

He gave her a nod before turning and walking away, saying a final good day to Kathleen as he passed by her.

Helen Summerville's voice whispered in Kathleen's mind. *"Go after him, Kathleen. Ask him to walk you home. If you would just show some interest in him ..."*

Show some interest in him? That was almost laughable. She'd all but thrown herself at Colin Murphy, and he hardly knew she was alive. No, that wasn't fair. He knew she was alive. He just had no interest in her.

Kathleen felt like crying, and it wasn't because she'd lost her heart to Colin. Oh, he was the nicest of men. A man of integrity. A good father. Looked up to in the community. Unquestionably handsome. But those weren't her reasons for wanting him to notice her. No, her reasons had to do with her mother-in-law. It was Mother Summerville who'd decided it was time for Kathleen to find herself another husband, and it was Mother Summerville who'd decided Colin should be the stepfather to her granddaughters. And Mother Summerville was not one to have her wishes thwarted.

"Mrs. Summerville ... Kathleen?"

She turned to face Felicia, hoping the other woman wouldn't see how close to tears she was. "I'm sorry. I was woolgathering. Would you mind terribly if I went home? Mother Summerville wasn't expecting me to send Charity over to play with my girls, and I really should be there."

"Of course it's all right." Felicia rose from the floor. "You've been a tremendous help. I'm grateful to you."

"You're most welcome." Kathleen removed her apron from around her waist and draped it over her left arm. "I'll see you at the picnic on Sunday, if not before."

"Picnic?" Confusion flitted across Felicia's face.

"Oh, for heaven's sake. Hasn't anyone told you? I thought for certain Mr. Swanson would have. The women of Frenchman's Bluff are planning a welcome picnic for you after church on Sunday."

"They are?" Something in Felicia's voice revealed more than she probably would have liked—her uncertainty, her trepidation, perhaps even her loneliness.

Kathleen's heart went out to her. "You must think we're terrible for not giving you a bigger welcome on the day you arrived, but this is why."

"No, I—"

"You'll be the guest of honor on Sunday, and everyone from miles around will be there to welcome you. I promise, we really are delighted you've come to Frenchman's Bluff." *Almost everyone, anyway.*

Relief filled Felicia's gaze. "Thank you, Mrs. Summerville."

It wasn't often that Kathleen felt sure of herself, sure of what the future held, sure of others. At least not since her husband's death. But she felt sure about this: she and Felicia would become friends. Mother Summerville might be predisposed to dislike her, but that wouldn't sway Kathleen's feelings in the least.

"Please, call me Kathleen," she said, smiling.

Felicia returned the smile. "I would like that very much."

"I look forward to introducing you to others on Sunday, Felicia. Now I'd better go." She gave a little wave as she hurried from the classroom.

Felicia walked to one of the desks pushed against the wall and sat down. She allowed the silence of the room to wrap itself around her as she considered the sweet news Kathleen had delivered. A potluck after church to welcome her.

Felicia hadn't realized until that moment how worried she'd been because of the absence of a welcoming committee on her arrival. But it seemed they'd been waiting for Sunday, and that made perfect sense. Sunday was when those who lived on the farms and ranches came to town to attend church, the day of the week when everyone took off to honor the Sabbath, to rest and be with their families.

"I'm sorry, Lord. I let myself worry too easily, don't I? How much better it would be if I relaxed and trusted in You to make it all work for my good."

She put her hands on her thighs, ready to push up from the chair, but the crinkle of paper reminded her of the letter in her pocket. A letter from Gunnar. Her stomach tightened. Why had he written to her? What more could her "cousin" have to say? They hadn't parted on the best of terms.

Drawing a deep breath, she opened the envelope and removed the single sheet of paper.

Felicia,

I write to you, hoping you have come to your senses. Rolf remains willing to take you for his wife. There is no need for you to be alone. You belong here with us. It was the wish of both Uncle Lars and Aunt Britta that you stay and marry Rolf. You know this to be true. After their many kindnesses to you through the years, we cannot believe you have chosen to repay them this way.

Are you so ungrateful for the life they gave you? You were nothing but a dirty little orphan when they took you in. You never wanted for anything after they brought you home. They even paid for your education. But you know as well as I that they meant you to teach the Kristoffersen children who would be born to you. Not to go off to teach strangers. Come back where you belong. Rolf is waiting.

Gunnar

Felicia wadded the paper into a ball and shoved it into her pocket, along with the envelope. Cousin Gunnar could await her reply until doomsday for all she cared. As if she would consider marrying any of his sons. Especially not his foul-tempered eldest. The idea made her stomach turn. Rolf Kristoffersen didn't want a wife. He wanted a slave. He wanted someone who would silently and obediently keep his home tidy, cook his favorite dishes, and warm his bed during the cold Wyoming winters. She shuddered at the thought of Rolf's large, sausage-fingered hands on her body. Never. She would rather starve to death. She would rather go unloved her entire life than tie herself to the likes of him.

She drew in a deep breath and straightened her shoulders. She wouldn't starve to death. She had a position that would allow her to support herself. She had a cozy home to live in. Although she wouldn't grow rich working as a schoolteacher, she wouldn't go in want either. And as a teacher, she would know the love of children—of many, many children—without needing to give herself in marriage to someone she couldn't love and respect. She would chart her own path. So help her, she would.

With new resolve, she rose from the desk and finished her cleaning chores in no time at all. Then the supplies went back into the storage closet, the desks went back into their neat rows, and everything was in readiness for the first day of school. The satisfaction she felt made her wish the school year was starting tomorrow rather than next week.

She'd made the right decision coming to Frenchman's Bluff. She would make a home for herself here. She would win the children's affection, and she would teach them far more than they expected. That was her promise to herself—and to God.

As she left the schoolhouse, she paused on the steps and closed her eyes. "Bless this building, Lord, and all who enter it to learn. And help me be the very best teacher these children could have."

FIVE

Colin stood in the doorway of his daughter's bedroom, listening as she said her bedtime prayers, hands folded and eyes tightly closed.

"... and God bless Mama, who's with You in heaven, and Papa, who's with me right here on earth. Amen." She got up from her knees and slipped between the sheets.

Colin went to the bedside, leaned down, and kissed her forehead. "Goodnight, pumpkin."

"Goodnight, Papa."

"Sweet dreams."

She turned onto her side and closed her eyes. "You too."

Colin turned out the lamp on her bedside table and left the room with silent footsteps, knowing his daughter would be sound asleep before he finished descending the narrow staircase to the ground floor. He envied her ability to fall asleep so quickly. It seemed to him that he'd spent more time tossing and turning in his bed than sleeping in it. Especially in the years since Margaret died.

In the parlor, he settled into his chair and picked up the envelope that held the letter from his mother-in-law. He turned it in his hand several times but didn't remove the letter. He knew what it said.

Olive Day was nothing if not consistent. He supposed he

couldn't blame her for wanting him to return to Ohio. Her husband and only child were dead. It was natural that she would want to be close to her granddaughter. And maybe he was wrong for refusing to leave Frenchman's Bluff. Maybe it would be better for Charity to be near her grandmother. Olive would dote on her, there was no doubting that.

Still, there were more reasons to stay in Idaho than there were incentives to move back to Ohio. He'd tried to explain them to Olive when she visited Frenchman's Bluff a few years back. Obviously he hadn't explained well enough, for her letters were always the same.

He returned the envelope to the table next to his chair, then rose and walked to the kitchen, where he ran water from the pump into a glass. Taking the glass with him, he went out on the stoop and sat on the top step. It was cooler outside than it was indoors. Although the days were still hot, he was grateful for the falling temperatures at night. A hint of fall was in the air, although it would be several more weeks before it arrived in earnest.

The screen door outside of the cottage's kitchen opened and closed — it had a distinctive squeak — and a moment later, he saw the shadowy form of Miss Kristoffersen following the path toward the outhouse. He considered calling out to her, but better judgment prevailed. It was easy to imagine the blush that would rise in her cheeks were he to stop her on the way to the privy.

How long would she remain the schoolteacher in Frenchman's Bluff? Miss Lucas had stayed only six months before she married that merchant from the capital. At least Miss Andrews, the teacher before Miss Lucas, had been with them for a year and a bit before she nabbed herself a husband and was required to resign from the position.

Not that Colin had anything against marriage. His own had

had its rough spots, to be sure, especially in the early years, when Margaret's heart had looked back instead of forward. Still, he and his wife had found contentment with each other, and their union had given them Charity.

Thoughts of his daughter brought a smile to his lips.

From the moment she was born, Charity Estelle Murphy had wrapped her papa's heart around her little finger. He'd loved her with a fierceness that took his breath away, as it did now. And with everything within him, he wanted the best for her—including a good education. If she'd had a better teacher at the start, maybe she wouldn't struggle so today. The same way he'd struggled.

The privy door closed—that too had a distinctive sound, even when closed carefully—and moments later, he watched as Felicia made her way back along the path to the cottage.

Maybe she would prove him wrong. She might turn out to be a good teacher. She might stay more than a few months or a year. He could hope so anyway.

Felicia carried the lamp from the parlor into her bedroom. After setting it on the chest of drawers, she freed the buttons of her shirtwaist. But when she began to remove her skirt, she heard the whisper of paper from within the right pocket. Gunnar's letter. She stepped free of the skirt, leaving it in a black puddle on the floor, and sat on the side of the bed.

A little more than six months ago, Britta and Lars Kristoffersen had died within hours of each other. Britta in the morning, Lars just after sunset. Felicia had been at their bedsides, without reprieve, for two days, but nothing she'd tried had brought down their high fevers or saved their lives.

She'd donned deep mourning attire at once. She'd seen them

laid to rest beneath a large cottonwood near the creek that ran through the homestead. The Kristoffersens had been her parents for sixteen years, and she had honestly grieved their passing, despite the loneliness she'd felt, despite the lack of affection shown her.

Then Gunnar and his sons had swept in like a swarm of locusts, and she'd learned that she was not only parentless but penniless and homeless too. That nothing besides her clothes were hers. That even the name she'd worn for sixteen years wasn't hers by right. She wore it now only because it was the name on her diploma from the normal school. Otherwise . . .

Tears filled her eyes, but she blinked them away. In that instant, she decided she was finished with mourning. She didn't care what convention said was the proper length of time for mourning one's parents. She would not wear the awful black shirtwaists and skirts and wraps another day, nor would she change gradually from black to gray to white to colors.

As a girl, Felicia had asked God why her adoptive parents couldn't love her. Why had they taken her into their home if they hadn't really wanted her? She would never know the answer to that question, not in her lifetime anyway. But it was time to let go of the wound it had left on her heart.

Eyes closed, she pictured herself holding in cupped hands the hurt and pain that came from being unloved and lonely. Then she lifted those hands toward the heavens.

I forgive them, Lord. I don't want to carry this hurt with me any longer. Will You carry it for me?

She sat in silence for a long while, waiting for a touch from her Savior, from the Friend who had faithfully walked with her for so many years, from the One who had promised to never leave her nor forsake her—a promise kept.

She envisioned, like a whisper in her heart, walking through a beautiful meadow, wildflowers of every color and hue in abundance. At first she was clad all in black. But then Someone joined her and walked beside her. She couldn't see His face, but she didn't need to. She knew Him well. When He took her hand in His, she saw her dress turn from black to red to white.

Forgiveness extended. Forgiveness received. Washed clean in the blood of the Lamb.

Amen.

She rose, folded the black shirtwaist and skirt—leaving the crumpled letter from Gunnar in the pocket—and carried them to the trunk at the foot of her bed. There was something satisfying about putting the clothes into the empty chest, followed soon by the remaining items of her mourning clothes from the wardrobe.

God willing, she wouldn't need them again until she was an old, old woman.

SIX

"Miss Kristoffersen's going fishing today, Papa. I told her I'd show her the way to the river. Remember? Can I stay and fish too?"

Colin looked across the breakfast table at his daughter. "I'm not sure that's a good idea, Charity."

"Why not? I know how to get there, and I'll make sure I don't go any closer to the water than that old log. Just like when I'm with you. I promise."

"Does it occur to you that she might not want you around all the time? She'll be with you every weekday once school starts."

Charity looked at him as if he'd spoken in a foreign language.

"No," he answered himself as he spread butter on a thick slice of bread. "Of course that doesn't occur to you."

"I told her she could use my fishing basket since she doesn't have one of her own yet."

His wife, Colin thought, had chosen the right name for their daughter. The child was always charitable toward others. Almost to a fault. "That was a nice thing for you to do."

"Then I can go fishing with her?"

He shouldn't relent. He should be stricter. But how could he say no when she looked at him the way she looked at him now? "I suppose. If she doesn't object."

"She won't! I know she won't!" She hopped up. "I'll go right now. She's probably ready to leave already."

With a sigh, Colin pushed his chair back from the table and headed outside. He'd best make certain Charity was welcome on this fishing expedition. He was halfway between the back door of his home and the side door of the cottage when Felicia stepped into view. Her appearance caught him by surprise. She wasn't clad in black. Instead, she wore a dress made from brown and white striped fabric. On her upswept hair sat a straw hat with a wide brim adorned with brown satin ribbons. The perfect outfit for a morning spent by the river, fishing pole in hand.

"Miss Kristoffersen."

A smile curved her mouth when she looked his way. "Good morning, Mr. Murphy."

Was it just the light-colored dress that made her seem ... what? Younger? Prettier? Utterly fetching? "Charity tells me the two of you are going fishing."

"Yes. It seems so."

"You don't mind if she tags along? Because I could give you directions easy enough. The river isn't hard to find."

"I like your daughter's company, Mr. Murphy. But if you don't want her sharing your favorite fishing spot, do tell her so."

His daughter had mentioned the log, but he hadn't immediately considered that's where she meant to take the teacher.

"Perhaps I should find my own way after all," Felicia said, breaking the momentary silence.

His daughter might be charitable by nature, but he obviously wasn't. At least that wasn't his first reaction, and it shamed him. Clearing his throat, he said, "Not necessary, Miss Kristofferson. Plenty of fish to go around, and Charity would be disappointed not to go with you."

"Papa." His daughter scurried into view. "Why don't you come with us?"

"Afraid not. I've got a store to run."

"Please, Papa. Jimmy could take care of things 'til you get back."

Colin was more than a little tempted. He hadn't gone fishing in a couple of weeks. It wouldn't be long before the weather turned cold. Another couple of months at most. And his daughter was right. Jimmy could take care of things for a few hours. The boy had done it numerous times since he started working at the mercantile. He was a trustworthy kid and one who didn't shirk his duties. Maybe—

"I'm sure your father is much too busy to join us."

Felicia's words were like a splash of cold water, bringing him to his senses. What was he thinking? When he went fishing, he wanted to be with his daughter, just the two of them. There was no room for anyone else. Especially not a husband-hunting schoolmarm.

He pinned the woman in question with a hard gaze. "Charity needs to be back by noon. She has chores to do."

The smile that had lingered disappeared in an instant. "I'll make certain of it, Mr. Murphy. You can depend on me."

❦

Felicia and her young companion walked at a brisk pace, the trail taking them down the steep north slope of the bluff and through a long, narrow canyon. Throughout the journey, Charity peppered Felicia with questions: Did she like horses? Charity loved to ride better than almost anything. Did she ever have a dog? Charity wanted one, but her papa didn't think she was ready for the responsibility yet. Why did Felicia want to be a teacher? It seemed to Charity that going to school *forever* would be *awful*. What was the train ride like? Charity had never gone anywhere on a train. What was Felicia's favorite dessert? Charity's was chocolate cake or maybe cherry pie; she couldn't decide for sure. What was her favorite color? Charity didn't have one yet, although yellow was sure pretty.

The mouth of the gorge opened onto a surprisingly different landscape than the arid one they'd left above. Here, tall trees grew beside the river, their branches providing blessed shade from the sun, while crystal clear water gurgled and splashed over stones and boulders.

"Not many folks come this way," Charity told Felicia, "'cause you can't bring a buggy down that trail. It's more fit for deer, sheep, and dogs, Papa says. But that makes it better for us. We get it all to ourselves."

Felicia nodded, letting the melody of the river wash over her, bringing with it a feeling of contentment. She would come here often, she knew, to sit in the verdant underbrush. She would come here not just to fish but to think, to pray, to seek God's face and wait upon His will.

"Come on." Charity motioned with her hand for Felicia to follow. Then she started off, half skipping, half running, as she led the way toward a bend in the river.

Felicia remembered herself at the same age. An absent father and poverty had made her early childhood in Chicago difficult, but she'd been happy nonetheless. Everyone she'd known had lived just like the Brennans, in a few small rooms in one of the many tenement buildings. She'd never considered that there was any other way to live, and the streets of Chicago had been as familiar to her as this trail to the river was to Charity.

If she closed her eyes, she could smell the scents that had permeated the staircase of their tenement building: cabbage, bacon, sauerkraut, onion, garlic. To this day, whenever she smelled cooked cabbage, she was transported back in time and melancholy would sweep over her. She missed her mother. She missed her brother and sister.

"Are you coming?" Charity called from a copse of cottonwoods ahead of her.

"Yes." Felicia pushed away thoughts of the past. "I'm coming."

A few minutes later, she found herself looking across a wider, deeper section of the river. The beauty of it took her breath away.

Charity sat on a log and put a fat grub on a hook. "Papa says fishin' for trout's best when the water's cold. In the summer, we try to be here right after sunup, before it gets so hot out."

"I'll remember that for next time." She sat next to the girl and began to bait her own hook.

"Papa makes me stay on this old log." Charity patted the tree trunk. "He's afraid I'll fall in the river." She flipped her legs to the opposite side of the log. "I'm not a very good swimmer yet, and Papa says the water's too ... too swift."

"Your father's a wise man."

"Can you swim, Miss Kristoffersen?"

"Yes," she answered as she got to her feet and moved closer to the riverbank. "Although I didn't have the opportunity very often where we lived. But I'm a strong swimmer."

"That's good. I was gonna say Papa could teach you if you couldn't."

The image that popped into Felicia's head alarmed her. She saw herself standing hip-deep in the river, wearing a bathing costume, with Colin Murphy standing behind her, his hands closed around her waist. The mental picture was so real she could almost feel the warmth of those hands as he kept her from being swept away by the current. The very idea of such intimacies!

Whatever is wrong with me?

Rather than answer Charity, she cast her line into the river.

⑥

The air in Colin's small office was still and close, and he thought again of his daughter and the schoolmarm, standing at the river's edge, the moving water cooling the temperature by several degrees.

Lucky them.

He rose from his desk chair. When he entered the storeroom moments later, he found Jimmy assisting Helen Summerville with a bolt of cloth while Miranda Reynolds, wife of the town's postmaster, added some canned goods to a basket on her arm.

"Good day, Mrs. Reynolds," he said as he approached the woman.

"Good day, Mr. Murphy."

"Are you finding everything you need?"

She turned to face him. "Do you have any fresh eggs?"

"I do indeed. Mrs. Dowd brought me three dozen this morning."

"Wonderful. I'm baking some cakes for the community picnic on Sunday."

"Picnic?"

"Gracious. Didn't anyone tell you? We're all eating together after church to welcome the new schoolteacher. I would have thought you'd know, being on the school board and all."

Colin would have thought the same. But then he remembered. He *had* been told. The day before Felicia arrived in Frenchman's Bluff, Walter had told him about the ladies' plans. Only Colin had been too busy expressing his doubts about hiring another female as their schoolteacher to make note of it.

"Well, no matter," Miranda said. "You know now. And you

60

needn't worry about bringing anything." She glanced over her shoulder at Helen. When Miranda looked at him again, she lowered her voice, saying, "I'm sure Kathleen will bring enough food for you and Charity."

Colin's jaw tightened. It seemed, despite how careful he'd been not to encourage Kathleen, that others in town were pairing them off. He'd feared such might be the case, but this was the first time anyone had said something about it to his face.

"Let me get those eggs for you." He turned. "How many do you want?"

"I'll take half a dozen. No. Better make that a dozen, if you would, please."

Just after the postmaster's wife left the store with her purchases, Colin heard laughter coming from the family living quarters. His daughter had returned, obviously in good spirits. He trusted that meant trout for dinner.

Before he could move toward the connecting door, it opened and there stood Charity, holding a string of fish up high for inspection. Her cheeks were flushed, and her eyes were bright with glee. Behind her stood Felicia, looking almost as excited and pleased as his daughter did. Not to mention even more beautiful.

"Look, Papa!"

He glanced toward the table where Jimmy was cutting another length of fabric from a bolt. As he'd suspected, his daughter's excited voice had drawn Jimmy's and Helen's gazes. But at least they couldn't see Charity. Or Felicia. Especially not Felicia. Last thing he needed was more gossip. Bad enough he'd been paired off with the widowed Kathleen when there was no truth in it. Worse yet if anyone tried the same with a never-married female who was new in town—and living in the cottage next door.

He moved quickly toward his daughter, forcing both her and

the teacher to take several steps backward. Then he closed the door behind him.

"Look how many we caught!" Charity exclaimed.

"I see." His tone was curt. "But you don't have to announce it to the customers."

The pleasure faded from Charity's face. He looked beyond her to Felicia. Her smile had disappeared too.

"Thanks for having her back before noon," he said in the same abrupt tone.

Felicia's eyes narrowed slightly. "I told you I would have her back on time." She bent forward at the waist. "Charity?"

His daughter turned to face the teacher.

"Thank you for taking me fishing. I had a wonderful time. I know I'll enjoy my dinner even more because of you." She straightened. "Good day, Mr. Murphy." With a curt nod, she turned and left through the kitchen.

He should go after her. He should apologize. But for what? For wanting Charity to remember he had a business to run? For correcting his own child? Or for that matter, for shielding Miss Kristoffersen from the tittle-tattle of other women?

No, he'd be hanged if he would apologize to her.

He looked at Charity. "Better take your catch into the kitchen. We'll fry them for supper tonight."

"Okay." There was no enthusiasm in her response.

Regretting his earlier reaction—and especially taking it out on his daughter—he said, "I'm glad you had a good time, pumpkin. Sorry if I sounded gruff."

She brightened a little. "It's okay, Papa." She turned toward the kitchen. "Did you know Miss Kristoffersen likes to swim? I told her that if she couldn't, you could teach her like you've been teaching me."

Colin shook his head. *That* would be the day.

When he returned to the storeroom, he found Helen Summerville, purchase held in the crook of her left arm, standing near the cash register while Jimmy counted out her change.

"There you go, ma'am." The boy dropped the last coin into the palm of the woman's right hand.

"Thank you, Jimmy." She looked at Colin. "Charity certainly sounded excited about something."

"We're having trout for supper."

Helen raised an aristocratic eyebrow. "My word. All that noise over fish for supper? I thought it was something earth-shattering." She smiled, but there was condescension in her eyes. "Charity is quite the tomboy, isn't she? She could use a woman's touch."

His jaw tightened and released, tightened and released.

"My dear Mr. Murphy. I'm sure you do the best you can, but a girl needs a mother."

He pressed his lips together. *And I suppose you have someone in mind for the job?* He knew the answer to that question.

"You don't want her growing up a hoyden, Mr. Murphy. She needs a mother to mold her into a young lady, to teach her manners and how to dress and how to speak. You may not realize the importance of those virtues now, but you will eventually. One can only hope you won't realize it too late, for her sake."

"I appreciate your concern, Mrs. Summerville." Somehow he managed to speak the words without choking on them. He even sounded halfway sincere.

She leaned her head to one side, a gesture that seemed to say, *Naturally, you appreciate my concern. I know better than you.*

Colin hoped she would leave before he lost his temper.

"And what are your thoughts on our new schoolteacher?"

At the last school board meeting, Helen Summerville had been the only person to agree with him. Strangely enough, that didn't sit well with him right now. He shrugged. "I guess we'll know more once school begins."

"I suppose we shall." She sniffed dismissively. "Well, I had best get home. We'll see you in church on Sunday."

"Yes, see you in church. Good day, Mrs. Summerville."

SEVEN

Outside the drugstore on Saturday morning, Felicia stepped into the borrowed buggy and took up the reins.

"Maybe I'd best go with you," Walter Swanson said as he watched from the sidewalk. "Don't want you to get lost."

"I wouldn't think of taking you away from your business another day, Mr. Swanson. You have provided me with an excellent map. I won't get lost."

"Well ... if you're sure." He sounded unconvinced.

"I'm quite sure."

Not wanting to prolong the discussion or give him the opportunity to insist he accompany her on her home visits, she slapped the reins against the horse's rump and drove away, headed south on Shoshone Street. In a matter of minutes, she'd left Frenchman's Bluff behind.

Smiling to herself, she drew a deep breath, taking pleasure in the fresh breeze on her face.

Yesterday afternoon she'd called on the students who resided within the township. Her visits had been brief, just long enough to let each child become comfortable with her. At least she hoped that had been the outcome.

Today she would visit as many of her students as possible who lived on farms and ranches outside of Frenchman's Bluff. Based on Walter Swanson's map, she should be able to call on all of those who lived south and west of town. The remainder would have to wait until Monday of next week.

With another slap of the reins, she urged the horse into a fast trot, eager to reach the first home. Until then, her thoughts were free to drift where they willed.

Unfortunately, what—or rather, who—came to mind first was Colin Murphy as she'd seen him yesterday, scowling at her and his daughter. How quickly he'd wiped away the pleasure of that morning's fishing excursion. How much he'd reminded her of Lars Kristoffersen, so curt, so unable to express anything but disapproval.

But then, perhaps she wasn't being fair to Mr. Murphy. Charity seemed to be a happy, loving child. Surely her father must have some redeeming qualities. Although Felicia didn't know what those redeeming qualities might be at present—other than his rugged good looks.

The thought brought her up short. Did she truly think him handsome? Well ... yes ... she supposed she did find him so. But a person's physical appearance was beyond their control. If they were born with good looks, that was nothing due to them. Their character, on the other hand, was their responsibility. By the grace of God, they could change their less stellar traits into something better.

She felt a nudge in her spirit. Was she judging another when she should be judging herself? Was she pointing at the sliver in Colin Murphy's eye when there was a log in her own?

"You must grow tired of correcting me, Lord."

The sun fell warm on her face, like a smile from heaven. Comforting. Familiar.

Those first years in the Kristoffersen home had been especially difficult ones for Felicia. She'd often felt sorry for herself. Sorry and completely alone. She'd missed her family so much. It was then, in those early years, that she'd begun talking to Jesus, times when she'd learned to lean into Him when the nights were dark and cold. And He'd sustained her. He'd become her best and dearest friend when she had no other. Then. Later. Now. Forever.

The horse and buggy crested a rise, and a house and barn came into view. A quick glance at the map told her this must be the Anderson farm. Two of her students lived there — Bernard, age thirteen, and Ola, age twelve.

She said a quick prayer for the visit to go well and for both the children and their parents to like her. Then she slapped the horse's rump with the reins once again, urging him into a faster trot.

Colin carried a large sack of flour and another of sugar to the back of the wagon and dropped them into the bed, next to a box of canning supplies. Brushing his hands together, he turned toward Charity. "You sure you don't want to come along?"

"I'm sure. I promised Tommy I'd help him with his tree house. We're gonna build a whole 'nother level."

"Charity is quite the tomboy, isn't she? She could use a woman's touch."

He shoved Helen Summerville's critical words aside and grinned at his daughter. "No falling out of the tree and breaking your arm."

"I won't."

"Tell Mrs. Bryant I'll be back before suppertime."

"Okay."

Colin stepped onto the wagon seat. "You mind Mrs. Bryant."

"I will, Papa."

With a nod, he clucked to the team and drove the wagon away from the mercantile. He didn't make many deliveries. Most folks came to the store and carried out their own purchases. But there were a few customers, like Widow Ashton, who needed some extra help on occasion.

Madge Ashton—not quite five feet tall, with life etched deeply into each wrinkle and line of her face—had lived alone on her forty-acre farm for more than twenty years, ever since her husband Albert's heart failed him at the age of sixty while walking behind a plow. Fiercely independent, Widow Ashton maintained her home and tended her chickens and her milk cow by herself. The farmland she leased to one of her neighbors. When weather permitted, she walked into town to attend church services or to do some shopping. She no longer owned a horse to pull a buggy.

Which was why Colin was driving out to her place now. The widow had been in the mercantile earlier in the day and bought more items than she could carry. He'd invited her to wait until Jimmy came to work so the lad could mind the store, then Colin could drive her home in the wagon with the supplies. But she'd declined.

"Too much to do at home to dillydally around here," she'd said. "Besides, it's good for me to walk. Keeps the blood flowing through these old veins. But I'll be much obliged if you would deliver those things to me when you can. Doesn't have to be today. First of the week would be fine."

But Colin didn't want to wait until Monday. He'd learned a thing or two about Madge Ashton over the years, and one was that if she bought canning supplies today it was because she was ready to begin canning today. She was a sweet old soul, but she did tend to be impulsive.

One of the horses snorted and bobbed his head. Colin looked

up and saw someone riding toward him. A woman. And if he wasn't mistaken, she was riding astride without a saddle. He leaned forward, narrowing his eyes.

Felicia Kristoffersen?

He drew back on the reins, stopping the team, and waited for the horse and rider to reach him. It was indeed Felicia, and the bay gelding she rode, he was certain, belonged to Walter Swanson.

"Miss Kristoffersen," he called as she drew closer, "what happened?"

"Mr. Swanson's buggy lost a wheel."

That explained the harness on the horse.

Colin looped the reins around the brake and hopped down from the wagon. "How far back?"

"I'm not sure. Five or six miles, I suppose."

Her complexion was rosy from the heat of the day, and a fine sheen of perspiration had beaded across her forehead and down her nose. Long strands of honey-brown hair had pulled loose from their pins to float about her neck, begging Colin to imagine what it might look like flowing over her shoulders and down her back. Riding astride had tugged her dark blue skirt several inches above the top of her boots, revealing more of her shapely calves than she probably realized.

He cleared his throat. "You'd better get down and come along with me." He put his hand on the gelding's neck. "I've got a delivery to make first, but then I'm going straight back to town. We'll tie your horse to the wagon."

Her gaze rose longingly toward Frenchman's Bluff.

Colin could tell she was about to refuse him. Quickly, he said, "I'm not sure it would be a good thing for most folks to see the new schoolteacher ... like this."

At first she seemed confused by his comment. Then came

understanding. The color deepened in her cheeks, this time from embarrassment. "I must be a sight." She slipped off the horse's back in a fluid motion, pulling down her skirt as soon as her boots touched the ground.

Yes, she was a sight, but not an unattractive one. Any red-blooded man would—

He turned away, leading the bay to the back of the wagon. By the time he turned back, Felicia was seated in the wagon, and her hands were busy tidying her hair. He was sorry for that.

He stepped up to the wagon seat and took the reins in hand. "Ho there!" The wagon jerked into motion. "Mind if I ask what you were doing out here?"

"Calling on my students."

"Ah." He nodded. "And the wheel?"

"I'm not sure what happened to make it fall off. The buggy didn't hit a rut or any obstruction."

He looked at her. "Were you hurt?"

"No." A momentary smile played across her lips. "I'm not all that fragile, Mr. Murphy."

Now would be a good time to apologize for the way he'd barked at her and his daughter yesterday. Then again, maybe it was best to leave things alone. He hadn't been wrong ... exactly ... in chastising Charity. And besides, it didn't seem as if Felicia was holding his gruffness against him.

Yes, he would leave it alone. Like she'd said, she wasn't all that fragile.

❦

Right up until the buggy wheel fell off and Felicia was dumped on the ground, it had been what she considered a perfect day. She'd called on four families, forming preliminary opinions about the students' strengths and weaknesses. Most of the children seemed almost as eager for school to begin as she was.

The two notable exceptions were Bernard Anderson and R. J. Franklin. Bernard, she suspected, was a lazy student. Not unintelligent, simply uninterested. She also suspected he was a prankster. Instinct told her that if he could stir up trouble in the classroom, he would. She would have to stay on her toes around him. As for R. J., he thought himself—at fifteen—too grown up to continue with schooling. He was eager to live as a man, to work beside his father on their dairy farm, to earn a living wage. Would she lose him before her first year of teaching was up, or could she change his mind, make him want to go on learning? And would she have to change his parents' minds as well as his?

The Murphy wagon turned off the main road, bringing Felicia's thoughts back to the present. Soon they were following a narrow track down a steep incline. Felicia braced her feet and held on to the seat with her hands until the wagon leveled out again. When it did, she was facing a field of tall corn. Green stalks and beige tassels waved in the warm breeze of midday.

"How beautiful," she whispered.

"Irrigation makes a world of difference to this land. Soil's rich. All it needs is water."

She glanced his way. "Have you a secret yearning to be a farmer, Mr. Murphy?"

"Me? No. I like what I do. Running the mercantile suits me."

Questions swirled in her mind. Things she would like to know about him, about the wife who'd died, about Charity. She found Colin a confusing man. Sometimes he seemed warm and caring, and just about the time she thought she might learn to like him, he turned gruff.

But perhaps her confusion had more to do with her lack of

experience with men. There had been few of them in her life. And those few hadn't been the sort who invited one to know them better. Her father had been a drunkard and a rare presence in their tenement flat. Lars Kristoffersen had been old, withdrawn, and a man of few words. As for Gunnar and his sons? Well, she'd rather not think about them at all.

"I've wondered the same about you, Miss Kristoffersen."

She met his gaze again. "About me?"

"Do you have a secret yearning to be something other than a teacher?"

"No."

"Then why did you wait so long to teach after getting your certificate?"

She turned her gaze away from him. "I was needed at home. My ... parents ... were growing old and couldn't do without my help. They passed away in late winter, and by this summer, it became clear that I ... I couldn't stay on their farm any longer. I had to begin teaching to support myself."

"Is that why you never married? Because you were caring for your parents?"

"I don't wish to marry, Mr. Murphy. I wish to teach."

The horses turned between a break in the cornfields, and up ahead, Felicia saw a farmhouse and barn. Colin eased back on the reins, slowing the team from a jog to a walk. Only after the wagon rolled to a stop did he speak again.

"I hope you mean that, Miss Kristoffersen. It would be good for the children to have the same teacher year after year."

Rolf Kristoffersen's image flashed in her mind. She suppressed a shudder, saying, "I promise you, sir. I do mean it."

EIGHT

Felicia sat on the stool before the dressing table, running a brush through her hair. Although her eyes stared into the mirror, it wasn't her reflection she saw but the memory of having her hair brushed by her mother as they sat near the stove in the kitchen of their tenement flat.

"Don't ever ... be forgettin' ... that I ... love you ... me dear ones."

Felicia lowered the hairbrush and set it on the table, her vision blurred by tears. Still, after all these years, she could hear her mother's voice—her *real* mother's voice—whispering those words to her children.

"Oh, Mum. I miss you. I wish—"

She swallowed the rest of the sentence. It was useless to want to change the past. She'd done enough wishing as a child, and it hadn't changed a thing. It hadn't brought her mother back to life or brought her brother, Hugh, to rescue her or made Felicia happier in her situation with the Kristoffersens.

I don't mean to be ungrateful. Truly, I don't.

She wiped away the tears with a handkerchief, then took up the brush a second time, using it to sweep her hair onto the top of her head, where she secured it in place with hairpins. Satisfied with her reflection, she rose from the stool and went to the wardrobe, where she withdrew a pale blue and white percale shirtwaist and a solid blue wool skirt. She'd ordered them both from the Sears, Roebuck & Company catalogue soon after she'd begun seeking a position as a schoolteacher, spending just over two dollars for the new outfit. This would be her first opportunity to wear them.

Hopefully, no one in Frenchman's Bluff would judge her for the abrupt change from black to lighter colors. Forgoing gray in between wasn't considered proper mourning etiquette, but for women of limited means, etiquette often took a backseat to practicality. Besides, Felicia looked ghastly in gray.

Pushing away the somber direction of her thoughts, she quickly donned the new outfit, placed a simple straw bonnet on her head and, with her Bible held in the crook of one arm, headed out the door of her cottage.

The Frenchman's Bluff community church was located on the south side of town, but even if she hadn't known the location already, it would have been easy to guess from the number of people walking in that direction on this Sunday morning—including Colin Murphy and his daughter, who happened to reach the corner of Main and Idaho at the same time Felicia did.

"Hi, Miss Kristoffersen," Charity said with her usual exuberance.

"Good morning, Charity." She looked up. "Mr. Murphy."

Colin nodded. "Miss Kristoffersen."

They fell into step together, Charity walking between them. For a time, no one spoke, which suited Felicia. But at least her time with Colin yesterday afternoon had eased her fear that he disliked her. By the time they'd returned to town from Mrs. Ashton's farm, Felicia had begun to feel almost comfortable with him.

Well, *comfortable* might not be the right word.

"How'd you like your trout?" Charity asked, intruding on her thoughts. "Did you eat it Friday night like you said you were gonna?"

"Of course. And I liked it very much. What about yours?"

The girl licked her lips. "Mmm, mmm."

Felicia laughed softly.

"Papa fried potatoes and onions to go with it, and for dessert, we had some cookies that I helped bake over at the Summervilles' house the day we cleaned the school. They had frosting on 'em."

"Oh my. That does sound good."

"It was. Wasn't it, Papa?"

"It was very good," he answered.

"I like your dress, Miss Kristoffersen. It's really pretty."

"Why, thank you, Charity. It's kind of you to say so."

"I think blue's my favorite color instead of yellow."

Felicia smiled at the child. "Mine too."

"Doesn't Miss Kristoffersen look pretty in her blue dress, Papa?"

Several seconds passed before he said, "Yes, she does."

The reply caused an odd sensation to swirl inside Felicia. He thought her pretty? She wasn't sure she wanted that. But perhaps he was merely being polite. He hadn't spoken with great feeling, and what else could he answer to his daughter's question when Felicia was walking right beside them?

"Papa, there's Phoebe and Suzanne. Can I go on ahead?"

"Okay," he said. "But try not to get your clothes dirty."

"See you inside, Miss Kristoffersen." Charity raced off to join her friends.

Felicia tried to think of something to say once they were alone: *Charity's a bundle of energy ... She's a delightful girl ... You must be so proud of her ... You've done a good job raising her ...*

But she said nothing.

His daughter was right. Felicia Kristoffersen did look pretty in that blue dress. So much more flattering than the bleak mourning attire she'd worn her first few days in Frenchman's Bluff. And the color matched her eyes to perfection, making them seem even bigger and brighter.

It bothered Colin that he was so aware of her appearance. It wasn't like him to notice. It was better to resist such thoughts, about *any* woman. Better for him, better for his daughter. Allowing a female past the barriers he'd constructed would put the careful order of his life — his and Charity's — in jeopardy.

They made the rest of their way to church in silence, and as soon as they arrived at the entrance to the narthex, Colin went to look for Charity, the perfect excuse to separate himself from Felicia's company. By the time he and his daughter entered the sanctuary, he saw Felicia was seated with Ann Dowd and her family.

Good. He didn't want the gossips to have a heyday because he and Miss Kristoffersen had happened to walk to church together this morning.

Colin and Charity took their usual place in the last pew. He hadn't always sat at the back of the church. That started after Margaret died. Back then, he hadn't wanted to be surrounded by people. He'd wanted to be able to leave at any time. He'd wanted to avoid more words of sympathy from well-meaning folks. Now he stayed in the last pew out of habit. Or maybe he stayed because he didn't want others to guess how little confidence he had in the messages given by Reverend Hightower.

For instance, all things *didn't* work together for good, not even for those who loved God. They never had. They never would. Hard things befell people, *good* people, and changed their lives for the worse. That's how it had been throughout the history of mankind, and no nice religious platitudes would change that fact.

Colin wondered if his wife could look down from heaven and see him. He wondered if she could read his thoughts as he sat there in that pew. He hoped not. Heaven was supposed to be a place where sorrow and sighing didn't exist.

If he even still believed in heaven. He wasn't sure he did, wasn't sure he didn't.

The pump organ at the front of the church bellowed a few opening chords, and the congregation rose to their feet, hymnals in hand. Colin stood and joined in the singing, but only for the sake of his daughter and the promise he'd made to her mother.

At the outdoor picnic that followed the Sunday service, Felicia was introduced to so many people that it left her head spinning with names and faces. Her cheeks hurt from smiling for such a long time, but she couldn't stop, even if she wanted to. Her heart was too filled with joy. For the first time in her life, she felt she'd found a place to belong. The fear that had dogged her heels on her way to Frenchman's Bluff was gone.

Felicia was particularly glad to see so many of her students, most of whom she'd met in their homes over the past two days. Some were shy. Some were bold. Some were short and slight, others tall and broad. They were the children of the shopkeepers in town and the children of the farmers and ranchers who worked the land beyond the borders of Frenchman's Bluff. The youngest was six, the oldest fifteen, and she thought it possible that she loved each and every one of them already.

After the tables had been weighed down with the offerings of the womenfolk, Walter Swanson took a moment to officially introduce Felicia and welcome her into their midst. Then Reverend Hightower said a blessing over the food. Following the "Amen," others quickly moved to get in line to fill their plates, but before Felicia could do the same, Iona Bryant told her to sit down on one of the blankets.

"Let someone else bring you food," the woman added. "You're our guest of honor."

Felicia felt a flush of pleasure warm her cheeks. Truly, she'd never been this spoiled nor felt this welcome anywhere. Still, she wasn't sure she wanted others to think she expected to be waited on. But before she could protest, she saw Charity hurrying toward her, holding a plate with both hands, mouth skewed in concentration.

"Here's your food, Miss Kristoffersen," the girl called as she came near. "Hope you like what I chose. I got Mrs. Dowd's fried chicken and Mrs. Bryant's bean salad and Mrs. Summerville's corn bread. Don't know who made this other stuff, but I thought it looked good."

"My goodness, Charity. I don't think I can eat that much."

"Sure you can. I heard Phoebe's grandmother say you're awful thin and could use some meat on your bones."

As she took the plate from Charity's hands, Felicia laughed, certain that Helen Summerville hadn't meant for that particular comment to reach her ears. "Thank you, Charity. I'll try to eat every bite."

The girl nodded before dashing off to fill a plate for herself before her favorites were gone. Then others settled onto blankets and chairs around Felicia and soon they began to ask questions. Where did she grow up? Did she have any brothers or sisters? What were her favorite subjects when she was a student? How long had she been at the normal school in Laramie? Did she like Frenchman's Bluff? Wasn't the food good?

"For pity's sake!"

Felicia glanced up to find Kathleen standing nearby, her hands on her hips as she frowned good-naturedly at the inquisitors.

"Can't you let the poor woman take a few bites? Give her a chance to eat before you ask anything else."

"I don't mind," Felicia answered.

Kathleen smiled. "But I do." She joined Felicia on the blanket, then lowered her voice to say, "Mrs. Dowd's fried chicken is the best. You should take the time to enjoy it."

Apparently, the others nearby decided to heed Kathleen's orders and began talking among themselves. And as soon as Felicia had a chance to bite into the fried chicken, she was glad for her new friend's aid. "Oh my. This *is* good."

"Didn't I tell you?"

Felicia nodded.

"You're going to do wonderfully, Felicia. I can tell. I was watching you with the children, and you had such a look of excitement on your face." Kathleen's gaze turned toward a small group of people seated in the shade of another tree. "I told Colin ... Mr. Murphy ... that he needed to give you a chance before being so sure you wouldn't be a good teacher. Everyone has to begin somewhere."

Felicia's throat tightened, and she swallowed hard, the food suddenly tasteless.

"All I know is that I'm glad the board didn't hire a schoolmaster. I think a man in that position might frighten Phoebe half to death, no matter how kind he was. She can be timid around men. I suppose because she lives in a house full of women, excepting her grandfather, and he spends most of the time at the bank. But *you* don't frighten her. She likes you already."

"I'm glad," Felicia answered softly. "I like her too."

She took another bite of the food on her plate, but the pleasure had gone out of the day with the knowledge that Colin Murphy believed she wouldn't be a good teacher. That somehow seemed even worse than when she thought he simply didn't like her.

⑥

Kathleen felt awful. Why had she allowed Mother Summerville to convince her to say anything to Felicia about Colin's opposition?

"Miss Kristoffersen deserves to know. She mustn't think she has unanimous support. It might make her feel so secure that she will disregard the wishes of the board in school matters."

It shamed Kathleen, knowing there'd been a small part of her that wanted Felicia to be worried. Not for the reasons Mother Summerville stated—which Kathleen didn't quite believe—but because she didn't want Felicia setting her cap for Colin. He was, after all, one of the few eligible *and* acceptable men in Frenchman's Bluff; her mother-in-law was right about that. And if Kathleen was ever to be free of Mother Summerville's control, she needed to marry a man who could afford to take in a wife and two stepdaughters.

Her guilt increasing the longer she sat next to Felicia, Kathleen excused herself, rose, and went to check on her children. She found them seated with a number of friends on the shady side of the church. Giggles and laughter were carried to her on the soft, warm breeze. She adored the sound, yet it was one that should be shared … with the man she loved. Loneliness swept over her.

She'd thought her life would be so different from what it was. She'd expected to grow old with Harold, living in the same house year after year after year. She'd expected they would be together to watch their daughters get married and give them grandchildren. She'd thought they would live comfortably always, supporting each other, encouraging each other, caring for each other.

But life, she'd learned, was rarely what one expected.

"Good day, Miz Summerville."

Recognizing the voice, Kathleen forced a small smile onto her lips as she turned toward Oscar Jacobson. "Hello, Mr. Jacobson. Are you enjoying the picnic?"

"Sure am. We don't get grub like this on the Double G. Not all at one sittin' anyway."

"No, I don't suppose you would."

The cowboy tipped his head in Felicia's direction. "The new schoolmarm seems right nice."

"She is." Another twinge of guilt caused her to take a quick breath. "Very nice."

"Pretty too."

"Yes." She wondered how long it would be before Oscar or one of his friends called on Felicia. After today, she wouldn't expect it to be long.

"I guess Suzanne and Phoebe must be eager to get back to school."

"Yes."

"Wish I'd been able to go further with my schoolin'." He moved a couple of steps closer. "The boys give me a hard time about it, but I'm right partial to poetry."

"You are?"

He grinned. "Don't have to sound so surprised."

"I'm sorry. I didn't—"

"I know you didn't, ma'am. I don't suppose I look much like the poetry type nor sound like one either."

No, he didn't, but she'd already been careless with her words. She wouldn't be so again. "Who do you like to read?"

"Whatever I can find. I like Shakespeare's sonnets. Henry David Thoreau. John Milton. I memorized a couple of his poems this summer."

"Can you say one for me? I love poetry too."

"Reckon I could give it a try." His grin widened. "I might get a bit nervous. Never quoted a poem to a lady before." His cheeks became flushed, something else she wouldn't have expected from him.

"Would it help if I didn't look at you?" she offered.

"I imagine it would help some."

She turned away from him, once more looking toward the group of children eating their picnic lunch in the shade of the church. "All right. I'm listening."

"It's called 'On His Blindness'." Oscar cleared his throat. "When I consider how my light is spent / 'Ere half my days in this dark world and wide, / And that one talent which is death to hide, / Lodged with me useless, though my soul more bent / To serve therewith my Maker, and present / My true account, lest He returning chide. . ." He paused to clear his throat a second time.

Never in her wildest dreams would she have imagined to hear such words coming from a cowpoke who spent his days on horseback and was better acquainted with cows and rabbits, coyotes and ground squirrels. And that he was quoting the John Milton poem so well, here in this public place, amazed her even more.

Oscar continued, " 'Doth God exact day-labor, light denied?' / I fondly ask. But Patience, to prevent / That murmur, soon replies, 'God doth not need / Either man's work or his own gifts. Who best / Bear His mild yoke, they serve Him best. His state / Is kingly: thousands at His bidding speed, / And post o'er land and ocean without rest; / They also serve who only stand and wait.' "

Silence stretched between them for several seconds. Then she looked his way, and the crowd seemed to recede, leaving them alone in a small bubble of affinity.

"That was lovely, Mr. Jacobson."

His grin returned, along with heightened color. "I'm right glad you liked it, Miz Summerville."

She felt a sudden warmth in her own cheeks.

"Maybe sometime we could read poetry together."

"I would like that," she responded without hesitation, surprising herself.

Mother Summerville would never approve.

NINE

The first day of school began with an overcast sky and a noticeably cooler temperature. Hopefully it meant the children would be alert and eager to learn rather than lethargic due to the heat.

Felicia arrived at the schoolhouse more than an hour before time to ring the bell. Although she'd done a thorough cleaning the previous week, she quickly swept the floor and ran a cloth over the desktops to clean away more recent dust. Then she wrote her name on the blackboard in large letters. Ah, the satisfaction she felt at seeing it there. She'd waited too many years for this moment not to want to savor it.

"I told Colin ... Mr. Murphy ... that he needed to give you a chance before being so sure you wouldn't be a good teacher."

"I *will* be a good teacher," she said aloud. "I *am* a good teacher. And I'll make certain Mr. Murphy changes his tune."

Felicia moved to a different section of the blackboard and wrote some math problems on it. This week, she would take the time to get to know her students better, to discover more of their strengths and weaknesses. If she understood them, it would help her impart to them a love of learning, a desire for knowledge. Perhaps she could help one of them become a great scientist or a revered physician or even a famous musician. Perhaps another would become a renowned theologian or a sought-after orator. Education was the open door to a life they'd never before imagined.

After writing the day's arithmetic lesson, she wrote reading words on a third section of the blackboard, starting with the simplest for the young children and working her way to the most difficult words for the older students. She prayed Miss Lucas had been a good teacher. She hoped her students would remember what they'd learned in this classroom prior to today.

According to Walter Swanson, Frenchman's Bluff would be the first school in Idaho to adopt a nine-month school term. Among the first in the nation too. One more thing for Felicia to worry about. Many people were skeptical about the change, especially farmers who needed their sons at home during planting and harvesting. Would the parents and school board blame her if the children didn't do as well under the new term? Well, she simply wouldn't give them the chance to blame her. She would make certain *all* of her students thrived in their studies.

She set the chalk in the tray and brushed her hands together to wipe away the lingering white dust. Turning to face the classroom, she drew in a deep breath, checked the watch pinned to her bodice, and headed outside to ring the bell. Many children were already in the yard; others were hurrying toward the schoolhouse, lunch pails and slates in hand.

With a smile on her face, Felicia rang the bell for several seconds. All conversations ceased as the children fell into two orderly lines, one for boys and one for girls. For the most part, they stood in order of age and size, shortest in the front, tallest in the back.

"Come in, girls," Felicia said.

As the girls filed past her, they made their manners with small curtsies. Whatever else Miss Lucas might or might not have accomplished as schoolmarm, it was apparent she'd instilled the proper decorum upon her students.

The boys came next, each of them bowing slightly at the waist as they went by, and once all of their lunch pails were on the shelves in the cloakroom and all the students stood beside their desks, Felicia made her way to the front of the class.

"Good morning, boys and girls."

"Good morning, Miss Kristoffersen."

She heard several children, especially the younger ones, stumble over her name. Perhaps she would do well to shorten it for their sakes. The sooner the better.

Turning toward the flag in the front right corner of the classroom, she placed her hand over her heart, waited a second for her students to do the same, then began reciting the Pledge of Allegiance. It was immediately followed by the Lord's Prayer, all heads bowed and eyes closed.

As the "Amen" echoed around the room, Felicia told the children to be seated and then sat in her own chair. A quick glance confirmed that only two of the desks were unoccupied. That meant all nineteen of the students on the roster were present. It felt like a personal victory of sorts.

Thank You, God, that they all came. Help me to teach them well.

When she had completed taking the roll, Felicia rose to her feet once again and stepped to the side of her desk. "First of all, children, you have my permission to address me as Teacher or as Miss K." She smiled at the younger students. "Today I want to learn more about you, more about how you are faring with your studies. And because I'm new to Frenchman's Bluff, I want you to have an opportunity to get to know me as well. Much of what we cover today may seem simple and repetitive, but I hope it will prove helpful for all of us throughout this new school year." She turned toward the blackboard. "We'll begin with reading."

The Franklin dairy farm was located southwest of Frenchman's Bluff, an easy half-hour ride on horseback. Marcus Franklin had come west in the late 1860s. Failing to make his fortune panning for gold in the mountains of Idaho, he'd returned to the plains, bought land near the new township of Frenchman's Bluff, and started his farm with half a dozen cows and a field of spring wheat. Many years later, his son, Randall, inherited one of the largest dairy farms in the state.

When Colin arrived at the Franklin place that afternoon, he found Randall on the shady side of the barn, cutting a board set on a pair of sawhorses. The moment he recognized Colin, Randall set aside the saw and walked toward his guest, wiping his hands on his overalls.

"Come to see that little mare I told you about on Sunday?" he asked.

"Thought it wouldn't hurt to look. Charity's been wanting a horse of her own, and her birthday's coming up." Colin stepped down from the saddle and wrapped the buckskin's reins around a nearby hitching post.

"She'd be perfect for your girl." Randall motioned for Colin to join him. "She's around this way."

The two men walked around to the opposite side of the barn. In a corral by herself was a small dun-colored mare with a long-flowing black mane and tail. At their approach, the mare lifted her head to look at them, ears cocked forward.

"How old is she?" Colin slid the gate lock back and stepped into the corral.

Randall stepped onto the bottom rail of the fence. "Eight years."

The dun stood just shy of fourteen hands high, a good size for his daughter now and in the years to come. Colin ran his hand over the mare's withers and along the black stripe on her back. "How'd you come by her?"

"Took her in payment on a debt. But she's too small for my boys, and my wife's already got herself a good saddle horse. No point me keepin' her. Figured I'd give you first look before I put her up for sale to all comers."

"Appreciate it." Colin walked around the back of the horse, eyeing the well-developed muscles of the mare's hind quarters.

Randall stepped off the fence rail. "Let me get a halter, and you can see how she goes."

"Thanks." Colin moved to the mare's head and stared into her dark eyes. She nickered softly as he stroked the bridge of her nose.

Charity would like her. There was no doubt about that. His daughter was partial to buckskins and duns, probably because he was. So unless he discovered something unexpected, he would buy the mare for Charity.

Half an hour later, Colin was the new owner of the dun. To seal the deal, the two friends settled onto a couple of chairs on the farmhouse's front porch, with glasses of lemonade that Randall's wife brought to them on a tray.

"So you're taking the mare?" Ellen asked as she sat on a chair beside her husband.

Colin nodded. "Yep. She's mine now. But I'm leaving her here until Charity's birthday. I want it to be a surprise."

"Perfect. She'll be so excited."

"That she will."

"And we won't mention to the boys that you came to look at the mare. We don't want them spoiling the surprise by letting it slip at school."

"Thanks." He took a sip of lemonade. It was the perfect blend of sweet and tart. Holding up the glass, he said, "This is good, Ellen."

"Glad you like it." She smiled, then took a deep breath and released it. "Oh my. I never can get used to how quiet it is around here when the boys are in school. I hope Miss Kristoffersen is managing well."

Randall said, "It's the last year for R. J. After this one" — he shrugged — "we've got a farm to run, and he's old enough to learn what it means to run it. Not just help out."

"You and R. J. think he's ready to leave school." The smile left Ellen's face. "I'm not so sure. When Miss Kristoffersen visited us last week, she mentioned the possibility of college."

Colin felt the friction between husband and wife. He suspected they'd argued more than once over this topic. Better be on his way, just in case they were about to argue again. He drained his glass with several big gulps and rose to his feet. "I'd best get back to the store instead of lollygagging around here. Thanks for the lemonade, Ellen. Randall, I'll plan to bring Charity out after church on Sunday. I'll tell her we're coming for her birthday."

"Why don't you plan on Sunday dinner with us?" Ellen stood and took the empty glass from his hand. "I'll bake a cake, and we'll have a little celebration. I should have thought of it before."

"If it wouldn't be too much trouble. I wasn't wrangling for an invitation."

"I know you weren't." She laughed, the anger gone from her eyes. "Besides, you and Charity aren't any trouble. You're practically family. You know that."

Yes, he knew that. Without Randall and Ellen, he didn't know what would have happened to him and Charity after Margaret died. They were the rocks he'd leaned on throughout those dark days. They'd been his friends before. Afterward, they'd been so much more.

"Thanks, Ellen." He gave her shoulders a quick squeeze. "We'll plan on it, then."

Felicia stood on the landing outside the school entrance and watched as her students scattered in all directions. Most of them left on foot, but some rode away on horseback. The latter were the boys and girls who lived farthest from town.

She couldn't keep from smiling as she stood there, tired but happy. The first day had been, in her opinion, a complete success. She'd worried needlessly. She was going to get along famously with her students. Even Colin Murphy would be impressed if he could see her teach.

At the thought of her landlord, she tilted her chin in the air. He would have to eat his words to Kathleen. So help her, he would. Before this year was finished, he would be glad the school board had hired her to teach the children of Frenchman's Bluff.

She returned indoors. Starting next week, she would assign some cleanup tasks to various students. But today she wanted to do it herself. There was nothing quite like mundane chores, such as cleaning blackboards, to allow one's mind the freedom to be creative. And she wanted to be a creative teacher, one who made her students eager and excited to learn. Education could be so much more than memorization, recitation, and ciphering.

She would have little time to inspire her older students, such as Randall Franklin Jr., better known as R. J. A tall, good-looking boy of fifteen, R. J. had informed her on her visit to the Franklin home that this was his final year of formal schooling. He'd said it with pride, as if announcing he was a man, fully grown.

But he isn't a man. He's only fifteen. There's so much more I could teach him if he'll give me a chance.

Her thoughts shifted to the younger Franklin boy. Twelve-year-old Edward was a carbon copy of his older brother, although a good four inches shorter. But they had the same sand-colored hair, the same dark blue eyes, and the same cocky smile. Perhaps Edward had a dash more mischief in his nature. Would he be influenced by his brother's decision to forgo more education? She hoped not.

Kathleen Summerville's daughters, Suzanne and Phoebe, were likable children, almost as pretty as their mother. Suzanne was outgoing, however, while her younger sister was painfully shy. Felicia would need to do all she could to instill confidence in little Phoebe.

Certainly, Charity Murphy didn't suffer from shyness, nor was she in need of a boost in confidence. But she did struggle with her reading — far more than Felicia had expected, despite the girl's own admission on the day Felicia arrived. Both teacher and pupil would have to work hard to improve Charity's reading skills and bring up her grades.

Felicia continued through the list of her students until she'd made mental notes to herself on all nineteen of them. Then, done with her tidying, she took up her handbag and lesson books and left the schoolhouse.

It wasn't a long walk to her home — a little more than a block away — and the sidewalk on the south side of First Street was shaded by mature trees, their leaves rustling in a gentle breeze. She was almost to her destination when she saw Colin stop his horse in front of the stable that stood behind and to one side of the Murphy living quarters. He dismounted, his movements relaxed, at ease. As he began to loosen the cinch on the saddle, he glanced over his shoulder, and his gaze met with hers. He stopped and took half a step back, waiting for her to draw closer.

"Good day, Mr. Murphy."

"Miss Kristoffersen."

Her gaze shifted to the tall buckskin beside him. "What a beautiful horse."

He patted the gelding's neck, a silent acknowledgment of her praise. "I saw the Franklin boys on my way back to town. They seemed to think the first day in school went all right."

Felicia doubted that R. J. or Edward had volunteered the information. Colin must have asked — hoping, no doubt, that the boys would indicate she'd failed as a teacher. She stood a little taller. "Yes, it went well."

"I imagine Charity will tell me everything as soon as I get inside." He began to loosen the cinch again.

"Yes, I imagine she will." Should she bring up Charity's reading skills? No, not yet.

As he yanked the saddle and blanket off the horse's back, his biceps flexed beneath his rolled-up shirtsleeves. An odd sensation fluttered in the region of Felicia's heart. How strong he looked. How rugged. How—

For pity's sake!

He turned toward her, and somehow she managed to drag her gaze from his strong arms to his face. His handsome face. His—

What on earth is wrong with me?

Thankfully, he didn't seem to notice the confusion that roiled inside her. With a brief nod, he bid her good day and headed into the barn, allowing her to escape to her cottage, where she could examine these unusual feelings in private.

TEN

On Saturday, the one morning of the week when Felicia was not required to arise early, she awakened just as the sky outside her window turned from black to pewter. Even before she was fully conscious, she began making a list in her head of things she needed to accomplish before Monday morning.

Lesson plans for the coming week must be prepared. She would begin those immediately after breaking her fast.

In the afternoon, she would speak to Mr. Swanson about purchasing a large wall map. How was one to teach about America, other nations, history, or current affairs without a decent map of the world? The schoolroom didn't even have a globe. A shameful oversight.

There was also the matter of her limited wardrobe. Until she could purchase or make some new shirtwaists, she would have to do laundry more than once a week.

She sat up and lowered her legs over the side of the bed, pushing her unruly hair behind her shoulder.

Tomorrow was Charity Murphy's birthday. Would it be improper to give the girl a present of some sort? She couldn't afford to do so for all of her students, but then, none of the other students' fathers was her landlord. Before she could again picture

Colin, muscles bulging beneath rolled-up shirtsleeves—something she'd done too frequently these past few days—she determined she would *not* set a bad precedent. If she could not give gifts to all of her students, she would give none at all.

That settled, Felicia rose from the bed and made quick work of her morning ablutions. It wasn't long before she was dressed, her hair caught in a tidy bun at the nape. Breakfast was an even quicker affair. Coffee, a fried egg, and a slice of bread spread with orange marmalade—the last guilty pleasure for a single woman of limited means.

Several hours later, the breakfast dishes washed and put away, her lesson plans completed for the coming week, and her laundry now clean and hanging on the line, Felicia set off for Walter Swanson's place of business, the Idaho Drugstore. A tiny bell above the door—like the one in the mercantile—announced her arrival. A moment later, Mr. Swanson welcomed her with a hearty handshake.

"Miss Kristoffersen. How delightful to see you. I hope you haven't come to the pharmacy because you're ailing."

"I'm almost never ill, Mr. Swanson. No, I came to speak to you about something for the school."

The man cocked an eyebrow.

"We are in desperate need of maps of the world or, at the very least, a globe. The maps are more expensive, of course, but they are superior because of their size. Rand McNally has an excellent series of seven large-scale school maps that can be placed on a wall of the schoolroom and pulled down as needed."

"What's the cost?"

Felicia felt her cheeks grow warm. Why hadn't she thought to ascertain the exact amount before coming to see Mr. Swanson? In normal school, she'd been told the cost, but that had been too many years ago to say for sure. Well, she would have to hope the price hadn't changed much. "I believe not more than twenty-five dollars."

"Twenty-five dollars?" His tone made it sound as if it were a million.

She stood straighter. "It's an investment in the children of Frenchman's Bluff, Mr. Swanson. You cannot expect them to learn history and geography without maps of our nation and the world."

He shook his head slowly. "The school's managed without them 'til now."

Felicia fixed him with a determined gaze, refusing to give in on the matter.

The man sighed. "Well, I suppose you're right."

"Then I may order them?" She couldn't keep the note of excitement from her voice.

"Yes, Miss Kristoffersen. You may order them." He cleared his throat. "But spend no more than twenty-five dollars without speaking to me."

"Naturally. I won't spend a penny more without clearing it with you first."

She bid him a hasty goodbye and left the drugstore. She decided to go straight to the mercantile and place her order, before Walter Swanson could determine the purchase was too expensive. Which was nonsense; it was quite reasonable. Besides, with the low salary they paid her, they could certainly afford to spend a little more on the children.

She felt a check in her spirit. My, her thoughts had turned peevish. When she'd accepted the town's offer of employment, she'd been thankful for the salary. As she should be. God had provided for her. Things could have been so much worse for her after the death of the Kristoffersens.

She drew in a slow breath and let it out, whispering, "Yet I will rejoice in the Lord, I will joy in the God of my salvation."

There. That was better. So much better to be grateful than to complain. So much better to look to the Lord than to her own frustrations.

"Talking to yourself, Felicia?"

She looked behind her, recognizing Kathleen's voice. With a laugh, she answered, "I do that on occasion. Either to myself or to God."

"Where are you off to?"

"Murphy's Mercantile. I need to order maps for the school."

"I'm headed that way myself." Kathleen held up her basket, as if for proof. "Mind if I walk with you?"

"Of course not. I'd enjoy the company."

They fell into step beside each other.

After a brief silence, Kathleen said, "I want you to know how happy you've made Phoebe. She was always nervous around Miss Lucas, who could be rather sharp at times. But not you. You put her at ease."

"That's good. I would hate to frighten any of my students."

"What about you? Are you afraid of any of *them*?" Her tone was teasing.

Felicia laughed again. "Maybe a little."

Kathleen tipped her head slightly to one side as she looked at Felicia. "I'm not sure I believe you. I suspect you're fearless."

"Me? Not hardly."

"My husband always said the definition of courage is to be afraid and to proceed anyway." Kathleen smiled. "So if you aren't fearless, then you are certainly courageous."

Felicia felt a surge of affection for the woman walking beside her, and again she thanked God, this time silently. For she had wanted a friend, and the Lord had provided one for her.

Jimmy Bryant leaned over the desk, his mouth skewed to one side, a pen in his right hand.

"Make sure to order the copper kettle Mrs. Reynolds requested," Colin told him from the doorway.

"Yessir. Already on the list."

"We'll need more flour, sugar, and coffee too."

Jimmy nodded.

The sound of a customer entering the store drew Colin around.

Felicia walked toward him down the narrow aisle, a sense of purpose in her step. "Good day, Mr. Murphy."

"Miss Kristoffersen." Only then did he see that Kathleen had followed Felicia into the store. "Hello, Mrs. Summerville."

"Mr. Murphy."

"What can I do for you ladies?"

Felicia answered him, "I'm in need of an item for the school. Something you'll have to order, no doubt."

"And what would that be?" He moved toward the counter.

"A series of large maps. Wall maps."

"Yes, those would have to be ordered." He looked over his shoulder toward the office. "Jimmy, come out here, will you? And bring the catalog with you."

"Yessir."

Colin returned his gaze to Felicia. "Is this to be billed to the school?"

"Yes."

"I assume you obtained permission from Mr. Swanson for the purchase?"

Her cheeks turned pink. "Of course. I came here straight from the pharmacy." She lifted her chin, an indignant spark in her eyes. "You may ask him yourself if you choose."

He hadn't meant to insult her, but it looked as if he had. And he was almost glad he had. The heightened color in her face was quite attractive.

Jimmy arrived with the thick catalog in his hands.

"Look up maps," he told his clerk.

The boy placed the book on the counter and opened it to the back, running his finger down the columns of words until he found what he wanted. Then he flipped through the pages to the desired one. Colin glanced at the book, noting the illustrations of world globes, books on stands, and what appeared to be wall maps. He took the catalog from Jimmy and turned it toward Felicia.

"Is this what you want?" he asked, pointing at the illustration.

She plucked her new pair of reading glasses from her pocket and set them on her nose as she leaned toward the catalog. "Yes. That's exactly what we need." Her gaze followed her finger across the page. "And the cost?" Then she straightened, smiling, her earlier irritation forgotten. "Twenty-three eighty for all seven. Perfect."

She should have looked prim and spinsterish with those glasses perched on her nose, but she didn't. Not at all. Not with that smile making her eyes sparkle.

"How long before I can expect delivery, Mr. Murphy?"

He resisted the urge to clear his throat. "Next week, more than likely."

She removed the glasses and slipped them back into her pocket. "I suppose the wait can't be helped. If the school has managed without maps for this long, another week or so won't make a difference. I shall simply concentrate on other subjects than history until they arrive."

"History is Charity's favorite subject."

"I know. She told me the day I arrived in town."

"That's right." He nodded, wondering at his reason for drawing out the conversation unnecessarily. "I remember now. She wanted you to quiz her."

"I'm glad she's enthusiastic about history. I would hate for her to grow to dislike school." She paused and then added softly, "Charity *is* behind other students her age in reading. And arithmetic as well."

This wasn't news to Colin, of course. Miss Lucas had told him the same thing more than once. In fact, the former teacher had gone so far as to suggest Charity wasn't capable of learning to read well.

"Best be sure she acquires good homemaking skills, Mr. Murphy," the woman had said. *"You know, sewing and knitting and such. She'll never be a scholar. Not that it matters. Unless she never marries, education will be wasted on her. And since she isn't unattractive—"*

Felicia's voice broke into his memory. "I don't want you to worry, Mr. Murphy. Charity is a bright child. I'll find a way to improve her reading and arithmetic skills. I promise you that."

Miss Lucas hadn't thought Charity bright. She'd thought education was wasted on her. And Colin had accepted the opinion as fact, having no way to dispute it. But if Felicia was right?

He felt a spark of hope spring to life in his heart—and a surprising affection for the woman standing opposite him.

Kathleen liked Felicia, but she wasn't sure the schoolteacher was right about Charity Murphy. After all, Kathleen had helped with the teaching duties after Miss Lucas married and moved away. She'd personally worked with Charity on her reading. It had been a frustrating exercise for them both. Phoebe, who was the younger by two years, read almost as well as Charity. Maybe even better.

But Kathleen was wise enough to keep her thoughts to herself, especially when she saw the look that crossed Colin's face. He doted on his daughter. Too much, according to Mother Summerville, who thought Charity spoiled and unruly.

Kathleen didn't agree with her mother-in-law completely. Yes, Charity was tomboyish and undoubtedly would benefit from a woman in the home, but Kathleen would never criticize the way Colin raised his child. Besides, Charity was happy and carefree and bighearted. How many mistakes could he have made? Not many. Probably fewer than Kathleen had made with her own daughters.

Colin turned to look at her. "And what can I help you with, Mrs. Summerville?"

For a moment, she couldn't answer. She'd almost forgotten what had brought her to the mercantile beyond accompanying Felicia. Oh yes. Needles and thread and a pound of sugar.

"I can find what I need," she answered him at last. "Thank you."

She moved down the aisle toward the dry goods, the voice of Mother Summerville whispering in her head. *It wouldn't hurt you to let him wait on you, Kathleen. Instead, you left him at the counter with Miss Kristoffersen. How do you ever hope to win his attention if you make no effort?*

Her thoughts drifted back in time to when she'd first met Harold. He'd been a student, and she'd been visiting a cousin in the same town. The moment they were introduced, her heart had been lost to him. She hadn't worked to win his affections or his attentions. She hadn't planned and schemed. She'd simply loved.

But things were different when one was a girl of nineteen than they were when one was a widow of thirty and the mother of two. And if she didn't want to go on living in her in-laws' home and depending on them for everything, including the money to buy a few needles and some thread, she would have to do whatever was necessary to get herself another husband.

Dropping a packet of needles into her shopping basket, she looked toward the counter in time to see Felicia bid Colin a good day, then turn to leave the store. When their gazes met, Felicia waved her fingers. "See you in church tomorrow, Kathleen."

"Yes." She returned the small wave.

"Are you sure you don't need any help, Mrs. Summerville?" Colin asked, his attention returning to her.

Grabbing a couple of spools of thread, she replied, "I'm sure." She walked toward the counter. "The only other item I need is a pound or two of sugar."

"Jimmy, can you help Mrs. Summerville with the last of her order? I need to check something in the stockroom."

"Sure thing, Mr. Murphy."

Colin gave Kathleen a distracted glance before disappearing through the doorway into the back room.

I might as well be invisible for all he notices me. She drew a deep breath and let it out on a sigh. *At this rate, I'll live with Mother Summerville until I'm a hundred.*

Returning home, Felicia removed her straw hat and left it on the kitchen table. Then she took a basket outside and removed the clean laundry from the clothesline. Before she went to bed, she would have to iron her clothes for Sunday, but she would wait for the day to cool before she heated the iron on the stove.

"Hi, Miss K."

Felicia glanced over her shoulder as she removed the last shirtwaist from the line. "Hello, Charity."

Perhaps that morning the girl's long hair had been tidy,

captured at the nape, but now most of it had pulled free from the ribbon. It hung in loose curls over her shoulders and down her back. Her cheeks and the skirt of her dress were smudged with dirt.

"What have you been up to?" Felicia asked, smiling.

"Tommy Bryant's dog Goldie was missing, so I helped look for her."

"And were you successful?"

"Yes'm. We found her and her new puppies too."

"Puppies?"

Charity nodded. "Twelve of 'em."

"Gracious. Twelve puppies. That's a large litter."

"That's what Mrs. Bryant said. Tommy wanted to keep 'em in his room, but his mother said dogs don't belong in the house. I don't see why not. Do you?"

Britta Kristoffersen hadn't allowed any pets, let alone any pets in the house, but Felicia liked to think her real mother would have allowed it, had they had the money to feed an extra mouth.

Sadness pulled at her heart.

"Something wrong, Miss K?"

She forced another smile. "No, Charity. Nothing's wrong. I was remembering something from my childhood."

"Want me to carry that basket inside for you?"

Felicia's sadness disappeared like a vapor, and she laughed. "You, Charity Murphy, are an amazing child."

The girl cocked her head to one side, obviously wondering why her teacher had said such a thing.

"I've never known anyone—child or adult—so quick to help others as you've been to help me."

Charity grinned. "That's 'cause I knew I was gonna like you right from the start. Even before you got here. Don't know why. Just knew I would. And I want you to like me too."

"I do like you, Charity. Very much. I like all of my students."

"And do you like Frenchman's Bluff?"

"Yes, I do."

"Good. Then you're gonna stay. Papa said if you didn't like it here, you'd wanna leave and not be the teacher anymore."

"Well, I do like it, so neither you nor your father need be concerned about that." She picked up the clothes basket, balancing it on her hip, and started toward the door to her cottage.

Charity followed. "I'm gonna ask Papa if I can have one of Goldie's puppies. He told me I could have a dog when I was old enough to take care of it on my own. Nine's old enough for that. Don't you think, Miss K? I'm gonna be nine tomorrow. That oughta be old enough to take care of a dog. Don't you think?"

Felicia set the basket on the kitchen table, once again refraining from comment.

"Maybe you can get one of the puppies too." Charity flopped onto a chair. "I bet Mrs. Bryant would let you have one if you asked her."

"I'm sure she would." No doubt Mrs. Bryant was eager to find new homes as quickly as possible for Goldie's entire litter.

"We're going to the Franklins' tomorrow after church." Charity leaned her elbows on the table and rested her chin on her knuckles. "Mrs. Franklin's making me a cake for my birthday. She makes really good cakes. I hope she makes mine chocolate. That's my favorite. What's your favorite?"

"Lemon."

The girl's nose wrinkled. "Lemon? You mean like lemonade?"

"Mmm." Felicia sat on a chair opposite Charity. "Maybe it's my favorite because I couldn't have it very often. Lemons were a rare treat when I was your age."

The girl's gaze roamed from the kitchen to the small sitting room. All of a sudden — presumably when she saw the time on the clock in the parlor — she hopped up from the chair. "Gotta go! I was supposed to be home before now." She dashed out of the cottage as fast as her legs could carry her.

Felicia leaned back, a smile once again slipping into place. That child was a delight. It was going to be terribly hard not to make a favorite of her.

ELEVEN

Ellen Franklin lifted the crumb-scattered plate from the table. "And here I thought there might be some cake left over for you to take home." She shook her head. "Silly to think so, considering my boys."

"Just as well. It would've been too much temptation." Colin patted his stomach. "Best chocolate cake I've ever eaten."

"Thanks." She carried the plate into the kitchen. When she returned, she had a package in her hands. "Happy birthday, Charity."

His daughter's eyes lit with excitement. "Thank you, Mrs. Franklin." She took the package, wrapped in plain brown paper and tied with string. "You didn't have to do nothin' more than the cake."

"Maybe not, but I wanted to." Ellen sat on her chair again. "Go on. Open it."

A few seconds later, the string was untied and the paper folded back to reveal the gift inside.

"A book." Charity's voice was soft, but her disappointment was obvious all the same.

Colin felt like scolding her but managed to hold his tongue. But when they got home, they would discuss the matter at length.

Ellen said, "It's *Alice's Adventures in Wonderland* by Lewis Carroll. I can't tell you how many times I've read it since I was a girl. It's a wonderful story."

Charity glanced at her father, then turned her eyes on their hostess. "Thank you, Mrs. Franklin. Mr. Franklin."

"You're very welcome." Ellen leaned forward and patted the cover of the book. "Maybe you'll come over sometime and we can read the book together. My boys were never as taken by Alice as I am, but I'm sure you'll love her."

Colin's irritation with his daughter turned to empathy. He knew she was ashamed because she couldn't read as well as her friends. Miss Lucas had said she needed to try harder, to apply herself to the task with more diligence, to stop daydreaming, stop talking, and make herself read. The schoolmistress had told Charity she would never excel in her studies as long as she was lazy. But Colin didn't believe his daughter was lazy.

He rose from his chair. "Charity, come with me."

The last traces of excitement drained from her face. He hadn't meant to do that to her, hadn't meant to make her think she was in trouble.

He put his hand on her shoulder. "This won't take long."

Eyes locked on the floor, shoulders slumped, expression dejected, Charity fell into step beside him. Once they were outside, she said, "I didn't mean to sound like I didn't like the book, Papa. Honest, I didn't."

"I know." *If I was a better pa, you'd probably read better.*

They walked across the yard toward the barn, but before they reached the entrance, an idea occurred to him. He steered them to the left, stopping just before the corral came into view. Then he lifted his daughter into his arms.

"Tell you what." He resumed his walk. "You read two pages in that new book of yours every night before bed, and I'll do something for you in return."

Suspicion replaced dejection in her dark brown eyes. "What?"

He stopped, set her feet on the ground, and turned her toward the corral where the dun mare stood, a bright blue ribbon — courtesy of the Franklins — tied around her neck. "Well, how about I give you your own horse."

Charity seemed momentarily frozen in place, her mouth agape.

"Happy birthday, pumpkin."

She let out an ear-piercing squeal of excitement that probably carried for miles. The mare tossed her head and moved to the farthest part of the corral.

"She's mine?" Charity looked up at him. "She's really *mine*?"

"She's yours. That means you have to feed and water her and brush her and take care of her every day. No exceptions."

"I will! I will!" She jumped up, throwing her arms around his neck. "Oh, Papa! Thank you! Thank you! This is even better than one of Goldie's pups."

He barely had time to return her hug before she was out of his arms and rushing to the corral, slipping through the bottom two rails.

"What's her name?" she called back to him.

"That's up to you." He strode to the corral, opened the gate, and entered. "You could call her Alice, like in the book Mrs. Franklin gave you."

"Don't be silly, Papa. She doesn't look like an Alice."

Although he couldn't see her face, Colin was fairly certain she rolled her eyes.

"She looks more like a ... a princess. That's what I'll call her. Princess."

Colin loved his daughter more than he could express with

words, but she often puzzled him. Charity liked to ride horses and climb trees and go fishing and play baseball. She wasn't afraid to get dirty and could hold her own with most of the boys at school. But she also liked to dress up and put ribbons in her hair ... and pretend a horse looked like a princess.

"Hello, girl. Hello, Princess." Charity held out her hand, palm up, and began moving toward the mare. "Aren't you a pretty girl. You're mine now. Did you know that? We're gonna have the best times together. Just you wait and see if we don't."

Colin grinned. His daughter was fearless around horses. She'd been that way even as a toddler. He used to put her in the saddle in front of him and take her for long rides. He'd planned to buy a pony for her third birthday, but then her mother got sick, and ponies and most everything else had been forgotten. Many other things had been forgotten too in the months, and years, that followed Margaret's death.

He watched Charity stroke the mare's head and neck. *I shouldn't have waited so long to get her a horse of her own.*

He'd become overly protective of his daughter after her mother died. He'd tried to control where she was and what she was doing every minute of the day. He'd tried to make certain she was never in any danger, that there was no chance of her getting hurt. If she so much as sneezed, he'd put her to bed and sent for the doctor.

But a year or so ago, Ellen had taken him aside and told him he had to stop, that he had to allow Charity to be herself, to be a child, to play and fall and skin her knees. Ellen had been right, of course. He'd known that, although he hadn't wanted to admit it immediately. It hadn't been easy, but he'd begun to change after that. He'd started to loosen his tight grip on his daughter.

Not that there weren't times when he fell back into those old habits. But for the most part, he'd succeeded. Now if only he could succeed in making Charity a better student so she didn't grow up to be like him.

◎

George and Helen Summerville, Kathleen's in-laws, owned the largest house in Frenchman's Bluff, and it was apparent to Felicia from the moment she stepped through the front door that they were likely the wealthiest citizens in town as well. It was apparent in the elegant draperies at the windows and the upholstered furniture that filled each room and the ornate rugs that covered the floors and the oil paintings that hung on the walls. Even the small statues, framed portraits, and varied knickknacks that filled nearly every flat surface—the mantelpiece, the piano, the side tables—spoke of money and influence.

Felicia was not the only guest invited to dine with the Summervilles that Sunday afternoon. Walter Swanson was there, along with Reverend Benjamin Hightower and his wife, Nancy.

It was a pleasant company, and the conversation around the dining room table was lively and enjoyable. All the same, Felicia felt uncomfortable. She had the distinct feeling her hostess didn't care for her. Helen Summerville's gaze, when turned upon her, seemed cool and condescending, which resulted in Felicia saying little and thus avoiding the woman's attention.

As the party rose from the dining room table at the end of the meal and retired to the parlor, Kathleen's oldest daughter tugged on Felicia's hand. "Miss K?"

"Yes, Suzanne."

"Did you know today's Charity's birthday?"

"Yes. I knew."

"Now we're the same age. Nine."

"Nine is a good age to be."

"Grandmother asked Charity and her father to come to dinner today, but they already were planning to go eat with the Franklins. So then she asked you."

"Suzanne!" Helen Summerville spoke in a whisper, but the note of displeasure could not be missed.

The girl glanced over her shoulder at her grandmother, then turned and went to stand before her. Felicia moved on with the others but still heard Helen telling Suzanne to please remember it was no one else's business who had been invited to dine with them.

No one's business, or just not mine?

Kathleen slipped her hand in the crook of Felicia's arm and drew her toward the parlor sofa. "I'm so glad you joined us today, Felicia."

"I appreciated the invitation."

Kathleen lowered her voice. "Mother Summerville always waits until Sunday morning to invite friends and neighbors to dinner. She says she wants the Spirit to move her." She smiled briefly. "I don't believe anyone has ever turned down her invitation until Colin ... until Mr. Murphy did so today. That's why she's out of sorts."

"Did you hear that, Miss Kristoffersen?" Walter Swanson interrupted.

As she sat on the sofa beside Kathleen, Felicia turned her attention toward him. "No, I'm sorry. I didn't."

Walter looked at Nancy Hightower. "Go on. Tell Miss Kristoffersen."

The reverend's wife seemed happy to oblige. "I was just telling Mr. Swanson that you'll have some new students in your classroom this week. Lewis and Jane Carpenter have brought home two orphan boys from New York. They arrived in Boise City yesterday by train."

For an instant, Felicia recalled her brother and sister and nearly two dozen other children as they sat in a railcar, dust and smoke blowing in the open windows as the train sped westward from Chicago. She felt again the fear of the unknown and the grief over her mother's death.

"My heart breaks for the Carpenters. They've buried five infant sons over the years. I suppose this is their only way of having a family now."

"Dear," Benjamin Hightower said softly, "we mustn't gossip."

His wife's eyes widened. "I wasn't gossiping, Ben. I was merely explaining to Miss Kristoffersen why Jane and Lewis have taken these boys into their home."

As if it were yesterday, Felicia remembered when the Kristoffersens had taken her home from the grange hall in Laramie. She no longer believed they'd wanted a daughter so much as they'd needed a housekeeper. It might have been worse, she supposed. They might have beaten her or abused her. In some ways, she almost wished they had. If they'd been cruel, she might have tried to leave. She might have run away. Instead, she'd lived in a house where emotions were never expressed, where love and anger and joy and sorrow didn't exist.

Please, God. Let the Carpenters be kind to those boys. Let them love them. She drew in a breath. *And if I can be of help, show me how.*

Colin couldn't recall a time when he'd seen a brighter smile on his daughter's face as the one she wore during their ride home that Sunday, Colin mounted on his buckskin gelding, Charity riding Princess, the dun mare. Most of the journey passed in silence, broken only by Charity's occasional questions: "Isn't she the prettiest horse ever?" "Do you think she likes carrots?" "Can I ride her to school tomorrow?"

The latter question caused him to laugh. "Ride her to school? We're hardly more than a stone's throw away."

"I know, Papa. But I want to show her to my friends."

"Maybe you'd better bring your friends home after school and let them see her in the stable."

"But Papa—"

"Charity."

His single word of warning caused her to swallow the rest of her protest, and he was glad. The day was ending too perfectly to spoil it now with a reprimand.

When they crested a rise in the road and Frenchman's Bluff came into view, he said, "Shall we canter the rest of the way home?"

"Yes." She kicked Princess's sides, and the mare jumped forward. Charity's laughter sailed back to him on the breeze.

He grinned. "Let's go, boy." The buckskin responded to the nudge of his boots, and in moments, they'd caught up with Charity and the dun. "Not too fast," he called to her.

What his daughter wanted was to let her horse break into an all-out gallop. He could tell that by the set of her mouth and the madcap look in her eyes. But she wisely chose to obey him, keeping the mare at a canter until they arrived at the edge of Frenchman's Bluff, where, in unison, they drew their horses to a walk.

"That was fun, Papa."

He grinned.

"I bet Princess could've beat Drifter if you didn't make us slow down."

"Not likely."

"She's small but she's fast. Faster than you think, I bet."

"Hmm."

"Can we go for another ride tomorrow?"

"We'll see."

They rode up to the small barn behind the mercantile living quarters and reined in. Colin dismounted first and looped the reins around the hitching post. Charity followed suit a moment later.

"I'll get a couple of brushes," she said and rushed into the stable.

Colin released a chuckle as he loosened the cinch. It had been a good day.

"Hi, Miss K! Come see what Papa gave me for my birthday. My own horse!"

He straightened and looked over the gelding's back. Felicia Kristoffersen seemed to have been about to enter the cottage, her hand holding the screen door partway open. But at Charity's invitation, she let it swing closed.

She wore the same dress he'd seen her in that morning at church, and he suspected she was only now returning from the Summerville home. Helen Summerville's Sunday dinners were elaborate and lengthy affairs, at least by the standards of most Sunday dinners in Frenchman's Bluff.

Charity ran to meet her teacher halfway, then took her by the hand and dragged her over to where her father stood with the two horses.

"Look! Isn't she pretty? I named her Princess. Doesn't she look like a princess to you? Her mane and tail are so long. That's why I think she looks like a princess. Papa thought I should call her Alice. Like in the book *Alice's Adventures in Wonderland*. That's what Mrs. Franklin gave me for my birthday. That book. Papa says I'm to read two pages of it every day. Do you think I can? It looks kinda hard to me, but Mrs. Franklin says it's her favorite book of all."

Felicia's gaze met with Colin's across the gelding's back, and a moment later, she smiled. As if to say, *Yes, she's a chatterbox, but I enjoy listening to her.* Colin couldn't help but return the smile.

"I don't think *Alice's Adventures in Wonderland* will be too hard for you," Felicia said to Charity. "But if it is, we'll work on it in school. All right?"

"I guess. Would you like to ride Princess sometime, Miss K? Do you know how to ride a horse? If you don't, I could teach you."

"I *do* know how to ride. I lived on a farm from the time I was ten until I came here. When I was not much older than you, I rode a big gray horse to and from school. I called him Soot."

"Soot. I like that. It's a good name for a horse. What kind of farm was it? Did you have milk cows, like the Franklins?"

"No. The Kristoffersens mostly raised wheat and barley."

The Kristoffersens. An odd way to refer to her parents, Colin thought, and it made him wonder about her family. There were many things he didn't know about the new schoolteacher, things he hadn't cared to know when he was still convinced she'd come to their town only to find a husband, like the teachers before her. He wasn't at all sure about that now.

Charity interrupted his musings. "I've gotta get Princess unsaddled and give her a good brushing. She's my responsibility to take care of. Isn't she, Papa?"

"Yes, she's your responsibility," he answered without looking away from Felicia.

"I'm sure you'll take very good care of your horse, Charity," Felicia said.

"I sure will." Grinning, the girl headed inside the barn.

Felicia looked up. "A horse is a wonderful gift, Mr. Murphy. She's a lucky girl."

Something strange blossomed inside of him in that instant. A feeling that had lain dormant for so long he couldn't put a name to it at first — attraction. And then when he could — attraction? — he had to reject the notion. Impossible! He wasn't attracted to this woman. He couldn't be. Given his primary reason for not wanting the school board to hire her, allowing attraction to grow between them was the last thing he wanted.

"I had better go inside," she said, her relaxed demeanor telling him she was unaware of where his thoughts had taken him.

Thank goodness for that.

She patted Princess on the neck. "Tell Charity happy birthday for me again." Then she turned and walked toward her cottage, a delightful feminine sway in her hips.

Colin felt his mouth go dry and found it impossible to look away until she disappeared inside.

TWELVE

Kathleen stood in the front parlor, staring out the window at the beautiful morning. In two or three more months, the peaks of the Owyhee Mountains, a good sixty miles to the south, would be white with snow. But for now, the skies were a gorgeous blue, and the sun still blessed the earth with warmth.

Voices drifted to her from the back of the house. Mother Summerville was giving Mrs. Hasting, the cook, the menus for the week. It happened at this time every Monday morning. Her mother-in-law was a woman who believed in schedules and routines. She was also a woman who lacked tact when it came to dealing with the household staff.

Mrs. Hasting would be in a foul mood the rest of the day.

Kathleen sighed as she moved away from the window and settled onto the piano bench. She brushed the ivory keys with her fingertips, and in her memory, she heard Harold playing for her and singing at the top of his lungs, *"Ta-Ra-Ra Boom-De-Ay!"* A smile came to her lips. Oh, how she'd loved those special times they'd shared.

His mother, however, had hated it whenever she heard him play such, as she put it, disgusting music. She hadn't raised him to enjoy the tunes of the lower classes.

But I adored it, Harry. I wish I could hear you sing it one more time.

Mother Summerville's crisp footsteps in the hallway gave Kathleen a brief warning before she appeared in the doorway. "Ah. There you are." Her mother-in-law stopped, her hands folded beneath her ample bosom. There was a spark of annoyance in her eyes, left over from her encounter with Mrs. Hasting, no doubt.

"I'm sorry, Mother Summerville. I didn't hear you call."

"I didn't call," she snapped. "But I did need to speak with you."

Kathleen rose from the bench. "You look upset."

"I suppose I am."

"With me?"

Her mother-in-law's eyes narrowed. "As a matter of fact, yes."

Kathleen said nothing, knowing she would learn the cause quickly enough.

"You're getting much too friendly with Miss Kristoffersen. You know how I feel about her. You know I don't believe she was the right choice for the position. We will be well rid of her when others realize their mistake, and I don't think it wise for you to align yourself with her."

You're being unfair. You're unkind and vengeful. I like Felicia.

"Hasn't it occurred to you that she's both attractive and single? She could end your hopes of marrying Mr. Murphy."

"My hopes," Kathleen whispered, too softly for her mother-in-law to hear. Were they her hopes or did they belong to Mother Summerville alone?

"You must be aware that you aren't a fresh-faced young debutante, Kathleen."

She didn't want the words to sting, but they did.

Mother Summerville pointed an index finger at her. "Mark my words. You'd best do something about this before it's too late."

Exactly what would you have me do?

As if she'd heard Kathleen's silent question, Mother Summerville released an exasperated sigh. Then she turned and disappeared down the hallway.

Kathleen sank onto the piano bench once again, tears welling in her eyes. Oh, how she wished she had a home of her own, a place for her and her daughters. How she wished she wasn't beholden to Mother Summerville for every little thing. And how she wished she could fall in love again. Not just to marry and have a home of her own, but to fall in love.

She couldn't help wishing for that most of all.

◌

"Ā, as in *ate*. Â, as in *care*."

Felicia softly read aloud with her younger students, who were seated on the recitation bench.

"Ä, as in *arm*. Å, as in *last*."

She noticed that Charity's eyes often went to the children to her right or left rather than staying focused on the book in her hands. It was easy to see that rather than reading the text, she was repeating a half second later what she heard her neighbors saying.

Felicia stepped off the platform and walked slowly down the narrow space behind the bench. When she reached Charity, she briefly touched her shoulder. The girl glanced up.

Read, Felicia mouthed.

Charity dipped her head.

"Ē, as in *eve*. É, as in *err*."

Felicia continued on, but her thoughts remained with Charity. The girl shouldn't be struggling this hard with the table of vocals in her reader. The exercises should be old hat to her by now. Assuming, of course, that Miss Lucas made use of them, and she believed she had. Otherwise, the other students wouldn't be performing so well.

"ŌŌ, as in *fool*."

The children reached the end of the table of vocals at the same moment that Felicia arrived at the end of the bench. She turned and said, "Phoebe, please read to us the short sounds at the top of page eight."

The girl stood and read the requested portion without making a single mistake.

"Very good, Phoebe. Thank you."

As she walked slowly toward the head of the classroom, this time in front of the students on the recitation bench, Felicia called on the boy seated beside Phoebe to read the next part of the lesson. He did so with equal ease.

Four students later, it was Charity's turn. The look on her face as she rose to her feet almost broke Felicia's heart. She stumbled over the words in the first half of the table of substitutes. It was as if she'd never seen them before. And with each mistake she made, her face grew more flushed, her expression more downcast.

So unlike the confident, vivacious girl Felicia had come to know outside of school.

"Thank you, Charity."

Charity resumed her seat.

Felicia stepped onto the platform and turned to face the class. Clapping her hands, she said, "Boys and girls, we'll take our recess now. Please rise and file out in your usual order."

Books closed. Papers rustled. Pencils clattered. But the children were quiet, except for a few whispers, until they reached the door of the school. Then the shouts began; it sounded as if the boys were choosing sides for a quick game of baseball.

Felicia sat at her desk, her thoughts churning as she stared down at the exercises in the reader. What was she to do about Charity? Of all the students to be struggling, why did it have to be her?

"Miss Kristoffersen?"

She looked up.

A woman stood at the entrance to the classroom, two boys right behind her. "I don't know if you remember me. I'm Jane Carpenter. We met at the church picnic."

Felicia rose from her chair. "Of course I remember."

"I apologize for not being here at the start of school." She glanced over her shoulder. "Go along, boys." She motioned for them to step in front of her, then the three of them approached Felicia. When they stopped, Jane Carpenter made the rest of her introductions. "This is Daniel and this is Keith. Daniel and Keith Watkins."

"How do you do?" Felicia said, making eye contact with both of the boys. "My students call me Miss K."

Neither of them responded.

Jane said, "The boys have come to live with me and my husband and will be attending your school from here on out."

"I'm delighted to have you in my class." Felicia looked at the taller of the two. "How old are you, Daniel?"

"Twelve."

He reminded Felicia of her brother, Hugh. Dark eyes, wise beyond his years. A stubbornness in his chin and in his stance. Perhaps a touch of defiance as well. "And how old are you?" she asked Keith.

"Ten."

Her heart went out to him. Ten. The same age she'd been when the Kristoffersens took her in. She wondered what tragedy had put these boys on a train in New York, sending them far from the life they'd known. Would Jane Carpenter love them as sons? Would

Lewis Carpenter be stern or gentle with them? Would other children in school tease them because they were orphans?

She gave her head a mental shake. "Daniel, why don't you take a seat over there?" She pointed to a desk in the first row as she stepped off the platform. "And Keith, you can use this desk." She touched the back of a nearby chair.

Jane waited until the boys had taken their assigned places. Then she asked, "What time will they be dismissed?"

"Four o'clock."

"I'll come for them then. They don't know where my shop is yet. I apologize again for not having them here at the start of school. They'll be on time in the morning. I promise you that."

"It's perfectly all right, Mrs. Carpenter."

Jane glanced from one boy to the other, then back at Felicia. "I trust they'll be well behaved."

"I'm sure they will be." Felicia smiled, hoping her confidence would ease the other woman's fears.

The ploy seemed to work, for Jane returned the smile before turning and leaving the classroom.

"Well," — she looked from one brother to the other — "can you tell me a little about yourself? Daniel, you first."

"Not much to tell."

"How about where you lived before you came to Idaho?"

"Me and my brother lived in an orphanage in New York, and that's where they should've left us. We never asked to come here. We hate it." Anger laced his words.

Felicia feared she would have trouble with this boy. Should she tell him she too had come west for placement? That she understood what it was like to be an orphan. No. At least not yet. His resentment was too fresh.

She turned toward the younger boy. "How about you, Keith? Can you share something with me?"

Tears glimmered in his eyes, and his chin trembled.

She gave him a gentle smile. "That's all right. Perhaps another time." Glancing at her watch, she added, "Recess is almost over anyway. We'll become better acquainted as time goes by."

Colin watched as Lewis Carpenter flipped through the catalog on the mercantile counter. Lewis was a strong man, tall and broad shouldered, his neck and arms thick, like a lumberjack. But his nature was gentle, his voice soft-spoken. Margaret had once said Lewis had the soul of a poet. Like Colin, he hadn't gone far in school. Unlike Colin, he loved to read. Rarely did he come into the store that he didn't peruse the selection of books available before buying more practical items.

Today he was in need of a couple of mattresses and a large bureau for the boys he and his wife had taken into their home. "Here's what the missus wants." He pointed at the catalog.

Colin made a mental note of the selection.

Lewis let the catalog fall closed as he straightened. "Should have done this sooner. The minute we learned they'd be bringing those kids as far as Idaho for placing out, I should have given you my order." He drew a deep breath and released it, shoulders rising and falling. "I guess I was afraid it would end in disappointment, and I didn't want Jane to get her hopes up. Or mine either."

"I reckon you two've got a right not to want to get your hopes up, Lewis."

The man shook his head. "I reckon not. The Good Book says, 'For I know the thoughts that I think toward you, saith the Lord, thoughts of peace, and not of evil, to give you an expected end.' I shoulda trusted He'd bring it about. After all, 'All things work together for good to them that love God, to them who are the called according to his purpose.'"

That was another thing about Lewis Carpenter. He could quote the Scriptures better than most preachers. And he didn't just quote them. He believed them. Lived them. Breathed them. Colin had to admire him for it, too. He couldn't say the same for himself. His faith, never very strong, had been shaken by the loss of his wife. Lewis's faith had seemed to grow stronger each time he'd buried an infant son.

"Jane was nervous as a cat near a rocking chair this morning." A grin spread across Lewis's face. "She wasn't happy with what the boys had to wear to school, and it took her longer to get them fed and ready to go than she thought it would. Never saw her get so flustered. But in a good way. Know what I mean?"

Yes, he knew what Lewis meant, and a sting of envy shot through him, catching him by surprise. For five years, he'd thought being a widower suited him. He'd been content to raise his daughter without anyone by his side. Many a man married two or three times, taking new wives to help raise the children of the wives who'd died before. Colin thought it better to leave things be.

But maybe he was wrong about that. Maybe he could use a partner, someone to share the burdens of day-to-day life. If he wanted, he could have a new wife within a short period of time. He need only ask Kathleen Summerville. She was willing. He knew that. It even made good sense.

"Not sure how much formal schoolin' the boys've had," Lewis continued. "I'd wager not much. Near as we can tell, they were on their own for about two years before they ended up in an orphanage. But if our new schoolteacher's worth her salt, she ought to be able to — "

Lewis kept talking, but Colin no longer listened, his thoughts having turned to Felicia. He pictured her standing at the front of her class, her hair captured in a bun at the nape, a pair of reading glasses perched on her long, narrow nose. Had he really expected the glasses would make her look prim? Because they sure didn't. They made her look smart. Not only that, her large blue eyes seemed even more noticeable because of them. Beautiful blue eyes. Maybe if he'd had a teacher as pretty as Miss K, he would have wanted to stay in school beyond the sixth grade. Perhaps he might have fared better in his studies.

As pretty as Miss K.

It wasn't wise, the way his thoughts had strayed to Felicia again and again today, the way he continued to think about the blue of her eyes or the sway of her hips.

No, it wasn't wise. If he must take notice of a woman, it should be Kathleen. She'd lived in Frenchman's Bluff almost as many years as Colin had. They knew the same people and shared the same friends. As a widow, she had no starry-eyed notions about marriage. She wouldn't expect love. Mutual respect would satisfy her. She would enter into a union of two families with the same practical view as he would.

If he would — and that was a big if.

That evening, as Colin finished washing the supper dishes, he heard a knock at the back door.

"I'll see who it is," Charity said, dropping the dish towel on the counter. A few moments later, she returned with Felicia in her wake.

Colin saw the teacher take in the apron tied around his waist. An instant later, a hint of a smile tipped the corners of her mouth.

"I hope I'm not intruding," she said.

"No." He untied the apron and hung it on a hook near the sink. "What can I do for you, Miss Kristoffersen?"

"I was hoping I could speak with you." Her gaze flicked to Charity and back again. "Alone."

Colin looked at his daughter. "You'd better take care of the horses before it gets any later."

"Now?" Reluctance was written on her face.

"Now."

She sighed heavily. "Okay." She headed toward the back door a second time.

"Better give them both a good brushing too," he called after her.

The screen door slammed shut in answer.

"Would you like a cup of coffee?" he asked Felicia.

"No, thank you."

He motioned toward the table. "Mind sitting in the kitchen while we talk?"

"Not at all." She moved to the nearest chair, pulled it out, and sat down.

Colin took a moment to pour himself a cup of coffee before sitting opposite her. "So,"—he took a sip of the hot beverage— "what's on your mind?"

"It's about Charity."

Interesting, the way the muted light falling through the kitchen window on the west side of the house seemed to gild her hair, especially the long wisps that had pulled free of her bun.

"I'm wondering. Do you ever read to her?"

He stiffened. "She isn't a toddler any longer."

"No, of course not. But she needs encouragement, and I thought—"

"What she needs is to apply herself if she wants to improve." He sounded like Miss Lucas and disliked himself for it.

Felicia sighed. "Yes. I agree, Mr. Murphy. That's why I hoped you could work with her in the evenings. Repetition can be a great teacher. I fear whatever skills she acquired last year were lost over the summer. She struggles with her reading, and she's embarrassed because of it. She knows she's behind the other students her age. If she got some help at home ..." Her voice drifted into silence.

He felt his daughter's embarrassment, wished he could rescue her from it. But he couldn't, and it made him angry that he couldn't. "I thought we hired *you* to teach." His exasperation made his voice sound harsh, which wasn't his intention. She wasn't at fault.

Felicia drew back in her chair, her eyes rounding. But she didn't attempt to defend herself as he would have done. "You did, indeed."

He should apologize. He hadn't meant to be rude.

The surprise left her eyes, replaced by determination. "Will you allow me to work with her in the evenings? If I had half an hour with her every weeknight, just the two of us without any interruptions, I'm sure we would see her reading skills improve. Perhaps I could come over after supper. She and I could work here in the kitchen, with your permission."

Strange, the way her offer made him feel. Trapped. Outmaneuvered. Exposed. And at the same time, grateful ... and perhaps hopeful.

"Please, Mr. Murphy. I believe it could make a real difference for Charity. It's so important that she not be left behind. What she learns in school now could alter her adult life more than she knows."

Margaret had read to Charity at bedtime, beginning when their daughter was no more than two years old. In his memory, he saw them together, their daughter's eyes wide with excitement. He'd often stood in the bedroom doorway, shoulder leaned against the doorjamb, arms crossed over his chest, listening to the stories and enjoying them almost as much as Charity had. Maybe if he'd been able to continue the practice after Margaret died—

"Mr. Murphy?"

He pushed away the old memories and his feelings of guilt along with them. "All right, Miss Kristoffersen. If you think this is best."

🍃

Felicia didn't understand Colin Murphy. Why was he unwilling to help his own child? Did he think a daughter less in need of an education than a son would be? No, she couldn't believe that. He didn't strike her as that type of man. Then, was he so busy that he couldn't take the time to give Charity half an hour every night? Perhaps. Yet he didn't seem to resent the time he spent with his child.

She remembered thinking, on the day she'd arrived in Frenchman's Bluff, that he was cool and reserved with his daughter. Only she'd changed her opinion about that over the past couple of weeks. He was strict, yes, but he was loving too. He wanted the best for Charity. Felicia didn't doubt that about him.

"Do you want to start tonight, or is tomorrow okay?" Colin asked, pulling her from her reverie.

"Tomorrow would be fine." She rose from her chair. "Shall we say seven thirty?"

"That'll be fine." He stood too. "I'll make sure Charity's ready for you."

She thanked him as she left the house. The screen door squeaked behind her, but she didn't hear it clack shut. She suspected Colin had stopped the door with his hand and that he remained there still, watching as she crossed the yard toward her cottage.

She wished he wouldn't do that.

THIRTEEN

Silence flooded the classroom as the last of Felicia's students headed for home. The blackboards were clean. Schoolbooks lined the appropriate shelves. No jackets or sweaters or lunch pails had been left behind in the cloakroom.

With a tired sigh, Felicia closed and locked the door to the schoolhouse. It had been a good week, all things considered. One of those "considered" things was Daniel Watkins. She'd had to discipline him several times. Daily, in fact. She'd warned him today that if he was involved in one more infraction, she would have to take the matter up with the Carpenters. He hadn't cared. That had been clear from the defiant look he'd given her.

As she walked toward home, her thoughts turned once more to her brother. The Hugh of her memories seemed so much like Daniel. Was that true? Were Daniel and Hugh really so much alike? Or had the passing time made the memories untrustworthy?

So many years. Hugh would be ... how old? Thirty at his last birthday. Long since a man. She tried to imagine what he might look like. Perhaps like their father, but Sweeney Brennan was even more of a blur than Hugh.

A sadness tugged at her heart. How different her life might have been had their mother lived. They might have been poor all of their lives, but they would have been together. She wouldn't have had to wonder what became of Hugh and their sister, Diana. She wouldn't have had to wonder what they looked like. She would know.

Arriving home, she pushed aside the melancholy thoughts at the same time she pushed open the door. She set her books, lesson plans, and lunch pail on the table, and her thoughts turned to supper preparations. It scarcely mattered. Cooking for herself held little appeal.

"Miss K?"

She turned toward the screen door. Charity stood on the other side, looking in.

"I've got a letter for you. Mr. Reynolds gave it to Papa."

Felicia made a mental note to herself: Speak to the postmaster about giving her mail to Colin. It wasn't her landlord's business, after all. And this was the second time since her arrival in French-man's Bluff that Mr. Reynolds had done it. Of course, that could be her fault. She had yet to visit the post office. But why should she? It wasn't as if she expected any correspondence.

Charity opened the screen door. "You want it?" She held the envelope toward Felicia.

Reluctance washed over her. Who would write to her besides Gunnar? She went to the door and took the envelope from Charity. "Thank you."

"Sure. See you later. I'm going for a ride on Princess."

The instant Charity disappeared from view, Felicia's gaze fell to the letter in her hand. Gunnar. As she'd thought. Who else? She was tempted to rip it to pieces without reading it, but she found she couldn't do so. She went into her small parlor and sank onto a chair. After drawing a deep breath, she removed the letter from the envelope, unfolded it, and began to read.

Felicia,

 Since there has been no reply to my first letter, I write again to persuade you to return to Wyoming. Have you no respect for the memory of those who took you in, no honor, no sense of obligation? You owe the Kristoffersens for the clothes on your back and whatever else you took with you to Idaho. Will you rob us? Come back and do your duty by the family.

Gunnar

Rage and hurt warred in her chest. She wanted to scream. She wanted to weep. How could he accuse her of robbing him and his sons? From the age of ten, she had worked alongside Britta and Lars. She'd cleaned the house and cooked meals and sewn clothes and weeded the vegetable garden and tended the livestock. Had Gunnar ever done a single day's work on the Kristoffersen farm? No, he hadn't. Not he or his sons. They were lazy and worthless and—

She drew herself up short, wishing to stop the torrent of unkind words in her head.

What would she have done with the farm if she'd inherited it? Sold it. She wouldn't have wanted to stay there. The Kristoffersens had done her a favor, really, leaving the farm to their nephew. Of course, it would have been nice to have a little money, to not feel she was on the edge of a precipice without a soft place to land should she tumble off.

Unto thee will I cry, O Lord my rock.

The whispered words in her heart shamed her even more than the bitter ones toward Gunnar. It wasn't a precipice on which she stood. She stood on *the* Rock.

He only is my rock and my salvation: he is my defense; I shall not be moved. In God is my salvation and my glory: the rock of my strength, and my refuge, is in God.

"You have brought me this far, Lord," she whispered. "I will trust You to take me into my tomorrows as well. Keep my mind set on You, and place forgiveness in my heart."

She folded the letter and slipped it back into the envelope.

Kathleen leaned down and kissed Suzanne's forehead, then repeated the same with Phoebe. "Goodnight, my darlings." She picked up the lamp and carried it out of the bedroom, leaving the door slightly ajar behind her.

Kathleen liked this time of the day. She enjoyed the silence that blanketed the house and the town. Her in-laws went to bed at the same time that her daughters did, but she was never ready to retire this early. Perhaps because this was when she missed her husband the most.

She went down the servants' staircase and set the lamp on the kitchen table. Afterward, she retrieved her white knit shawl from the hook near the back door and stepped outside onto the porch.

Frenchman's Bluff was mostly dark, lamplight spilling from windows here and there. Overhead, stars glittered in a cloudless sky, and a night breeze rustled leaves. The air was quickly cooling, causing Kathleen to pull her shawl closer about her shoulders. Moving slowly, she followed the porch around the side of the house to the front, where she stopped beside a post and leaned her shoulder against it.

Faint music from the saloon reached her ears. The tune made her smile. Another of those scandalous songs Harold had liked to play on the piano.

The moon was just beginning to rise when she heard the sound of a horse coming down the street. *Clip-clop. Clip-clop.* She wondered who it might be. Perhaps Dr. Young, their neighbor, returning from visiting a patient. Or perhaps the horse was headed in the other direction, carrying a man to the saloon. No, the hoof beats were drawing closer.

Moonlight spilled over the tops of trees to the east, illuminating the street and, a moment later, the horse and rider. Then the rider pulled back on the reins. "That you, Miz Summerville?"

The sound of the male voice, coming out of the silence of night, speaking her name, startled her, and she straightened away from the post.

He nudged his horse forward. "It's me. Oscar."

Her pulse quickened even more. "Mr. Jacobson."

"Surprised to see you there." He stepped down from the saddle. "You looked a little like an angel with the moonlight on your white shawl."

His comment made her laugh. "I'm not an angel. I assure you."

"Mind if I come up and sit a spell? I know it's kinda late, but I'm headed back to the ranch, and I'd just as soon let the moon get a bit higher."

Mother Summerville wouldn't approve. It was night. They were unchaperoned. "I don't mind. Please come join me."

Oscar tied his horse to the hitching post near the front gate. "I shoulda got an earlier start back." He walked toward her, a jingle of spurs accompanying his steps. "But I was helpin' the pastor fix the roof on the parsonage. Wouldn't do to have it leakin' when winter sets in. Time just got away from me."

She liked this young cowpoke. It was pleasant to have his company here on the porch, surrounded by the soft night. Perhaps five or six years her junior, Oscar Jacobson had a quiet, unassuming manner. And it still surprised her that he liked to read and recite poetry.

After he climbed the steps to the porch, they moved in unison toward the chairs. He waited for her to be seated first, then sat in the closest chair to her right.

"Nice weather," he said.

"Yes."

"Always have liked the end of summer—days still warm but the nights cool. Air smells good this time of evenin'."

She drew a deep breath through her nose. "Mmm."

A period of silence followed. A peaceful one, when neither person present felt the need to fill it. That surprised Kathleen too, that she would feel that way in this man's company. It wasn't as if they were longtime acquaintances, yet it felt as if they were.

Oscar removed his hat and held it between his hands. "I finished readin' Rudyard Kipling's novel *Captains Courageous* this week. Have you read it?"

"No."

"I could loan you my copy if you wanted. It's a good story." He paused, then added, "It's not poetry, but I think you'd like it."

Her mother-in-law thought reading novels was a horrid waste of time, but Kathleen liked nothing so much as a good book. "I should like to read it, Mr. Jacobson. Thanks for the offer."

"I hear there's gonna be a barn dance at the Dowd place in a few weeks." He cleared his throat. "You plannin' to go?"

"Yes. My girls and I are looking forward to it. We didn't attend the last two. We were ... we were still in mourning."

Another silence stretched between them before he said, "I reckon you know I'm sorry for your loss, ma'am. I've heard your husband was a fine man."

"Yes." She smiled, not for his benefit but for her own. "Harry was a fine man."

"Wish I could have known him."

"Me too."

Oscar cleared his throat. "If you'll be dancin' this year, I hope you'll save one of 'em for me."

Warmth rose from her neck into her cheeks. She felt more like a schoolgirl than a widow and mother of two. The urge to giggle nervously was hard to resist, but somehow she did.

"You think that might be possible, Miz Summerville?"

Her smile broadened. "Yes, Mr. Jacobson. I do think it's possible."

Although the moonlight couldn't reach his face, seated as they were beneath of roof of the porch, she knew he grinned. Knew it as surely as she knew her own name.

"I'll be lookin' forward to it." He stood. "Guess I'd best be ridin' on. I'll be gettin' back to the ranch mighty late as it is."

"Do ride carefully."

Oscar set his hat on his head. "I will, ma'am."

She rose and followed him as far as the porch steps, then waited until he rode away before going inside. She was still smiling half an hour later when she slipped between the covers on her bed and went happily to sleep.

FOURTEEN

Felicia awakened before dawn on Saturday morning with a desire to take a long walk. Laundry and other chores could wait. She ate breakfast, put a mason jar filled with water into a canvas bag along with her Bible and a small writing tablet, and then set off in the direction of the foothills before the sun had crested the mountains in the east. She walked quickly at first, following the same trail she had taken with Charity the day they'd gone fishing together. Once she reached the river, she turned and followed its winding path, north and east, north and east. At one point, she came upon a broken tree branch that made a good walking stick. She was glad for it as the trail slowly but steadily climbed.

Close to two hours had passed before she decided to stop. A giant boulder presented an ideal resting place. She sat on it, facing the river, the sun warm on her back. After taking a drink of water from the mason jar, she opened her Bible, letting it fall open, then put on her glasses and began reading in the first chapter of Mark. Two chapters later, she came to the passage that said, "And he goeth up into a mountain, and calleth unto him whom he would: and they came unto him." She stopped reading, lay back on the rock, and imagined herself among the throng who had followed Jesus that day.

There she was, moving along the dusty pathway in her simple tunic, a scarf draped over her head. She was trying to find a place where she could see the young rabbi. She'd heard that Jesus of Nazareth had done many great things, healing the sick of all sorts of diseases. Not only that, He was able to cast out demons. Who wouldn't want to see Him with their own eyes?

And finally there He was, making His way up the hillside. Was there anything remarkable about the way He looked? Not really. Not as she'd expected there to be. Shouldn't a man who could heal the sick and turn water into wine have a look that set Him apart?

Wait! He was looking at her. Not just *at* her. He *saw* her. He seemed to see inside of her. She held her breath. Would He speak? Would He announce aloud to the world what He saw in her heart? She hoped not, for suddenly she was ashamed of what He might find there—anger at the Kristoffersens, especially Gunnar; resentment over what might have been but never was; fear over the unknown future.

But then His gaze moved on, and she felt both relieved and sorrowful.

"Come," He said. "Peter, come to Me."

Oh, how she wished it was her name He called.

"James, come here. And John, you too."

She imagined what it was like for Jesus to call His disciples to Himself, and then she pondered how amazing it was that He had called her too. Not as one of the inner circle of three, or one of the twelve closest to Him, or even one of the five hundred who witnessed Him after the resurrection. But He had called her as one of those for whom He prayed almost two thousand years before.

With eyes still closed, she whispered the words, "Neither pray I for these alone, but for them also which shall believe on me through their word." Jesus had known her even then. He'd known she would trust in Him and want to serve Him. "That the world may believe that thou hast sent me." She inhaled deeply. "That the world may know that thou hast sent me, and hast loved them, as thou hast loved me."

Felicia smiled as she realized — as if for the first time, although it was not — that Christ's prayer *had* been answered. All of these centuries later, *she* knew the Father's love, and she would never be alone. No matter what happened to her in Frenchman's Bluff, she wouldn't be alone or cast aside. She need not fear tomorrow. Of that she could be sure.

She began to speak aloud those things for which she was most thankful: for her small cottage; for the comfortable bed that welcomed her at night; for each of her students, from the youngest to the oldest; for the opportunity to cook for herself, especially because she could make whatever she wanted; for the warm sun on the rock; for the music of the river flowing by; for the songbirds in the trees. On and on she went.

Once she had exhausted her list of thanksgiving, she stretched her arms above her head and cried, "Thank You. Thank You. Thank You, Lord." Then she laughed for joy.

Colin knew he should ride on. He should disappear back into the trees that lined the river. When he'd first heard Felicia's voice, he hadn't realized she was praying. How could he? It was unlike any prayer he'd heard before. But now that he'd realized it, he should leave. Yet he couldn't make himself go. She looked so ... peaceful ... stretched out on that rock, bathed in the morning sunlight. Peaceful and joyful.

And beautiful.

Drifter shifted his weight beneath the saddle and snorted his impatience. Felicia sat up, a startled gasp carrying to Colin.

"It's only me, Miss Kristoffersen," he called before riding forward.

"Mr. Murphy." She stood, clutching a book against her abdomen.

"Didn't mean to intrude."

"You didn't. I mean, I was just … just …"

"Praying?" he finished for her, half hoping she would correct him.

"Yes." She nodded. "I was praying."

Colin dismounted and moved to stand beside the horse's head. "Never heard Reverend Hightower pray like that."

Her face grew pink.

He surprised himself by adding, "I liked it."

The blush deepened.

Colin couldn't recall knowing another woman who blushed as easily as Felicia. He found it almost as attractive as the blue of her eyes.

"I didn't expect to see anyone out here," she said. "It's so far from the main road."

"I was hunting." He motioned with his head. "It's a bit early in the season, but I thought I might find a deer or two up through the canyon that way. Both Charity and I are partial to venison stew."

She nodded, as if saying she liked venison also.

"Mind if I join you for a moment or two?"

Uncertainty filled her eyes. "Well, I—"

"Drifter would like a rest."

Apparently she was more prone to take pity on his horse than on him. She nodded again. "Of course. If you like. Please join me."

Colin turned the gelding loose to graze, then climbed onto

the boulder. By that time, Felicia was seated again, her legs tucked beneath the skirt of her outing costume. He sat beside her. "Beautiful spot."

"Yes."

There were plenty of other things Colin might have said next. He could have talked about the weather. He could have brought up Charity. He might even have discussed the cost of school supplies. What he said instead surprised him. "Do you pray like that often?"

"Not often enough, I suppose." The corners of her mouth slipped into a smile.

"Do you think God hears you?"

"Of course." The smile disappeared. "Don't you think He hears when you pray?"

Tipping his head back, he looked at the unbroken expanse of blue overhead. "I'm not sure."

She didn't say anything in return, and he was grateful for that. He didn't know why he'd been so forthright in the first place. He'd never even expressed his doubts to his best friend. He'd hardly admitted them to himself.

"I'm not much of a Christian," he added after a lengthy silence.

"That could be said for most of us."

Her reply drew his gaze.

"We're all sinners, Mr. Murphy. We all stumble at times. Even those in His church. Our faith grows stronger under fire and testing."

"My wife said something like that, toward the end."

Her eyes invited him to say more.

"Margaret wasn't happy for a long time." Why was he telling her this? Why didn't he keep his business his business? "But it seemed like after she got sick, she trusted God more, and she was happy again." *And then He let her die.*

"Tell me about her."

What could he say about Margaret? Time had changed his memories of her, softened them, made him wonder what might have been if she'd lived longer.

Felicia said, "Charity says she looks like her mother."

"Yes, she does. Same brown eyes. Same color of hair." That much wasn't forgotten. He pictured his wife, her dark hair falling down her back in soft waves. "Same smile too. We grew up near each other back in Ohio. Even as a little girl, she was fearless. If she wanted something, she would work like the dickens to get it. Even when I was only about fifteen or so, I knew she was the girl I wanted to marry."

"How romantic."

Romantic? No. Practical. Sensible. He and Margaret were good friends. He liked spending time with her. She was smart and wanted to get ahead in life, same as he did. No, he couldn't be accused of being a romantic.

There'd been no romance, and no love either. Certainly not on his wife's part. At seventeen, Margaret had fallen hard for Broderick Hazleton, a handsome but feckless fellow of whom her parents strongly disapproved. They'd insisted she marry Colin, and she'd obeyed them—but only after some terrible rows.

"What brought you from Ohio to Idaho?"

"Margaret's uncle. He owned the mercantile here in Frenchman's Bluff. After he took sick, he offered to sell the store to us at a good price when the time came if we'd move out here and take care of him until he regained his strength. So that's what we did."

He didn't bother to tell Felicia that Margaret's parents had thought it best for the newlyweds to move away, for Colin to take Margaret to a place where she wouldn't risk running into Broderick. It turned out to be good advice.

"He kept his word," Felicia said. "You bought the store."

"Actually, he didn't sell us the store. He left it to us in his will. He died six months after we arrived."

"How tragic."

Colin acknowledged her words with a nod. "I wasn't sure about owning the mercantile, about staying here for the rest of my life. But Margaret loved Frenchman's Bluff right from the start, and she had a good head for business too."

In Colin's opinion, this town and the mercantile had kept his marriage from going completely sour. Because Margaret loved the town and the store, she had time to learn to care for Colin again. Maybe she'd never loved him. Maybe he'd never felt more than affection for her. But they'd become close again. They'd been good friends, and friendship wasn't a bad basis for a marriage.

"You still miss her, don't you?" Felicia said into the silence.

He shrugged, then nodded. "It isn't the same as it used to be, but yes, I still miss her. Especially when I catch a glimpse of her in Charity. Or because she'd know how to do something that I can't do or know what to say when I haven't got a clue."

"You surprise me, Mr. Murphy."

"I do?" He cocked an eyebrow.

"I was under the impression you were a man who never doubted himself or his decisions."

Never doubted himself? Never doubted his decisions? Not hardly. But he wasn't surprised to hear that's what she thought of him. He worked hard to project an image of self-confidence to others.

If they only knew—

With a shake of his head, he pushed up from the rock. "I'd better go. The store's open by now, and Jimmy and Charity will wonder what's keeping me. Shall I see you back?"

"No, thank you. I'll stay here and enjoy nature a while longer."
He bent his hat brim at her. "Good day, Miss Kristoffersen."

"Good day, Mr. Murphy."

Felicia lay back against the boulder once again and closed her eyes.
But it was no longer a prayer of thanksgiving to God that filled her
mind. Instead, she thought of Colin, pictured him as he'd been a
short while before, seated beside her, near enough that she could
have touched him. Perhaps too near.

"You still miss her, don't you?"

"It isn't the same as it used to be, but yes, I still miss her."

She felt a strange twinge in her chest. It was almost painful.
Suddenly she felt alone — and lonely — and she wanted to weep.

FIFTEEN

Colin had no reason to decline Helen Summerville's invitation to dinner for a second week in a row. Which is why he found himself that Sunday at two o'clock seated next to Kathleen at the large dining room table in the Summerville home. Across from him sat the town's physician, Patrick Young, as well as Noel and Iona Bryant and their middle son, Samuel. The Bryants' oldest son, Jimmy, sat on the other side of Kathleen, while their youngest, Tommy, had gone into the kitchen along with the two Summerville girls and Charity to eat their meal apart from the adults.

After George Summerville spoke a blessing over the food, Kathleen picked up the platter of roast beef and passed it to Colin. "Mrs. Hasting knows how much you like her roast beef," she said softly.

Colin thought the Summerville cook probably knew the food preferences of almost everyone in and around Frenchman's Bluff. She'd once owned a restaurant in town. Then, half a dozen or so years ago, it had burned to the ground. Without insurance, Victoria hadn't had the money to rebuild. So she'd taken the job offered her by the Summervilles and had been cooking for them ever since.

He forked a slice of roast beef and passed the platter to his hostess.

"We're so glad you could join us today, Mr. Murphy," Helen said as she accepted the plate. "We missed your company last week."

"Always a pleasure to be here, Mrs. Summerville." His reply, though polite, wasn't entirely true. It wasn't always a pleasure to spend time in her company. Helen held herself a little too highly in her own estimation. She enjoyed too much her self-appointed role as leader of Frenchman's Bluff society.

"I understand you gave Charity a horse for her birthday," she continued.

"Yes."

"What do you think of that, Kathleen?"

"Of what, Mother Summerville?"

"Of a girl of nine having a horse of her own."

There it was. That note of criticism. Of disapproval. A tone that said Colin had made a grave mistake.

Kathleen's gaze flicked from her mother-in-law to Colin. "Charity showed Princess to Suzanne and Phoebe and me earlier this week. I've never seen her so excited." She smiled briefly. "I think that horse was the perfect gift for her."

Colin returned the smile. It wasn't easy for anyone in town to stand up to Helen. It must be doubly difficult for Kathleen, who was dependent on the older woman.

"Perhaps if she were a boy, Mr. Murphy, it would be different. But a girl?" Helen clucked her tongue. "Charity could use a mother's tender guidance."

Her comment wiped the smile from his lips.

"Some potatoes, Mr. Murphy?" Kathleen held the large serving bowl toward him.

"Thanks."

Noel Bryant chuckled. "I should've promised Charity one of Goldie's pups for her birthday. That was a missed opportunity if ever I saw one."

Noel's comment was enough to cool Colin's growing irritation with their hostess, and he laughed along with the others.

"How about you, George?" Noel continued. "You could use a huntin' dog, couldn't you?"

"Well, I—"

Helen cut off her husband's reply. "I should say not."

There was an awkward silence before George said, "I don't do much hunting anymore, Noel."

Colin wished he could join the children in the kitchen.

"Samuel," Helen said, "are you glad to be back in school?"

The boy—at fourteen a slightly shorter version of his brother Jimmy—shrugged. "It's all right."

"And what do you think of your schoolteacher?"

"Miss K? She's all right."

Helen turned her gaze toward Colin. "I understand she asked for more expenditures for the school. After only a few days of teaching. I don't think Mr. Swanson should have given in to her request without talking to the rest of the school board first."

"It seemed a reasonable request," he answered. "Some world maps is what she ordered."

"If Miss Lucas and those before her could get by without them, I can see no reason why Miss Kristoffersen can't do so as well." She shook her head. "You and I were right to vote against offering her the position. I hope the other board members will realize their mistake soon."

Colin's irritation returned. It would be one thing for Helen to make her comments to him privately. It was another for her to do it in front of people who weren't on the board—especially when one of them was a student.

But before he could form a response, Kathleen spoke up. "Suzanne and Phoebe love Miss Kristoffersen. They can't wait to go to school in the morning."

"That doesn't make her the best person for the job, Kathleen," her mother-in-law returned, her mouth tightening.

Kathleen sat a little straighter in her chair. "Perhaps not, Mother Summerville, but it doesn't disqualify her either. We have to give Miss Kristoffersen a chance to prove her capabilities." She drew a quick breath before adding, "I like Felicia. I like her a great deal."

⑥

Kathleen could scarcely believe those words had come out of her mouth. Here, in front of all of these people, disagreeing with Mother Summerville. She must be losing her mind.

Or perhaps she was beginning to find it.

She turned toward Colin. "Don't you think we need to give Miss Kristoffersen a chance, Mr. Murphy?"

There was something about the way he looked at her — was that admiration in his eyes? — that calmed her nerves and shored up her courage.

"Yes, I believe we need to give her a chance." He seemed to be fighting a smile. "Everyone deserves a chance."

When Kathleen dared to glance in her mother-in-law's direction again, she was met with a glare as cold as ice. But for some reason, she didn't care. She was tired of tiptoeing around this house, around her own opinions. She didn't use to be afraid to express her thoughts. How had she become the timid woman she was today? If Harold were to see her now, would he even know her? She feared he wouldn't.

The doctor changed the topic to a theater production he'd heard was coming to Boise City, and thankfully, Mother Summerville seemed content to let the previous conversation be forgotten. At least for the time being.

⑥

146

A breeze rustled the leaves in the nearby tree. As Felicia sat on her porch, that was the only sound she heard. The whole town of Frenchman's Bluff seemed to be napping, humans and animals alike, on this warm Sunday afternoon.

She found the idea of a nap a tempting one, but she didn't want to go inside. The day was too pleasant for that. Soon enough, it would turn cool. The leaves would change from green to red and orange, gold and yellow, and then they would fall to the ground to crunch beneath the shoes of passersby. Finally the snow would blow in from the west, blanketing her small corner of the world in white. There would be no sitting on her porch then. Better she enjoy it while she could.

Her thoughts drifted from the weather to the previous day when she'd sat beside the river on that rock—and to the moment when Colin Murphy had joined her there. Their brief exchange had been agreeable, but it troubled her spirit to remember the loneliness that had washed over her after he departed. Felicia liked her solitude. Often preferred it, in fact. And hadn't she been enjoying the Lord's presence only moments before Colin arrived? Those strange feelings of loneliness couldn't be because she'd come to like Colin, like him as a woman likes a man. Could they?

No, of course not. Ridiculous. He was her landlord, even her employer. But nothing more.

She drew in a deep breath and turned her attention to the round table at her side. On it lay her writing materials. As disagreeable as she found the task, it was time she answered Gunnar's letters. She picked up the pen and dipped it in the ink bottle.

Cousin Gunnar,
*   I am in receipt of your two letters.*
*   Surely you must know that I have no desire whatsoever*

to return to Wyoming, not to marry Rolf nor for any other reason. While I am grateful for the home I was given with Britta and Lars, my obligations to them, to the farm, to any other members of the Kristoffersen family, were fulfilled long ago. I took nothing with me that was not mine. For you to suggest otherwise is spiteful and untrue.

Please do not trouble yourself in my regard again. I have no intention of leaving my position as teacher in Frenchman's Bluff.

Sincerely,
Felicia

She laid aside the pen and read the letter one more time. It wasn't a warm letter, to be sure, but no less so than Gunnar's letters to her. For all the world, she couldn't understand why he wanted her for a daughter-in-law. He didn't like her the least little bit. And Rolf? If he felt anything for her, it was lust, and she couldn't be sure of even that.

She shuddered as she always did when she imagined herself joined in marriage to Rolf Kristoffersen.

"I'm not lonely," she whispered. "I'm not alone. The Lord is with me. I have my work, which satisfies me. I am educated and intelligent and able to take care of myself. If I am ever to marry, it will only be for love. Never for convenience or to satisfy convention. Never for that."

Drawing a deep breath, she folded the letter and slipped it into an envelope, which she quickly addressed and sealed.

"Hi, Miss K!"

She looked in the direction of Charity Murphy's voice and saw the girl and her father walking toward the rear entrance to their living quarters. But Charity promptly changed directions and ran over to Felicia. A moment later, Colin did the same, though at a slower pace.

As if to taunt her, her words of moments before repeated in her mind: *If I am ever to marry, it will only be for love.*

Her insides seemed to tumble, causing her to grip the arms of her chair.

Colin removed his hat. "Good afternoon."

She hadn't spoken to him at church that morning, although she'd seen him there, seated with his daughter several rows behind her. Now she was keenly aware of how handsome he looked in his dark Sunday suit. He was, without a doubt, one of the handsomest men of her acquaintance. Certainly more so than any of her Kristoffersen "cousins."

Again that strange tumbling sensation.

"We ate Sunday dinner at the Summervilles," Charity said.

"How nice." Felicia smiled at the girl and prayed her face revealed none of her inner turmoil.

"The food's always good," Colin said.

Something in his tone told Felicia he hadn't enjoyed the afternoon. Did Helen Summerville dislike him too? That was difficult to believe.

"Mr. Bryant said he should have promised me one of Goldie's pups for my birthday." Charity glanced over her shoulder at her father. "Maybe I could have one even though my birthday's over?"

Colin's eyebrows drew together in a frown. "We can discuss that later. And we need to get inside and change out of our Sunday clothes. Besides, we're intruding on Miss Kristoffersen's letter writing."

I don't mind. I'm finished writing. Although she didn't speak the words aloud, she felt her cheeks grow warm with embarrassment.

She could only pray that her eyes didn't reveal her wish for the two of them to remain and talk to her a little longer.

Colin placed his right hand on Charity's shoulder. "I'm sure your family will be glad to hear from you." With a nod of his head, he turned, drawing his daughter with him, and the two of them strode toward their home.

"I'm sure your family will be glad to hear from you."

She looked down at the envelope on the table. Gunnar wasn't her family. Yes, she addressed him as "cousin," but that was a designation of habit, not fact. He was no blood relation whatsoever.

But she did have a family. Somewhere.

Try again, her heart seemed to say. *Don't give up.*

It had been sixteen years since she and Hugh and Diana had left Chicago, and seven or eight years since she'd last tried to discover the whereabouts of her brother and sister. What were the chances that anyone could help her find them after such a long time?

Try again. Don't give up.

She reached for the pen and another sheet of stationery and began to write.

Dr. Cray's Asylum for Little Wanderers
Chicago, Illinois

Dear Sir,

My name is Felicia Brennan Kristoffersen. In the summer of 1881, your organization placed me with a married couple who lived on a farm near Laramie, Wyoming. Their names were Lars and Britta Kristoffersen, and they called me Felicia Kristoffersen from that time forward. In fact, I believed they adopted me until it was revealed otherwise after their deaths earlier this year.

I have an older brother and a younger sister, Hugh and Diana Brennan, who were also placed with families in the summer of 1881, but I cannot say for sure where those families lived. I know only that my brother and sister left the train before Laramie.

It is my desire to locate my siblings. Can you help me?

Sincerely,
Felicia Brennan Kristoffersen
Frenchman's Bluff, Idaho

As she folded the stationery, she whispered a prayer that this time God would send an answer. Still, she knew finding them would take a miracle.

SIXTEEN

The wall maps arrived at the mercantile on Tuesday afternoon, not long after school let out for the day. Colin knew Felicia would be eager to have them, so he left the store under Jimmy's watchful eye and carried the maps to the school.

When he entered the classroom a short while later, he found Felicia seated at her desk, grading papers, while a boy of about ten — judging by his height alone, for Colin couldn't see his face — cleaned the blackboards behind her.

Colin cleared his throat, and Felicia looked up.

"I have something for you," he said.

Her face brightened. "Our maps." She dropped the pencil on her desk and stood. "How wonderful!"

"Where do you want me to hang them? I brought a hammer and some nails with me."

Felicia pointed to the east wall. "Right there, next to the window."

Colin followed her to the designated spot.

"Keith," Felicia called to the boy at the blackboards. "Come and see what Mr. Murphy brought for us."

Keith? Colin couldn't place the kid, and he knew every family within fifteen to twenty miles in any direction of Frenchman's Bluff.

"Mr. Murphy, this is Keith Watkins, one of my new students. Keith and his brother live with the Carpenters."

Oh, that's why he didn't recognize the boy. He was one of the orphan kids from back East.

"Keith," Felicia continued, her hand on the boy's shoulder, "these are the new maps of the world for us to use when we study history and geography."

The boy's expression said it all: Unimpressed. Bored speechless. He'd rather be anyplace else than where he was at that moment.

It was Felicia's turn to clear her throat. "I think those black-boards are clean enough. You may go home now."

"Thanks, Miss K." Grinning, he darted for the exit.

"See you tomorrow," she called after him. Then she faced Colin again. "I suppose it was asking a lot for him to be as excited as I am about a set of maps."

"I reckon."

But to be honest, her excitement was contagious. The way she twisted her hands and paced back and forth on the platform while Colin hung the black case holding the seven pull-down, oil-colored maps made him want to pace with anticipation too. It made no sense. They were just drawings of the world that made it look flat and showed one country pink and another yellow and another green. No more exciting than any other teaching tool in the schoolroom.

When the case was fastened to the wall, Colin stepped aside, motioning with his hand. "Be my guest, Miss K."

The smile she sent in his direction did more than brighten her face. It seemed to brighten the entire room. Colin had to take another step backward and remind himself to breathe.

"It's wonderful," she said after revealing the first map. Then she spun around and hurried to the desk farthest away. She slid onto the seat, folding her hands on the desktop. "Absolutely wonderful. The children will love it."

To Colin, she looked more like a student than the teacher. Fresh, innocent, wide-eyed. Enthusiastic and untouched by the sorrows of life. What he wouldn't give to feel the way she felt, to look at the world the way she saw it now.

Her smile faded, and the joy vanished from her eyes.

He swallowed, realizing the longing that had gripped him as he stared at her. Heaven help him.

Felicia tried to draw a deep breath but couldn't. The air around her felt thick and uncomfortable. And that strange look in Colin Murphy's eyes made her weak and a little afraid, although she couldn't say why.

"I should get back to the store," he said.

She rose from the desk. "It was thoughtless of me to keep you so long. I should have tried to hang them myself."

"No." He moved toward the exit. Toward her. "I wanted to help."

She feared he must hear the rapid beating of her heart.

"I'll send the bill for the maps to Walter."

"Yes." She swallowed. "To Mr. Swanson. He'll be expecting it."

He stopped a short distance from her, and for one thrillingly frightful moment, she thought he might reach out and touch her. Instead, he bent the brim of his hat—a gesture already so familiar to her—and said, "Good day, Miss Kristoffersen."

"Good day." She remained standing until he was out of sight. Then she dropped onto the seat, her knees unable to keep her upright any longer.

What just happened?

She forced herself to take a slow, deep breath.

I'm being ridiculous. Nothing happened. He was being neighborly. That's all. He delivered the maps; he hung them for me—what any gentleman would do. What any good tradesman would do.

Not every tradesman, however, would look at her the way Colin had moments before—as if he could see into her mind and read her thoughts.

But he *couldn't* read her thoughts. That was pure silliness on her part. Colin could no more see into her mind than she could see into his. And neither of them would want—

"Felicia?"

She started, surprised by the sound of Kathleen's voice, and felt unprepared to face anyone. But what choice did she have? She could only hope she didn't look as confused as she felt. Drawing another deep breath, she rose and turned.

Kathleen stood in the doorway, and right behind her was her mother-in-law.

Felicia forced a smile of greeting. "Kathleen. Mrs. Summerville. It's good to see you."

"We're glad we found you still here," Kathleen said.

"I ... I'm usually here until four thirty." Did she appear flustered or uncertain? She hoped not.

Helen Summerville looked as if she'd been sucking on a lemon. "Was that Mr. Murphy we saw leaving just now?" Her tone dripped with disapproval.

"Yes." She motioned to the opposite side of the classroom. "He brought the new maps we ordered."

"*We?*" Helen said softly, then sniffed.

Kathleen moved forward. "As you know, Jane and Lewis Carpenter have taken in a couple of orphan children."

"Yes. They're fine boys." When Daniel wasn't misbehaving,

anyway. "I enjoy having them in my class." True, despite Daniel's resisting her authority.

"Well, the placement came up rather suddenly, and they don't have many of the kinds of things I'm sure they could use. You know, extra bedding, clothes for growing boys, balls and bats, and whatnot." Kathleen gave a little shrug. "I want to organize the women of our community to do something for them that might help with their new family."

"I'd be happy to participate."

"I knew you would. Could you come to my ... to our home on Saturday morning at nine?"

"Yes, I can."

"Good. We'll see you then." Kathleen turned around. "All right, Mother Summerville. We can go home now. I told you it wouldn't take long." As they moved toward the exit, she glanced over her shoulder. "See you Saturday."

Kathleen's parting smile was a balm on Felicia's rattled nerves. God was good to have given her the friend she'd hoped and prayed for. It strengthened her knowing she had someone she could confide in, a friendship she was sure would grow even stronger with time.

But what would Kathleen think of Felicia's odd reactions to Colin?

She inhaled deeply. What rubbish! She was imagining the look in his eyes and her breathless response. Neither were of any importance and certainly nothing she would share with a friend.

❦

The supper dishes had been washed, dried, and put away before Felicia arrived for her tutoring session with Charity. When the familiar knock sounded at the back door, Charity went at once to answer it.

Colin had been surprised by his daughter's eagerness to spend extra time studying with her teacher. Knowing that she struggled with reading, he'd expected her to resent the evening sessions, time taken away from more pleasurable activities. Instead, she seemed glad for them.

Not that he expected the tutoring to bear much fruit. As far as he could tell, listening from the parlor each evening, teacher and student weren't accomplishing much. Nothing that sounded like schoolwork, at any rate.

As Charity returned to the kitchen, her teacher right behind her, she said, "Papa says the new maps came today."

"Yes. He hung them on the wall so they'll be ready to use tomorrow." Felicia stopped just inside the doorway and her eyes lifted to meet his. "Good evening, Mr. Murphy."

"Evening."

"Am I too early?" A touch of pink colored the apple of her cheeks.

He shook his head. "Nope. Right on time. So I'll leave you two alone." He turned on his heel and strode into the small parlor, where he sat in a comfortable wing-backed chair that Margaret had brought with them from Ohio. He took the weekly newspaper from the side table near his left elbow and placed it on his lap. But he didn't look at it. Instead, he listened to the voices drifting to him from the kitchen.

"Twinkle, twinkle, little star," Felicia said. "How I wonder what you are! Up above the world so high, like a diamond in the sky!"

Silence, and then his daughter repeated the words, slower, with less confidence, sometimes stumbling, finally stopping before she'd reached the end.

"Sound it out, Charity."

"Di-"

He strained with her.

"-a-"

He tried to picture the word in his head but couldn't.

"-mond."

"Very good. *Diamond*. And where is that diamond?"

"In the sky!"

Laughter — the deeper tones of a woman, the lighter tones of a child — mingled together. He wished he could see their faces. He wished he could laugh with them.

"Now once more, together this time. 'Twinkle, twinkle, little star. How I wonder what you are ...'"

Colin put the newspaper back on the table and rose from the chair, making his way to the front entrance of their living quarters. He opened the door and moved to stand near the porch steps, leaning his shoulder against the post.

Frenchman's Bluff was quiet this time of evening. With the exception of the saloon on the west end of town and the restaurant to the east of the mercantile, the businesses that lined Main Street were closed, the workers gone home to be with their families. Already the shadows had grown long.

He shook his head. How quickly the seasons came and went. It didn't seem all that many years ago since he and Margaret had come to Idaho as newlyweds. How could he have foreseen that in little more than a decade he would be a widowed father, managing the mercantile on his own?

He heard another burst of laughter from inside the house.

Maybe he shouldn't be doing it on his own. Not managing the mercantile. Not raising his daughter. Maybe trying to protect both himself and Charity from pain, loss, or disaster wasn't the best way to live. For either of them.

But what was the best way?

His eyes lifted to the sky, where cotton-ball clouds on the eastern horizon had been brushed with shades of peach and lavender. He remembered Felicia's prayer beside the river, and he found himself wishing he could pray like that. He wished he could ask the Almighty what plans He had for Charity's future, for his future. Other people seemed to pray so easily. They seemed to trust in a good God without question.

I'd like to trust You again, Lord. I'd like to find my way back. Is that possible? Or is it already too late?

He almost laughed aloud, realizing that he'd just wished he could pray easily and then had found himself, indeed, praying.

Maybe it wasn't too late after all.

SEVENTEEN

Felicia adored hats. Straw hats with ribbons to match a dress. Velvet bonnets with ostrich plumes that fluttered in the breeze. Felt hats sporting a cluster of roses. Surely a woman could never own enough hats.

And that belief was one reason Felicia had stayed away from Jane Carpenter's millinery shop in the weeks since she arrived in Frenchman's Bluff. With her funds in short supply, she shouldn't go where she would be tempted.

But there was no avoiding the shop or the temptation today.

At 4:15 on Thursday afternoon, Keith Watkins ran on ahead of Felicia and his older brother, opening the door into his new mother's shop and shouting, "Ma! Miss K's here to see you."

By the time Felicia and Daniel stepped into the store, Jane had emerged from the back room, a half-decorated bonnet in her left hand, a concerned expression on her face. "Is something wrong, Miss Kristoffersen?"

"I'd like to speak with you. Alone, if I may."

"Of course." Jane looked at the boys. "You two get along home. Your pa will be waiting for you to help with the chores. Tell him I'll be home directly."

Before he turned to leave, Daniel cast a sullen glance in Felicia's direction. She made certain not to give him the satisfaction of a reaction.

As the door closed behind the brothers, Jane said, "Daniel's giving you trouble in class, isn't he?" She motioned toward the workroom. "There's a couple of chairs in the back. Let's go sit down. Would you like some tea? It wouldn't take long to heat the water."

"No, thank you. I'm fine."

Jane held aside the curtain that separated the front shop from the workroom and motioned for Felicia to go first. What met her eyes was not what she'd expected. While the front of the long, narrow building was tidy as a pin and sparsely furnished—two small tables with mirrors on them, two padded stools for the customers, a half dozen hats on display—the back room was an explosion of colorful disarray. Every table and shelf was covered with ribbons, feathers, buttons, and all kinds of other decorations, as well as several hats in varying stages of completion.

Jane quickly cleared off the seat of one of the chairs. "Please, sit down here."

"How long have you been making hats?" Felicia asked, her gaze continuing to roam about the room.

"I've had my shop nigh onto five years now. Lewis thought it a good idea ... when it seemed certain we wouldn't be blessed with children."

Felicia looked at the other woman then and saw the lingering sadness in her eyes. "I'm sorry for your losses."

"Well,"—Jane revealed a quivering smile—"we have our boys now."

Felicia wasn't fooled by the forced cheer. It couldn't be an easy thing, burying five babies. That kind of pain must always remain in a mother's heart.

Jane sobered. "You've come about Daniel."

"Yes."

"He's in trouble?"

Felicia nodded. "Yes."

"What did he do?"

"He got into a fistfight with another boy. There was some name-calling and cursing first, and the next thing we knew, the boys were rolling on the classroom floor."

"Oh dear." Tears welled in Jane's eyes. "He doesn't want to be here. I think he hates us, my husband and me."

"He doesn't hate you, Mrs. Carpenter. He's afraid, and he's trying to work up his courage the only way he knows how."

Jane dabbed at her eyes with a handkerchief.

Felicia leaned forward on her chair. "I know something about this." She reached out and took Jane's hand in hers. "After my mother died, I was placed out, just like your boys. I was Keith's age when I was taken from the only home I'd ever known and sent across the country and separated from my brother and sister. I was a girl who'd been raised in the tenements of Chicago, and suddenly I found myself living on a farm in the middle of nowhere. Everything seemed strange and vast and empty. I was terribly afraid, terribly lonely."

"I didn't know that about you."

"I don't talk about it much. Not that I'm ashamed to have been orphaned or placed out. I'm not. It simply doesn't seem very important to me now. But it does give me a unique understanding of what Daniel and Keith are going through."

Jane's shoulders sagged. "I'm sure you didn't get into fistfights with other girls at school, did you?"

She gave a brief smile. "No. I coped with my fear in a different way." She thought of Hugh as she released Jane's hand and straightened again. "I believe my brother was more like Daniel."

Jane used her handkerchief to blow her nose.

"Do you love these boys?" Felicia asked softly. "Does your husband love them?"

The answer came swift and strong. "Yes. We both do. Very much. From the first moment we saw them."

"Then just keep doing so. Keith already accepts it. I know he does. He calls you Ma and your husband Pa, and he's a happy child. It will take more time with Daniel. He's older, and he's used to taking care of himself and his brother. No one's wanted to look out for him in a long while. But if you're patient, he'll begin to trust you."

"Lewis will insist he be disciplined for fighting in school."

"Of course. But I hope he'll temper the discipline with love. As will I as his teacher." Giving Jane another squeeze of the hand, Felicia rose. "I must be going."

Jane stood too. "Thank you, Miss Kristoffersen. For telling me about your own placement. I don't know why, but it gives me hope."

"I'm praying for you and your boys, Mrs. Carpenter."

"Thank you," Jane said again.

Felicia walked out of the back room and across the shop to the entrance, Jane following right behind her. They bid each other a good day, and then Felicia left, walking toward home, a mixture of feelings swirling in her chest. Perhaps chief among those feelings was a touch of envy. Daniel might not accept it yet, but he'd been placed with a woman who wanted to love him as only a mother could. He had no idea how blessed he was, and she hoped he would realize it soon.

EIGHTEEN

Strong winds blew in from the northwest on Saturday morning, bending trees sideways and snapping branches. As Felicia made her way across town to the Summerville home, the sky grew dark with storm clouds. To keep her straw hat from being swept away, she placed the flat of her hand on its crown and hurried toward her destination, made easier by the wind at her back.

"Gracious, look at the weather," Kathleen said when she opened the door a short while later. "Come in. Come in before you blow away."

"Thank you." Felicia prayed she didn't look as disheveled as she felt.

"You're the first to arrive."

"I'm not too early, am I?"

Kathleen took her by the arm, a warm smile in place. "Not at all." She drew Felicia with her into the front parlor. "Mother Summerville is in the kitchen, speaking to Mrs. Hasting. Please sit down, and I'll pour you some tea. Or would you prefer coffee?"

"Tea would be lovely." Felicia removed her hat and sat on the upholstered settee.

"Milk?"

"Please."

A blast of wind and rain rattled the windows.

"Oh no." Kathleen twisted in her chair, looking toward the parlor window. Water ran down the glass in a thick sheet. "I hope the others don't stay home because of the foul weather."

"Maybe the storm won't last long." Judging from the darkness outside, Felicia didn't hold out a lot of hope for that.

Kathleen turned toward her again. "At least you made it here before you got a thorough drenching." She lifted the delicate cup and saucer and held them toward Felicia. "And you and I can have a nice visit, no matter what else happens."

Felicia nodded as she took the cup and saucer into her own hands.

"If I haven't already told you," Kathleen said as she poured tea into a second cup, "Suzanne and Phoebe have nothing but praise for their new teacher."

"They're both good students."

Kathleen laughed, but the sound wasn't merry. "Their grandmother would accept nothing less from them. High performance is required of all who bear the Summerville name."

Felicia sipped her tea, not knowing how to respond. It wasn't that she disagreed, only that—

"I'm sorry. I've made you uncomfortable."

"No. Not really."

"I envy you, Felicia."

She felt her eyes widen. "I don't know why you should."

"You're doing what you love to do. How very fortunate you are. There are so many people in the world who cannot say the same."

"I do love teaching. I love the children."

"I know. It's written all over your face whenever you're with them." Kathleen took a sip from her teacup. "So tell me. Why haven't you married and had a family of your own?"

Before Felicia could begin to form a reply, Helen Summerville sailed into the parlor. At first her expression was one of welcome, but it altered ever so slightly when she saw that their only guest was Felicia. "Oh. Miss Kristoffersen. You made it here before the storm." A strong wind rattled the house, as if to emphasize her comment.

"Just barely," Felicia answered.

Helen's gaze shifted to her daughter-in-law. "I'm afraid your party has been spoiled by the weather, Kathleen."

"It wasn't a party, Mother Summerville."

"Of course. I chose my words poorly." Helen took her seat in the chair farthest away from the two younger women. "Why don't we do some preliminary planning. That way we can tell the other women what we need from them, whether they come later this morning or we must wait until we see them at church tomorrow. It is our place, as leaders in our community, to lead the way in all things. The Carpenters are in need of our help, the sooner the better."

Felicia was certain that when Helen said "our place," she didn't mean to include the lone guest in the room. As far as the elder Mrs. Summerville was concerned, Felicia's place was undoubtedly the lowest in the community.

She pasted a determined smile on her lips. "What a wonderful idea, Mrs. Summerville. How may I assist you?"

The rumble of thunder drew Colin to the front window of the mercantile. The few horses tied at posts along the main street of town stood with rumps turned to the wind and rain, heads hung low. There wasn't a person in view. Folks thereabout had too much sense to be out in such weather.

"Never seen it rain so hard for so long," Jimmy said as he came to stand beside Colin.

"There'll be flooding by the creeks and rivers. Look what's happening to the street."

"Yeah. I can already hear my mom hollering at me to take my boots off before I come in the house." The kid laughed. "Dad says her floors don't stand a chance when she's got three sons and a husband set on tracking them up."

More thunder rolled in the distance. At least the heavy rain would lessen the likelihood of a range fire started by a lightning strike. After the heat wave of late summer, all could be thankful for that.

"I'll get the ladder and clean those top shelves like you wanted."

"Thanks, Jimmy."

Colin waited a moment, then turned and walked to the back of the store and into his living room. Much as he'd done moments before in the store, his daughter stood at the parlor window; her forehead was pressed against the glass as she stared out at the storm.

"Hey, pumpkin."

Charity looked over her shoulder. The expression on her face was pained. "We're not gonna get to ride, are we?"

"Doesn't look like it. Even if the rain stops soon, it'll be too muddy."

"Can I go over to Suzanne's and Phoebe's?"

He grinned as he shook his head. "No. The Summervilles don't want you coming over wet and muddy. You'll have to spend the day with me." He crossed the room to stand beside her.

"Miss K went over to the Summervilles' this morning."

"She did?"

"Uh-huh. She told me when we were reading last night. I wanted her to go for a ride with us. I figured she could borrow a horse from Mr. Daughtry. Don't you think he would've lent her a horse? But she said she'd be busy this morning."

Colin looked in the direction of the Summerville home, although he couldn't see the house from here. "Hope she went before it started to rain."

"She did. I saw her go."

"Not much escapes you, does it?" He ruffled his daughter's hair.

She shrugged. "What're we gonna do if we can't ride?"

"Why don't you read that book you got for your birthday?"

"I don't want to read."

He'd hoped the evening sessions with Felicia had changed that. Guess it was expecting too much for anything to change this soon.

"Can I go out to the barn to see Princess?"

He looked at the dark sky and pouring rain. "Not until the storm lets up."

Charity released a dramatic sigh.

"Come on. You can help me do the inventory while there're no customers in the store."

"Ah, Papa. I don't want to—"

"Charity."

"All right. I'm coming."

Because of the unrelenting rain, no other women came to Kathleen's meeting. But if it upset her, she didn't let on to her mother-in-law or Felicia. She proceeded to make a list of items she thought the Carpenters needed and another list of the women who could probably help and what items they might provide.

The Summervilles would buy denim overalls and a pair of boots for each boy. Also a couple of warm coats for winter, which would soon be upon them. Felicia volunteered to make the boys two shirts apiece. Kathleen thought Nancy Hightower could be depended on to provide two of the beautiful quilts she made. And on went the lists.

When they were finished, Kathleen informed Felicia that she must stay for lunch, and then they would have Elias take her home in their buggy.

"Oh, I couldn't let you do that. It's only a few blocks."

"In this rain?" Kathleen rose from her chair. "The hem of your skirt would be caked with mud as soon as you crossed the street. We wouldn't think of letting you walk home. Would we, Mother Summerville?"

The older woman hesitated a fraction of a second before answering, "Of course not."

"I'm going to check on the girls, and then I'll tell Mrs. Hasting to expect one more for lunch." Kathleen left the parlor.

Alone with Helen, Felicia felt the silence grow awkward. If only the rain would stop, she could insist that she must leave at once. But the rain didn't stop. It looked as if it might continue for forty days and forty nights.

"More tea, Miss Kristoffersen?"

She pulled her gaze from the window. "No, thank you."

"Such a dreary day."

"Yes."

"You know, Miss Kristoffersen, my daughter-in-law has grown quite fond of you in your short time in Frenchman's Bluff."

"I'm fond of her too. It's nice to have a friend."

"She thinks you're doing a fine job as schoolteacher."

Felicia heard what had gone unsaid—that Helen disagreed with Kathleen. She lifted her chin. "I'm glad she thinks so. Most of the children are doing well with their studies."

"I wish I knew what they will decide about the cottage and your living situation."

"I'm sorry. My living situation? To what do you refer?"

"Why, to Kathleen and Mr. Murphy, of course. Kathleen insists they can manage for a short time in the living quarters of the mercantile. But I believe it's much too small for a couple and three active girls. The cottage wouldn't be much better. I think they should wait until they build a new home before they marry. And if they choose to use the cottage, what will we do with you? The availability of a separate house has been a definite benefit to potential teachers, given the salary we offer. I hope the change won't make you want to leave us."

Marry? Leave?

"Oh dear." Helen glanced toward the hallway. "Listen to me go on. I shouldn't have said anything. Kathleen and Mr. Murphy don't want their engagement known as yet."

Engagement? Somehow, Felicia found her voice. "Why not?"

"The children. They don't want to get them all excited about a wedding until they decide where to live and when the wedding will be. Mr. Murphy is a proud man. He won't allow George to help with the expense of building a new home. He insists, if that's their decision, on doing it himself, even though we would be pleased to spend whatever is needed. Money is no object for us, as you must know. And after all, our granddaughters deserve to have a good home."

"I'm sure they'll have a fine one," Felicia said softly.

Helen leaned forward at the waist and whispered, "Please don't tell Kathleen I said anything. It was quite by accident."

"No. No, I won't tell her."

There was no reason a secret engagement between Colin Murphy and Kathleen Summerville should matter to Felicia, beyond hoping they would be very happy together.

And she did hope that for them.

Why wouldn't she?

NINETEEN

After four days of constant rain and black skies, the streets of Frenchman's Bluff were a sea of mud. Gloom spread over the whole town. Or so it seemed.

Charity's and Colin's moods were no better than their neighbors', and the last thing Colin wanted to do after the store closed on Wednesday was stand at the stove to prepare supper. "Grab your umbrella, Charity. We're going to eat at Miss Caroline's."

"Really?" His daughter brightened at once.

"Really."

The pair of them put on their galoshes and hurried across the street to Miss Caroline's, the one remaining restaurant in Frenchman's Bluff. They apparently weren't the only ones who'd thought dining out was a good idea. More than half of the tables were occupied when they arrived.

"Look!" Charity said. "There's Suzanne and Phoebe and their mom."

When Colin's gaze met with Kathleen's, she smiled and motioned to the two empty chairs at their table.

"Can we eat with them, Papa?"

A week or so ago, he'd asked himself if raising Charity alone was the best way, and the thought had stayed with him. Maybe this was God's subtle—or not so subtle—answer to that question. Maybe it was time Colin stopped caring about the gossips in town. Kathleen knew what it was like to lose a spouse. She knew what it was like to raise her children alone. He liked her, and that was a good place to start.

He nodded to Charity, then followed her to Kathleen's table.

"I'm surprised to see so many braved the rain," she said as he settled onto the chair opposite her.

"Must be feeling as closed in as I was."

The waitress came, and everyone ordered Miss Caroline's meatloaf special.

"It's my favorite," Charity told her friends.

"Mine too," Suzanne and her sister replied in unison.

Colin looked at Kathleen and shrugged. "What can I say? Mine too."

Kathleen laughed. "I guess we're all in agreement, then." She was a pretty woman, especially when amused. It made her brown eyes sparkle.

The restaurant door opened again, letting in a draft of cool, damp air. Kathleen looked past Colin's shoulder, and he thought he saw a subtle change in her countenance. She'd already looked happy and that didn't change. Her cheeks had already been slightly flushed from her laughter. Did they seem more so now? He was about to turn to see who it was that had drawn her attention when two men stopped at the end of the table.

"Evenin', Miz Summerville," one of them said.

Colin recognized the men as cowpokes who worked for Glen Gilchrist. The one who'd spoken to Kathleen had come into the store for supplies a number of times over the summer. Oscar something. Johnson. No, Jacobson.

The young man—Colin guessed him to be nine or ten years

his junior—nodded to him next, a slight frown furrowing his brow. "Evenin', Mr. Murphy."

"Jacobson." He looked at the fellow behind him, but he didn't look familiar, so Colin just nodded.

Kathleen said, "I'm surprised to see you in town with all this rain, Mr. Jacobson."

"Ranch work doesn't wait for the weather, ma'am."

"No, I don't suppose it does."

"Well,"—Oscar set his hat back on his head—"didn't mean to intrude on your supper."

"You aren't intruding, Mr. Jacobson. Mr. Murphy and his daughter came in just a short while ago, and we invited them to join us. My daughters and Charity are good friends."

The frown smoothed from Oscar's forehead. "Well then, you all enjoy." He and his friend moved to an empty table near the window and sat down.

Colin couldn't put his finger on it, but something felt different at the table after that. Kathleen focused her attention on her daughters, asking them questions about schoolwork, never once looking at Colin until the waitress brought out their food and it was time to say grace.

Kathleen was mortified. Absolutely mortified. What had possessed her to feel the need to explain her reasons for dining with Colin and his daughter? It was none of Oscar's concern, nor the concern of anyone else in the restaurant, yet the words had rushed out of her as if it were vital that he—and they—know.

"Amen," Colin said at the end of the blessing, and Kathleen realized she hadn't heard a word he'd spoken.

Another reason to be appalled at her behavior. And it wasn't helped by the voice of her mother-in-law playing in her head, telling her that she wasn't getting any younger, that she was going to miss her opportunity to make a suitable match, to have a home of her own.

A home of my own...

She looked at Colin and offered a warm smile, determined not to be distracted from him again.

TWENTY

"Very good, Charity." Seated in the kitchen of the Murphy residence, Felicia slid a paper across the table. "Now let's see how quickly you can read that list of words. Just like we've done before. Try to read them as fast as you can. Ready?"

Her pupil nodded.

"Okay. Go."

"He, that, on, but, with, was, she, they, at, all, out, have, there, be, am."

Felicia clapped her hands three times. "Yes! You got every one of them right."

"Did I really?"

"Yes, you did. Bravo!"

Charity beamed with pleasure. "Papa!" she called, looking toward the doorway into the living room. "Papa, did you hear that? I got all the words right."

Colin appeared a moment later. He too was smiling. "I heard."

Felicia's heart tightened in her chest, a reaction that had happened every time she'd seen him for the past week. She supposed it was because of the weight of the secret she carried, thanks to Helen's careless words. There could be no other reason for it. No reason at all.

Colin entered the kitchen, pulled out an empty chair, turned it toward him, and straddled the seat, leaning his arms atop the chair back. "Can I see the list of words?"

"Sure, Papa." Charity slid the paper toward him.

He was silent for a moment, his eyes scanning the page. "I timed you. Fifteen words in ten seconds."

"That's fast." Charity turned toward Felicia. "Isn't that fast, Miss K?"

She nodded. "Yes, Charity. It's fast. And not a single mistake." Felicia glanced in Colin's direction and found him watching her, eyes serious but the hint of a smile still on his lips. Her insides seemed to dip and twirl. She wished he would go back to the parlor.

He didn't move.

She looked at Charity again. "Why don't we stop early tonight? You've done so well this week."

"Okay!" The girl hopped up from her seat. "Are we still going fishing in the morning?"

Felicia knew better than to look at Colin again. "If it's all right with your father."

"Sure. Why not? The ground's dry. I'd go too if I could, but I'm expecting a big shipment in the morning."

Charity said, "Jimmy could handle it."

"Maybe so. But two can handle it quicker. I wouldn't feel right leaving it all to him. But fried fish sounds good for supper tomorrow night."

"Could Miss K come to supper?"

Her pulse quickened. "Oh, Charity. I'm not sure that I should. There's always so much to do on Saturdays."

"You have to eat." Colin shrugged. "Might as well join us. I'll do the cooking."

He was engaged to another. It wouldn't be right to join him

for supper. Would it? Of course, Charity would be there. Would it be any different than when she was tutoring and he joined them in the kitchen at the end of the lesson? Like now.

The room suddenly felt much smaller than it had moments before.

"Please, Miss K."

"Let's see if we catch any fish," she said, rising to her feet.

"Okay." Charity rocked back on the heels of her shoes. "See you in the morning."

"See you at six." Felicia gave the girl a quick smile before hurrying out of the Murphy kitchen and across the yard to her cottage. Once inside, she breathed a sigh of relief as she dropped her things on the table.

What's wrong with me? It's so foolish to react this way. He was being polite to Charity's teacher. Nothing more. I'm just anxious because I know his secret. But even that's silly. What he and Kathleen do doesn't affect me.

Well, that wasn't entirely true. It could mean she would have to leave this cozy little home, that she would have to live with the family of one of her other students, perhaps different families from month to month. But that wouldn't be so terrible. Teachers all around the country did it. If they could, so could she.

Kathleen is my friend. She likes me. That must be the reason why Colin ... why Mr. Murphy seems to have changed his opinion of me. See? It's for the best.

She stepped into the parlor, her gaze taking in the sofa and chair and small oval tables, the oil lamp, the painting on the wall, the little knickknacks that told her a great deal about the woman whose home this had been meant to be.

Was Kathleen anything like Margaret Murphy? Was that why Colin asked her to marry him? Did he love her?

She ran her fingers over a porcelain figurine.

Charity liked Kathleen and was a good friend of Kathleen's daughters. The three girls were as close as sisters. Charity would undoubtedly be delighted when she learned her father was to marry her friends' mother. An ideal situation for one and all.

Felicia's eyes blurred behind unshed tears. "Silly. I'm being silly."

She had no reason to cry. Not a single one. She'd come to Frenchman's Bluff to teach, to educate her pupils, to help her students succeed. She was doing so. Look at how much Charity had improved with her studies. And Daniel Watkins seemed to be settling down, seemed to be a little less defiant. She was succeeding where once she'd feared she might fail. Her life was ever so much better than it had been only a month ago.

"Not a single reason to cry," she whispered, wiping her eyes. "Not a single one."

Except for the ticking of the mantel clock, the house was quiet. Charity had headed to bed early, excited about the morning fishing trip with Miss Kristoffersen.

Miss Kristoffersen ...

Colin looked down at the sheet of paper on his lap. Charity's list of practice words. Fifteen of them. Fifteen words she had recognized in ten seconds. His eyes scanned the list.

He ... that ... on ... but ... with ...

Not all the words. Not fifteen seconds.

Was ... she ... they ... at ... all ...

But he knew them. Saw them. Understood them.

Out ... have ... there ... be ... am.

He could almost hear Felicia say, "You got every one of them right this time, Colin." He liked imagining her calling him by his given name. Perhaps liked it more than he should.

He reached for the Bible on the table beside him—Margaret's Bible, the cover and pages worn from use—and put it in his lap, on top of the sheet of paper with the practice words. He opened the book to the place where the letter was. A letter with his name on it. In the place where Margaret had put it many years ago. When, he couldn't say for sure. Nor could he say why she'd written it since she'd known the truth he'd tried so hard to hide from everyone.

He couldn't read.

He … that … on … but … with …

He hadn't thought he could learn to read, so why try? Hadn't thought he was smart enough to learn to read. That's what the teacher had told his father. *"Might as well keep him home, Mr. Murphy. He'll need a good trade. If he can't read by now, no point his staying in school."*

Words shouldn't hurt the way those had hurt him. The way they still hurt him. Not after so many years. Too stupid to learn.

Was … she … they … at … all …

In his mind, he heard Felicia's instructions to Charity, her words of encouragement, spoken time and again during their evening tutoring sessions. Felicia's patience seemed unending. When had he started to feel as if she were speaking to him as much as to his daughter?

He put the letter back into the Bible, closed it, and set it on the table. Then he rose from the chair and went upstairs, carrying the lamp with him. He stopped outside Charity's room. She lay on her stomach, arms flung wide, her face half hidden beneath her pillow. At this moment, he could pound on a bass drum and it wouldn't wake her.

He'd wanted to yell at Miss Lucas the first time she'd suggested

Charity wasn't as smart as other children her age. He should have told the woman to shut up rather than let Charity feel the same way he'd felt for the past twenty-five years.

I'm sorry, pumpkin.

He should thank God for Felicia Kristoffersen. He closed his eyes and did so: *Thank You, Lord, for Felicia Kristoffersen.*

How could he not thank God for the new schoolmarm? She'd stepped in and done what Colin couldn't — helped Charity discover the joy of learning to read.

He eased the door to his daughter's room closed and continued on to his own room. After setting the lamp on the bedside stand, he undressed, laying his clothes over the back of a chair. He washed his face and cleaned his teeth before slipping into his nightshirt and sliding between the covers on his bed.

Outside, the moonless night was as black as pitch. Along with the cool air, muffled music from the saloon drifted through the narrow opening in the window, a melody he recognized when the piano player reached the chorus.

After the ball is over ... after the break of morn ...

A sad song, that one, and suddenly the bed seemed too big and the room too empty.

TWENTY-ONE

Saturday dawned with clear skies overhead and frost in the air.

Felicia was glad for her coat and gloves as she and Charity set off for the river, fishing poles on their shoulders. As they walked, Charity kept up a steady stream of chatter, bouncing from one subject to the next. Felicia allowed the girl's merry spirits to lift her own. Whatever had brought her to tears the previous night, she was determined to put it behind her and not think of it again.

The heavy rains of earlier in the week had carved deep ruts in the steep parts of the trail, but thankfully, the ground was now dry, the earth hard beneath their shoes. Still, Felicia was glad when they reached the level pathway that led to the river.

"Wow! Look how fast the river's running, Miss K." Charity set her pole and basket next to the log, then stood with arms akimbo as she stared at the river.

"I see." Felicia stopped at the girl's side. "You be sure you stay back from the edge like your father says."

"I will."

Felicia didn't have the best depth perception, but it seemed to her the water was running several inches higher and much swifter than the last time she'd been there. Even more rain must have fallen in the mountains to the north than in the valley.

She sank onto the log and removed her gloves. Charity did the same. Then they both took worms from the tin can inside Felicia's fishing basket and readied their hooks.

"You stay here," Felicia instructed Charity. "I'll go up to that bend there." She pointed. "Call if you need me."

The girl rolled her eyes. "Miss K, you sound like Papa. I'm not a baby. I can fish on my own without any help."

Felicia subdued a laugh. "Pardon me." Carrying her pole and basket, stepping over tree roots, underbrush, and fallen branches, she made her way to the spot she'd selected. Minutes later, she cast her line into the river.

Morning sunlight played across the surface of the water and gilded her pole, almost blinding her with its brightness. Birds called from treetops as the world of nature awakened around her, and Felicia's heart and thoughts responded to its beauty, words of praise springing into her head.

One thing have I desired of the Lord, that will I seek after; that I may dwell in the house of the Lord all the days of my life, to behold the beauty of the Lord, and to enquire in his temple.

Oh, that she would daily remember what was most important in life: to know God and to do His will. That she would seek to behold His beauty and remember that, no matter the trials encountered, earth was her temporary home.

A memory came to her, of her mother sitting in a rocking chair in their small tenement flat in Chicago, the Bible open on her lap. Elethea Brennan had been a woman of unwavering faith who had attempted, in the short time allowed her, to pass along the same to her three children.

"Hold fast to God, Felicia, and you be remembering that He's holdin' on to you too."

"I remember, Mum," she whispered, the words whisked away by the sounds of the rushing river.

The expected freight arrived shortly after eight o'clock that morning, a good hour earlier than usual. Colin and Jimmy set straight to work, emptying boxes and barrels, filling shelves in the mercantile with merchandise, putting the excess into the stockroom at the back.

When they were done, Colin checked his pocket watch. If the fishing was any good, Charity and Felicia might still be at it. If he hurried—

"Jimmy, I'm going to be out for a few hours. Mind the store."

"Sure thing, Mr. Murphy. Anything special you need done while you're gone?"

"Nope. Just take care of the customers."

The fishing tackle was organized and his horse saddled and bridled in short order. Then he was on his way. He watched the trail before him, hoping he wouldn't see Felicia and his daughter returning from the river before he could get there himself.

"Miss K!"

Felicia looked downriver and saw Charity's pole bending in a big arch.

"My line's snagged on something. I can't get it free."

"I'll be right there." Felicia reeled in her line, then collected the basket—with three trout inside it—and the coat she'd removed a short while before. "I think it's time we start back anyway."

"So soon?"

"It's not all that soon." She made her way back to Charity. "Look how far up the sun is."

"But I've only caught two fish. That's not enough for Papa."

Felicia chuckled. "I'll give you one of mine." She set down her things. "Looks like you've caught a log at the bottom of the river this time."

"I know." Charity gave her pole a tug. "It won't come loose."

"Let me have a look." She stepped closer to the riverbank, reached up, and took hold of the pole, giving the line another hard yank. "I'm afraid we'll have to cut it."

"Are you sure?" The girl stepped to Felicia's side.

"Get back, Charity. You know your father doesn't allow you to get this close to the river's edge."

"Ah, Miss K. I'm okay here beside you."

"Listen to me. I can swim. You're still learning." Felicia looked down. "If you don't mind the rules, you might not be allowed to come with me next time."

Charity rolled her eyes before giving her pole a vicious yank. The line must have broken, for the rod whipped up, smacking Felicia across the side of her face. She cried out in pain, her eyes watering. She lifted her hand to her cheek.

"Miss K, I didn't—"

Blinded by her tears, Felicia started to turn. But instead of solid ground, her foot landed on a slippery rock and she was thrown off balance. Her arms flailed about, trying to find something—anything!—to grab hold of, but all her hands found was air. The next thing she knew, she hit the water.

Merciful heavens, it was cold!

As she bobbed to the surface, she heard Charity yelling her name. She wanted to answer her, to call back that she was fine. But before she could, the water pulled her down again, her sodden woolen skirt wrapping around her legs. The weight of it threatened to pull her to the river bottom and keep her there while the swift current swept her downriver. She smacked into a large rock and bounced to the surface as pain exploded in her hip. She sucked in air and opened her eyes, hoping to find something to grab on to. She moved her arms, trying to swim toward shore, but her clothes had become her enemy.

God, help me!

She went under again, smashing into more rocks and forest debris that had washed down from the mountains. She felt her body weakening. Was this how she would die?

She renewed her struggle against the current, fighting her way back to the surface. This time she saw a large tree limb, half submerged, stretched over the river a short distance ahead of her. She was going to hit it. There was no avoiding that. But if she could grasp it, if she could hold on to it, perhaps she could pull herself to shore.

❦

Colin heard his daughter's screams while he was still in the narrow canyon. Heart pounding, he kicked Drifter hard in the ribs. The gelding shot forward, galloping headlong down the trail. Colin leaned forward over the saddle horn. Whatever was wrong, his daughter was in great distress. He had to find her. He had to help her. He had to save her.

His horse shot into the opening. "Charity!"

She continued to scream, probably too loudly to hear his call. And then he understood what she was saying. "Miss K! Miss K!"

He caught sight of his daughter a few heartbeats later. She was pushing her way through the underbrush along the riverbank, still screaming her teacher's name.

"Charity!"

She heard him this time. "Papa!"

He reined in, and Drifter slid to a stop. Colin's feet hit the ground at a run.

"Papa, hurry! It's Miss K. She fell in the river."

Oh, God! Don't let her drown. Don't let that happen.

He grabbed hold of his daughter and pulled her against him— *Thank God it wasn't you; thank God it wasn't you*—even as his gaze searched the river for some sign of Felicia.

Charity pulled away. "She's over here, Papa. Hurry!"

He saw her then, arms wrapped around a tree limb, her face barely above the water, looking half drowned already.

<hr />

Felicia couldn't hold on much longer. She *was* going to die in the river. Perhaps she was already dead. She couldn't hear Charity screaming her name any longer. Poor Charity. She shouldn't have seen this. She might never enjoy coming to the river to fish again.

Water splashed into Felicia's mouth, and she coughed and choked as she fought for a breath of air. So she wasn't dead after all. There would be no coughing or choking in heaven. Nor would her limbs be numb from the cold.

If she just let go . . .

Strong arms went around her waist. "Miss Kristoffersen."

Felicia opened her eyes and looked up. Colin was beside her. Water dripped from his dark hair and off the tip of his nose and chin.

"Can you let go of the branch and hold on to me?"

She nodded, but she couldn't seem to make her arms obey.

Gently, he pried her grip free from the tree limb, and after he did, the last of her strength seemed to be swept away in the current.

In the next instant, she was cradled in his arms as he carried her to shore. Against her ear, she heard the rapid beat of his heart, above the sounds of the river.

"Charity," he called to his daughter, "leave everything. I'll come for it later. We need to get Felicia home and into some warm clothes."

She realized then that she was shivering. Shivering so hard her teeth rattled. "I'm ... all ... r-right," she managed to say. "You ... can ... p-put me ... down."

If he heard her, he pretended he didn't. Instead, he carried her away from the river. Shade and sunlight alternately fell on her face. The rapid flashes of dark and light made her dizzy, and she closed her eyes.

The next thing she knew, they were on horseback, Colin astride the saddle, Felicia still held against his chest. With his free arm, he grabbed hold of Charity and pulled her up behind him.

"Hold tight, pumpkin."

"I will, Papa."

"Let's go, Drifter."

The horse moved forward at a fast walk, following the trail, climbing out of the river canyon toward the bluff. Felicia tried once to open her eyes to see where they were, but the dizziness overcame her a second time. She kept her eyes closed for the rest of the way.

The horse stopped at last, and Felicia felt Colin swing his daughter to the ground. "Go get Dr. Young, Charity. Fast as you can. Run!"

"I'm ... all right," Felicia protested weakly.

He stepped down from the saddle. "You almost drowned." He carried her inside the cottage and into her bedroom, where he sat her on the straight-backed chair next to the bed. With Colin in the room, it felt half the size it had that morning. Small and airless.

He knelt, took her right foot in his hand, and began unlacing her boot.

"I can do that," she said.

"No, you can't."

She wanted to argue with him, wanted to tell him she was capable of taking care of herself. But that was a bald-faced lie. She could hardly manage to stay upright in the chair, let alone bend forward at the waist to remove her boots.

When his calloused fingers touched the skin of her foot, she jerked in surprise. No man had ever touched her bare feet. It seemed . . . it seemed strangely intimate.

"Miss Kristoffersen?"

I like it better when he calls me Felicia.

"What's wrong?"

She inhaled through her nose. "Nothing. I'm fine."

"The doctor'll be here soon, and we'll get you into bed."

We? The room began to sway.

"Miss Kristoffersen?" His voice came from a distance, beyond a roaring much like the sound of the river. "Felicia?"

The light in the room grew dim, and then everything went black.

Colin paced outside the cottage, waiting for a word from Dr. Young. Charity sat on a chair on the porch. At last the door opened, and Kathleen came outside. Colin moved toward her. "How is she?"

Kathleen took his hand and looked him in the eyes. "There is nothing seriously wrong with her, Mr. Murphy. She has a cut on her head and some bruises and has taken a chill from being in the river. But I'm sure she fainted because of fright more than anything. All she needs is to rest for a day or two, and she will be right as rain."

Colin released a breath as he withdrew his hand and leaned his back against the tree that grew near the side of the cottage. "When I saw her go under ..." He raked the fingers of his right hand through his hair. "I thought she was gone for good."

"But she wasn't. You saved her." She glanced over her shoulder toward the door. "The doctor will be out in a few minutes. I'll go back in and stay with her for the afternoon. She shouldn't be alone until she's steady on her feet again."

He gave Kathleen a brief smile. "It was good of you to come over and help Dr. Young."

"I was talking to Mr. Swanson outside the pharmacy when Charity came for the doctor. When I heard what happened ..." She allowed her words to drift into silence.

"You've been a good friend to Feli—" He cleared his throat. "To Miss Kristoffersen, right from the first day she got here."

"I've tried to be." Kathleen brushed her hands over her skirt. "Maybe after you've talked to the doctor, you should take Charity to play with my girls for a while. She's terribly upset. She says Miss Kristoffersen's accident was her fault."

"She did?" Colin straightened away from the tree and looked toward the porch again. "She didn't tell me that."

"When has she had time to tell you?" Kathleen's simple words felt like a rebuke, although there was no sting in her tone of voice. "And even if she'd had the time, she might not have said anything to you without some urging."

"I'd better talk to her now." He started to move away, but Kathleen stopped him.

"Wait, Mr. Murphy. Please."

"Yes?"

"I'd like you to know that I'm *your* friend too. You do know that, don't you? You could come to me any time. Whatever the need."

He felt guilty for some reason, although he couldn't say why. "Yes, I know." Then he walked toward the porch, leaving Kathleen behind.

TWENTY-TWO

"I'm fine, Kathleen." Felicia pushed her loose hair over her shoulder. "And I don't need to stay in bed."

"But you *will* stay in bed because that's what the doctor ordered."

Felicia sighed her frustration. "Well, you needn't stay. You've given up enough of your time already."

Kathleen sat down on the chair near the bed. "I'll stay and prepare your dinner. When I'm satisfied you can take care of yourself for the night, I'll go home."

"It's a lot of folderol over nothing."

"You almost drowned, Felicia. If Mr. Murphy hadn't come when he did . . ." Kathleen shook her head slowly. "I hate to think what would have happened to you."

Felicia shuddered. She hated to think about it too. When she closed her eyes, it seemed as if the water was sweeping over her again. She probably wouldn't sleep a wink tonight. All the same, she knew she didn't need anyone to fuss over her. The bruises would heal, as would the cut on her forehead near the hairline. The likelihood of her fainting again was slim to none. She wasn't the swooning sort. In fact, it embarrassed her to know she'd done so in front of Colin.

"Are you hungry?" Kathleen asked, drawing Felicia's attention once again.

"Not really."

"You should eat anyway."

"Perhaps a slice of bread with butter. With a glass of milk."

Kathleen frowned. "That isn't much."

"It's all I want. Truly."

"No wonder you're so thin." Kathleen rose from the chair. "But I suppose you know your own mind." She moved toward the door.

"Kathleen."

She stopped and looked over her shoulder.

"Thank you. I haven't seemed very appreciative of your help, and I'm sorry for that. You've spent almost the entire day with me, and I ... I fear I'm not a very good patient."

A small smile tipped the corners of Kathleen's mouth. "It's what friends do for one another."

"You've known me such a short time."

"Not all friendships take a long time to grow and deepen. Some are formed in an instant." Her smile broadened now. "From the moment we met, I knew we were destined to be good friends. I'm not sure why. It's just the way I felt."

Now Felicia was embarrassed. How did one respond to such open affection? With children, she knew what to do. But with a friend, woman to woman? It was foreign territory.

"I'll be right back with your bread and milk."

Alone in her bedroom, Felicia leaned against the pillows and quickly counted her blessings. She was alive. She hadn't drowned in the river. Charity hadn't been harmed—how much worse it would have been if Charity had gone into the river instead of Felicia! Colin had arrived before her strength gave out. She hadn't been badly hurt. She wouldn't miss any days in the classroom and wouldn't lose any pay. The doctor's fee wasn't terribly high. Kathleen was her friend, meaning Felicia no longer had to feel that she was all alone in the world. So much to be grateful for.

Thank You, Lord. I don't deserve Your many blessings.

A short while later, Kathleen returned with a tray. On it was a glass of milk and a thick slice of bread spread with butter. She set the tray on a small bedside table before settling once again on the nearby chair.

Felicia laughed softly. "You're going to stay until I eat every last crumb, aren't you?"

"You're learning."

Felicia took the tray onto her lap, then lifted the bread and took a bite.

Kathleen nodded her approval.

Swallowing, Felicia said, "I'm glad we're friends."

"Me too."

"When I first arrived in Frenchman's Bluff, I hoped I might become friends with Mrs. Murphy. I didn't know my landlord was a widower. Funny, isn't it? That it will happen that way after all."

Kathleen's head tipped a little to one side, a puzzled look pinching her brow. "What do you mean?"

"You and I are already friends, and when you marry, I shall, indeed, be the friend of Mrs. Murphy."

"What on earth? Oh dear."

Realizing her mistake, Felicia tried to think of something to say to cover her blunder. She drew a blank.

"The whole town must think I've chased after him shamelessly." Kathleen lowered her gaze to a spot on the floor, her expression distressed.

"No. I'm sure you're wrong. No one thinks that."

"Then why would you assume we're to marry?"

"Aren't you?"

The other woman shook her head.

"I wouldn't tell another soul if it were true."

"But it isn't true," Kathleen said softly.

What could Felicia say to that outright denial? She'd already betrayed one confidence. True, it was a confidence she shouldn't have been given to begin with, but she'd promised Helen Summerville she would keep the secret. She didn't want to be the cause of friction between Kathleen and her mother-in-law, nor did she wish to give Helen another reason to dislike her.

Finally, Felicia managed to say, "I didn't mean to upset you. I'm sorry."

"It isn't your fault. It's my own." Kathleen drew a shaky breath. "But let's not talk about it. Let's talk about you instead. Why haven't you married? Surely there must have been some young men in Wyoming who were interested."

She thought of Rolf and his brothers and subdued a shudder. "None I would wish to marry."

Her friend raised an eyebrow, silently encouraging her to continue.

"I did have some gentlemen callers when I was at normal school, but there wasn't anyone special. No one who made me want to give up being a teacher and making my own way." She shook her head. "It seems to me that most men—too many of them, anyway—want a wife to keep their house and give birth to their heirs and nothing more. But what about a woman's mind? Can't we think for ourselves? Can't we contribute to society? Why should we have to be subject to the whims of men simply because we were born female? I could never live like that."

"My goodness, Felicia. You have a rather harsh opinion of men."

She felt color rise in her cheeks.

"Haven't you ever been in love?"

The question brought an unwelcome image to Felicia's mind—Colin Murphy, holding her close as his tall buckskin cantered along a road. She shook her head, both in answer to Kathleen's question and in an effort to chase Colin from her thoughts.

"Never? Not even a little bit?"

Felicia sat a little straighter in the bed. "The farm where I grew up was remote. The only young men I saw regularly were my cousins." That was skirting the truth a bit.

"Well, if you ever *do* fall in love," Kathleen said, "I wager it will change your mind about men *and* marriage."

Colin and his horse tried to force their way back into Felicia's thoughts. She resolutely pushed them back.

As if in response, she heard his voice saying, "Hello inside. May I come in?"

Colin waited outside the back door until he heard an invitation to enter the cottage.

"Felicia's feeling much better," Kathleen said from the bedroom doorway as she watched him walk toward her through the kitchen.

Removing his hat, Colin stopped before entering the bedroom, and Kathleen took a step to one side. His gaze went to the bed, where Felicia was sitting up, her back against the headboard. She wore a blue robe that matched the color of her eyes, and her hair fell loose around her shoulders, like a honey-colored cloud. On the day she'd arrived, he'd thought her striking but not beautiful. He'd been wrong. Dead wrong. She was beyond beautiful in his eyes.

"Glad to hear you're all right," he said before clearing his throat. "You look better than the last time I saw you."

The instant the words were out of his mouth, he was sorry for them. But then a smile touched the corners of her mouth. He assumed that meant she hadn't been insulted.

He looked at Kathleen. "I'm going over to get Charity. Is there anything you need from home that I can bring back for you?"

Before Kathleen could answer, Felicia said, "She doesn't need anything, Mr. Murphy. But you *can* walk her home. I'm not an invalid. I'm able to take care of myself. Take her home so she can enjoy supper with her children."

The fragile, half-drowned female he'd brought back from the river that morning had vanished. Not a trace of her remained.

Colin cocked a brow at Kathleen.

She nodded. "I'll walk home with you."

"Okay." He set his hat back on his head. "Ready?"

Kathleen went to the bedside. "Are you sure there's nothing you need before I go?"

"I'm sure." Felicia took hold of Kathleen's hand. "Thank you for everything."

"I was glad to help. And if you do discover you need something, you need only send for me."

Colin led the way across the kitchen and held the screen door open for her to pass through, then he followed. They fell into step, Colin shortening his stride to match hers. Neither said anything for several minutes. Perhaps they would have remained silent all the way to the Summerville home if not for their many neighbors.

"How's the schoolmarm doin'?"

"Mighty scary."

"Came near to drowning, I heard. Thank God we didn't lose her."

Each time they were stopped on the sidewalk, Kathleen was quick to issue assurances that Felicia would soon be perfectly fine.

"A little rest is all Miss Kristoffersen needs. You'll probably see her at church tomorrow."

Colin felt another rush of relief each time Kathleen said those words. When he recalled the way Felicia had looked as she clung to that branch, her head barely above water, and later at home, sopping wet, strands of hair clinging to her damp skin, her face as white as a sheet, her eyes rolling back as her body went limp—the memory caused his heart to catch every time.

At last, they reached the Summerville residence. Colin put his fingers beneath the elbow of Kathleen's right arm as they climbed the steps to the porch.

"Mr. Murphy." She stopped and turned toward him. "There's something I think you should know."

If she was about to tell him there was more wrong with Felicia, then—

"Miss Kristoffersen was under the impression that you and I are to be married."

"*What?*"

Kathleen's hands clenched at her waist and tears flooded her eyes. "It's my own fault. I'm sure everyone in town knows that I'm fond of you and Charity. And that ... that I would be willing to be more than a friend to you."

Colin removed his hat and raked his fingers through his hair.

"I'm sorry," she rushed on. "I've been much too forward when in your company. You've never encouraged me, never led me to believe you felt anything more than friendship. But neither have you been cruel enough to publicly reject me." The tears slipped from her eyes to trail down her cheeks. "I'm sure the gossips have had a heyday over my behavior."

"Don't cry, Kathleen." He couldn't help but use her given name. Calling her Mrs. Summerville would feel too strange after her confession.

She dabbed at her eyes with a handkerchief.

"I won't pretend I didn't know you ... felt kindly toward me ... and that you'd be open to a union between our families."

A soft groan escaped her lips, and she cast her gaze to the floorboards between them.

"But the truth is, I don't know if I care to marry again. Only times I've considered it, it was because of Charity, because I think she needs a mother." He cleared his throat, uncomfortable with his words, hoping he wouldn't cause her more distress. "When I've considered marriage, Kathleen, I've known it'd make sense if I were to choose you."

"Thank you ... Colin," she said softly, raising her eyes to meet his. "It's kind of you to say so." After a moment's hesitation, she turned toward the door. "I'll go get Charity for you. Would you care to wait inside?"

"No. If it's all right with you, I'll just wait for her here on the porch." He hadn't lied to her. If he were to marry, it would make sense to choose Kathleen for his wife. Problem was, make sense or not, it wasn't her he wanted to be with. It was an entirely different woman who captivated his thoughts. One who'd felt so right in his arms when he carried her home from the river that morning.

"Of course. That's perfectly fine. I'll send Charity out to you." Without another backward glance, Kathleen opened the door. "Good evening, Mr. Murphy."

And just like that, they were back to more formal means of address.

"Good evening, Mrs. Summerville."

Long after the household had grown silent, Kathleen lay in bed, staring at the ceiling, remembering the events of the day.

"I won't pretend I didn't know you ... felt kindly toward me ... and that you'd be open to a union between our families."

She groaned as Colin's words repeated in her head. How mortifying—but not surprising. She'd known he wasn't looking for a new wife. But then, she didn't want to marry him either.

No, she really *didn't* want to marry Colin. She liked him. He was a good man, a good friend, but that was all. And to marry for no other reason except to escape living with her mother-in-law would be wrong. Wrong for herself. Wrong for her daughters.

How embarrassing that others had witnessed her attempts to win Colin's affections, especially since she'd done so to placate Mother Summerville, not because she truly cared for him. How awful it would have been if she'd succeeded. She'd loved Harry, and because of it, she'd loved bearing his children. Would she want to share the bed of a man she didn't love simply to appease Helen?

In her imagination, she pictured a crooked grin and heard another voice. *"If you'll be dancin' this year, I hope you'll save one of 'em for me."*

Her pulse quickened as her mind went a step further. She imagined herself lying in Oscar Jacobson's arms, pictured them snuggling close beneath warm quilts on a cold winter's night.

Oscar?

He was much younger than she, too much for her to think of him in a romantic way. He probably owned little more than his horse and saddle, assuming he owned even those. What were his prospects? They must be limited indeed.

One thing for certain, Mother Summerville wouldn't approve if Kathleen allowed Oscar Jacobson to come courting.

She rolled onto her side, hugged a pillow close to her chest, and closed her eyes. But sleep wouldn't come for several more hours.

TWENTY-THREE

A throbbing headache awakened Felicia before dawn. She wasn't surprised. Nightmares had tortured her sleep. Again and again she'd dreamed of water rushing into her nose and throat, of struggling for air, of longing for dry land when there was none. She'd felt her arms and legs and torso and head slamming against large, sharp river rocks, felt water rolling and twisting her in crazy circles, felt her clothes weighing her down.

Better to be awake, her head pounding, than to experience that panic rising up in her chest over and over and over again.

She discovered the location of every bruise when she got out of bed. Thankfully, the more she moved around, the less stiff she felt. By the time she left the house for church, she was able to walk normally. When she rounded the back of the mercantile, she saw Colin and Charity standing at the corner of the street. She wondered if they were waiting for her, and the thought brought a flutter to her chest.

Colin tipped his hat as she drew close. "Good morning." He looked extraordinarily handsome in his Sunday suit.

"How're you feeling, Miss K?" Charity reached for her hand.

"Quite myself again." Felicia gave the girl's hand a squeeze.

"I'm sorry about what happened. I never meant for the rod to hit you. If Papa hadn't come ..." The words trailed off into a guilty silence.

Felicia glanced at Colin.

"I already told her it was an accident."

"Of course it was an accident." Felicia's gaze returned to the girl. "Anyone's line could have gotten stuck. If I'd paid more attention to the ground beneath my feet, I wouldn't have slipped when the line broke. Besides, I'm none the worse for wear." She gave Charity's hand another squeeze before releasing it.

As if by mutual consent, the threesome turned and began walking in the direction of the church, Charity moving out in front, leaving her father to walk beside Felicia. Strange, the way she seemed to feel the heat of his body through her bodice sleeve, even though there was a good foot of space between his arm and hers.

His arm.

His arms around her. Her ear to his chest. The rhythm of his heartbeat. His long stride as he carried her into the house. His hands cradling her shoe ... and then her foot.

Merciful heavens!

She felt the heat rise in her cheeks.

Please don't let him look at me. Please don't let him guess my thoughts. Please don't let me faint again!

As they drew near the church, other congregants greeted Felicia and expressed their good wishes for a swift recovery. She assured them that she was already recovered and hoped the flush of embarrassment would give her cheeks a healthy glow rather than make her look feverish.

"Sit with us, Miss K," Charity said as they climbed the steps to the church entrance.

Each of the previous Sundays since her arrival in Frenchman's Bluff, she'd sat with a different family. It would be rude to refuse

Charity's request, even if Felicia wanted to. And she didn't want to, she realized as she stepped into the back pew, even though sitting elsewhere might have made her more comfortable—not to mention better able to concentrate on Reverend Hightower's sermon.

She had another reason to regret her decision when the Summerville family entered the sanctuary a short while later. Although Kathleen smiled in her direction, it seemed strained. And her mother-in-law's eyes had daggers in them. Helen Summerville must have learned that Felicia had broken her word.

I'll have to apologize.

The realization made her wish she'd remained at home in her snug cottage.

There was something right about Felicia sitting in the same pew with him, Colin decided as the congregation rose to sing the first hymn. A rightness he hadn't felt in church for years.

Not since Margaret died.

Was it because he'd begun to open his heart to God once again? Or was it because the Lord hadn't allowed Felicia to drown yesterday, that God had enabled Colin to reach her in time? Whatever the reason, he was glad she was there beside him.

He held the hymnal toward Felicia. She took hold, keeping the book low enough so Charity, who stood between them, could see the words. When she sang, he was taken by the pureness of her voice.

"O for a thousand tongues to sing my great Redeemer's praise. The glories of my God and King, the triumphs of His grace!"

Mixed in with Felicia's clear voice, he heard his daughter singing too. Their voices seemed to blend naturally together, and the sound moved his heart. Or was it the words of the hymn that moved him?

"My gracious Master and my God, assist me to proclaim, to spread through all the earth abroad the honors of Thy name."

Had Felicia ever entertained doubts about her Master and God? He was sure she hadn't, and he envied her that. But perhaps it would be possible for him to find his way back into a relationship with the Savior. Perhaps the day would come when he could sing the hymn with the same conviction.

"Jesus! the name that charms our fears, that bids our sorrows cease; 'tis music in the sinner's ears; 'tis life, and health, and peace."

As if aware he watched her, Felicia turned her head, and their gazes met above Charity. In that moment, he knew his world was about to change in more than a spiritual sense.

TWENTY-FOUR

Felicia closed the book and leaned back in the chair. "I think that's enough for tonight," she told Charity. "You're doing very well."

The girl beamed at the praise, and when her father appeared in the kitchen doorway, she jumped up, went to him, and hugged him around his waist. "Miss K says I'm doing good."

"Doing well," Felicia corrected, but she did so with a smile.

Colin smiled too, but it felt to Felicia as if she were the reason and not his daughter. Her heart began to gallop in response.

"How about a piece of apple pie before you go?" he asked, his gaze still locked with hers.

"Yes!" Charity released her hold on her father and returned to the table.

Felicia meant to decline the offer, yet somehow she found herself nodding.

"You two deserve a treat. You've worked hard every night for three weeks now." He went to the counter and removed a cloth from a pie tin. "Ellen Franklin dropped it off this afternoon."

Felicia could see the glitter of lamplight on the sugary crust and bubbles of pale juices around the edges. "It does look good."

"It's good," Charity said, removing plates from the cupboard. "Mrs. Franklin always makes good pies. I like cherry better, but the apple's really good too. You'll see."

"My daughter's a ... What's that word?" He paused, frowning. Then he grinned again. "Oh yeah. Connoisseur. She's a connoisseur of desserts."

Charity looked at him, obviously uncertain whether to be pleased or upset by what he'd said.

"The word means you're an expert judge of taste," Felicia informed her.

"Oh." The girl brightened. "I like that."

Felicia watched as Colin cut into the pie, dividing it into six rather large slices. She took pleasure in watching his hands, the way he held the knife, the way he scooped the dessert onto the plates, the way he looked at his daughter with such open affection. The whole room was warm with love, and it enveloped Felicia too. Made her feel almost a part of the family.

He turned, and their gazes met. Her mouth went dry, for she thought she saw something in his eyes that she shouldn't see, for his engagement to Kathleen was no less binding simply because it was as yet a secret.

Colin brought two plates to the table, setting one before Felicia. Charity carried her own dessert and three forks, one for each of them. Soon they were all seated around the table, the books and slate from their study session pushed aside.

As Felicia took the first bite of apple pie, she remembered a time as a little girl when her entire family had been seated around a table much like this one. The tenement flat had been smaller than the Murphy home. Colder too, the winter wind seeping through the walls and windows, overpowering the fire in the stove. But in her memory, she wasn't cold. In her memory, everyone was smiling, even her father. They were eating pie, a rare treat, for there was rarely enough money for sugar. She remembered her father rising from his chair and drawing her mother up from hers and dancing with her around that small kitchen, both of them laughing.

Tears came to her eyes, and she blinked several times to keep them from falling.

"What's made you sad, Miss Kristoffersen?" Colin asked softly.

She shook her head as she cut another bite of pie with the edge of her fork.

"Please, tell me."

She looked at him again. "I was remembering my family when I was a little girl in Chicago."

"Chicago?" Charity said with surprise. "I thought you came from Wyoming."

"I came to Frenchman's Bluff from Wyoming. But when I was your age, I lived in Chicago with my mother and brother and sister. My father was ... often away. After my mother died, we were placed out as orphans with other families. That's what took me to Wyoming."

The girl reached over and patted the back of Felicia's hand. "No wonder you're sad, Miss K. I'd be sad too."

Felicia was in danger of losing her battle against tears, and it didn't help to see the caring looks from both father and daughter. Except for Jane Carpenter, she hadn't told anyone in Frenchman's Bluff that part of her history. She hadn't wanted people's sympathy. It was the past and couldn't be changed. Better that she focus on the future and the life she wanted to have.

As if understanding her thoughts, Colin asked Charity something about her horse, and the girl's response filled the awkward silence, giving Felicia an opportunity to gain control of her emotions. *Thank you.* Though she didn't speak the words aloud, she hoped he would somehow know she was grateful to him.

It had grown late by the time Felicia rose from the table, the dessert plate before her now clear of any evidence of the apple pie.

"Pumpkin," Colin said to his daughter, "you get ready for bed. I'm going to walk Miss K to her door."

"That isn't necessary, Mr. Murphy," Felicia protested. "It's only across the yard."

She was right, of course. He hadn't walked her to her door any of the other evenings over the past three weeks. But tonight felt different. He couldn't say why. It just did.

"It's dark out," he answered. "I'd just as soon walk with you."

She looked at him for a long time before she said, "All right."

The night was cool but not cold, the sky hidden behind clouds. As they went down the few steps outside the back door, Colin took hold of Felicia's arm. What any gentleman would do. No more. No less.

"Charity's learned a lot since you started working with her." *So have I.* "Not sure I've told you how much I appreciate the extra work you're doing with her."

"She's a good student. She just needed someone to help her find her way."

They reached the door to her kitchen and stopped. He released his hold on her arm as he turned to face her. "I'm glad you came to Frenchman's Bluff to teach, Miss Kristoffersen. Not sure I've told you that either."

"And I'm glad you've changed your mind about me, Mr. Murphy."

So she knew he'd opposed her. He shouldn't be surprised. He'd voiced his opinion openly enough. It was bound to reach her ears sooner or later. "I'm sorry. It was unfair of me to oppose your hiring simply because you are a woman. It was only because I thought a schoolmaster with a family might bring more stability to the school. He wouldn't up and marry and move away like what's happened here in the past. And, of course, you hadn't any actual experience." His voice lowered, almost to a whisper. "But it turns out that didn't matter either."

Although it was dark, he could make out the contours of her face as she looked up at him. He didn't need light to see the high cheekbones or the strong jaw or the wildflower blue of her eyes. The desire to kiss Felicia washed over him, like a crashing wave upon the shore. He longed to hold her as he had when he'd carried her back from the river. He'd like to unlace her shoes and cradle her foot once again in his hand. He wanted —

Felicia drew in a quick breath, and only then did he realize that he'd leaned close to her, that his mouth was mere inches from hers, that his hands now rested on her shoulders.

Kiss her. Go on. Kiss her.

Somewhere in the dark, a creature moved. The branches of the nearby tree swayed. A twig snapped.

Felicia took a step back, out of his reach.

The moment to kiss her had passed.

"Good night, Mr. Murphy," she whispered.

"Good night." *Felicia.*

He watched as she turned and hurried into the cottage, closing the door behind her. He waited a few more minutes before walking slowly back to his own door.

TWENTY-FIVE

"Who can spell *frightened*?" Felicia asked the small group of students seated on the recitation bench.

Charity, the oldest in the group, glanced to her left and right, then raised her hand. Not with great confidence, but her willingness to try was a victory in Felicia's mind.

"Charity."

She stood. "F-r-i ... g ... h-t ... e-n ... e-d. *Frightened*."

"That's correct."

Joy spread across Charity's face like the sunlight spread across the foothills in the morning.

"The next word is *whisper*."

Two hands went up this time.

"Phoebe."

"W-h-i-s-p-e-r. *Whisper*."

"Very good. How about *mischief*? Tommy."

"M-i-s-c-h ... i-e-f."

"Correct. Very good, all of you. You may return to your desks now."

A feeling of pride welled in her chest. Every day she saw new progress in her students. Now that Charity was slowly but surely overcoming her reading difficulties, Felicia's two greatest challenges were R. J. Franklin and Daniel Watkins, although for very different reasons.

Her gaze drifted to the last row of desks, the last seat at the back, nearest the exit. Apropos, since R. J. was so anxious to leave school and start working with his father.

And what a waste that would be. The Franklins were prosperous dairy farmers. Surely they could afford to send their son to college. R. J. didn't need to settle for a mediocre education. He could study to become a professor or a doctor or a lawyer or a scientist. Or whatever it was that interested him the most. There must be something, other than milk cows, that interested him.

All I have to do is help him discover his passion.

She looked in another direction, to Daniel. Things had improved since their rough beginning, and he hadn't gotten into any more fistfights. Not since she'd talked to Jane. But Felicia still worried about him, still spent a great deal of time praying for wisdom, asking God to show her how best to deal with him.

With a mental shake, she turned and stepped onto the raised platform. A quick glance at her watch told her the lunch hour had arrived. She dismissed the students, one row at a time, and within a few minutes, she was alone in the classroom. The children's voices drifted to her through the open door as she retrieved her own lunch and sat down at her desk to eat.

She bit into a crisp slice of apple. The sweet-tart flavor burst in her mouth, and she smiled even as she chewed. Jimmy Bryant had promised her she would love these apples. And right he was.

"My mom makes great applesauce," he'd told her yesterday in the mercantile. "Mmm. She puts up all kinds of fruits and vegetables, startin' in the middle of summer and goin' right on into October. Been at it for weeks now. Tomatoes and pickles and cherries and peaches and all sorts of things."

Now, there was a young man whose life might have been changed by a college education. It was too late for Felicia to influence him, but it wasn't too late for his brothers. She still had a chance with fourteen-year-old Samuel and nine-year-old Tommy.

She almost laughed aloud at the thought of the youngest Bryant brother. If one of her students was ever born to be a salesman — or better yet, a politician — it was Tommy Bryant. He had been trying to convince her to take one of Goldie's puppies for several weeks, and she was afraid she wouldn't be able to resist much longer, even though she hadn't the time or the resources for owning a pet. He was full of blarney, that one.

Closing her eyes, she sent up a silent thanks to God for this new life He'd given her. She was succeeding as a teacher, most of her students seemed to enjoy school, and she was making friends in the community. Kathleen and Jane and ... and Colin ...

Colin.

Her heart fluttered. He'd almost kissed her two evenings before. She'd almost *let* him kiss her. And she'd *wanted* him to kiss her.

It had been wrong for him to think about it. It would have been just as wrong if she'd let it happen. He was engaged to another woman. Not just some other woman. To her friend.

Father, help me. I'm not strong enough on my own.

❦

"Mr. Murphy." Helen's arms were crossed beneath her ample bosom, and the set of her mouth was severe. "May I speak with you privately? It won't take but a moment."

It was all Colin could do not to groan. Instead, he nodded. "Of course, Mrs. Summerville. Come into my office." He motioned toward the door behind the counter.

The woman walked ahead of him, her body stiff, her head held high. The feather on her large, fashionable hat fluttered from side to side like the pendulum of a metronome.

Whatever she wanted to say, Colin decided, it wasn't going to be pleasant for him to hear.

He followed her into the office and closed the door behind him. "Please, have a seat."

"Thank you."

If Helen Summerville was any more rigid, she would snap in two.

"Mr. Murphy, I have come to you on a matter of some delicacy."

He nodded solemnly, resolved to say nothing until she was finished.

"About Miss Kristoffersen."

His eyebrows rose, but he held his peace.

"And you."

That jolted him from his resolve. "And *me?*"

"It has come to my attention that Miss Kristoffersen has been seen coming and going from your house in the evenings. Frequently. And after dark."

Anger coiled in the pit of his stomach.

"You can imagine the concern this has caused among the other members of the community, especially those of us on the school board."

"No, Mrs. Summerville. I *can't* imagine why it would cause anyone concern. Miss Kristoffersen has been tutoring Charity in the evenings, helping her with her reading."

"Mr. Murphy, *you* are a single man and *she* is an unmarried woman."

"That's true, ma'am, but she is a teacher working at the kitchen table with her pupil, and I have other things to do while they are so employed. And if anyone doubts it, they can ask my daughter. There is nothing inappropriate about our dealings with one another."

"That's not what I heard. You were seen by an acquaintance of mine holding and . . . and kissing that woman outside her home just two nights ago."

Who'd seen him? In the dark? Then he remembered the sound of the snapping twig. Had someone been watching them? Had this busybody put someone up to it? No. Surely not. Even Helen Summerville wouldn't sink that low. It must have been by chance.

"Well, Mr. Murphy. What have you to say for yourself?"

"You were told wrong. Whoever your *acquaintance* is was mistaken. I walked Miss Kristoffersen home. That's all. I didn't kiss her." *But I wanted to badly enough.*

The woman rose from her chair. "I'm disappointed in you, Mr. Murphy. Appearances matter. I was certain you would wish to preserve the reputation of both yourself and Miss Kristoffersen. I see I shall have to resolve this matter in another way."

"What do you mean by that?" He stood too.

"I shall have her dismissed, of course."

The simmering anger boiled over. "Dismissed? For doing her job? For teaching my daughter on her own time?"

"Dismissed." Her chin jutted forward as her eyes narrowed.

"Mrs. Summerville, you are not only narrow-minded; you are unkind."

"And you obviously have no concept of the decorum of polite society. I was mistaken about you, Mr. Murphy. Gravely mistaken." She turned toward the door, sweeping the skirt of her gown behind her with one hand. "Good day."

Colin wanted to punch something.

He waited several seconds after the woman left his office before he moved to the doorway. Thankfully, there wasn't another customer in the store. No one, with the exception of Jimmy, had heard the altercation, and Jimmy was trying hard to look as if he hadn't.

"Jimmy," Colin said, a growl in his voice, "I'm going to deliver that anvil Randall Franklin ordered last week. I'll be gone most of the afternoon. Tell Charity to do her chores when she gets home from school."

Jimmy, probably afraid to say anything, nodded.

Colin strode into his living quarters, out the back door, and across the yard to the barn.

Another school day done, another week of teaching behind her, Felicia closed the door to the schoolhouse, holding a satchel of books and papers in her left hand while turning the key in the lock with her right. As she descended the steps, a light breeze tugged at her hair. Leaves in the nearby trees, turning from green to gold, made a sound similar to a baby's rattle.

She walked swiftly toward her small cottage, eager to get home. Tomorrow night there was to be a barn dance at Yancy and Ann Dowd's farm, and she wanted to finish making a new dress for the event. She'd purchased the material with money from the first wages she'd drawn and had been working on the skirt and shirtwaist for a number of evenings already. Of course, she wouldn't have the courage to dance, even if someone asked her. Her friends at normal school had taught her a few steps, but that had been years ago. No, she would be content to help with the refreshments and to watch others dance. Still, she wanted to wear something pretty for the occasion. Not that the new gown was anything fancy. It would be perfectly suitable for a schoolteacher to wear any day of the week.

Felicia had just laid her satchel on the kitchen table when Charity appeared on the other side of the screen door.

"Hi, Miss K."

"Hello, Charity."

"Can I come in? Papa's gone to make a delivery." She pressed her face against the dark mesh. "Jimmy says he won't be back for a while yet, and I don't want to wait in the store. It's boring."

"Don't you have chores to do after school?"

"Uh-huh. But I did 'em already. Just finished brushing and feeding Princess. That was the last thing I had to do."

"Well, I have chores to do myself. I don't think it will be any better here than in the store."

"Pleeeeease."

She should tell Charity that it wasn't polite to beg, but she didn't. What was it about this particular little girl that made it impossible for her to be as strict as she knew she should? Almost from Felicia's first day in Frenchman's Bluff, Charity Murphy had taken hostage her schoolteacher's heart. Perhaps it was the charm of the Irish.

And her father possesses the same charm.

Not that she'd always thought he did.

She turned her back to the door. "Come in if you wish. You can get our book off the bookshelf and read to me while I sew."

"Ah, Miss K."

"If you read to me now, we can skip our tutoring session this evening."

"Oh . . . okay."

Felicia retrieved her sewing basket and settled on the sofa, the skirt of the new outfit on her lap.

Charity found the book and sat on the chair opposite Felicia. "What're you makin'?"

"A new dress."

"I like the color. You gonna wear it to the barn dance tomorrow?"

"Yes, if I finish it in time."

"Papa thinks you look pretty in blue."

Oh, that horrible-wonderful fluttering heartbeat. "Did he tell you that?" She tried to sound disinterested in the answer.

"Nope. I just know."

Felicia drew air into her lungs as she put needle to fabric. "You're prevaricating, Charity." *And so am I.*

"Pre-var-i ... what?"

"Prevaricating."

"What's that?"

"You're being evasive."

"Evasive?"

"Never mind. Just read to me."

Charity sighed. "Okay." She opened the book on her lap and flipped it open. "Chapter Three."

"She wants her fired, Randall." Leaning against the wagon, Colin peered at the sun, which rode low in the western sky.

"Mrs. Summerville likes to think she runs everything in Frenchman's Bluff, Colin. You know that."

"Yeah, I know. And I don't mind for myself, but Felicia ... Miss Kristoffersen ... she doesn't deserve this."

"You like Miss Kristoffersen, don't you?

Colin grunted, a sound of acknowledgment and frustration at the same time.

"Folks have taken to her," Randall continued. "I don't think you have to worry about Mrs. Summerville having her way this time."

"Maybe not, but she can sure make things uncomfortable." He removed his hat and raked his fingers through his hair. "All she … all Miss Kristoffersen's done is to help Charity. You wouldn't believe how much better my girl's doing since they started working together in the evenings. And she didn't have to do tutoring on top of everything else. The town sure doesn't pay her enough to expect it."

Randall was silent for a long spell before saying, "Maybe you'd best send Charity over to the teacher's house for the tutoring. That'd take care of Mrs. Summerville's complaints."

Colin mulled over the suggestion and decided his friend was right. Sending Charity to the cottage each evening would solve the matter. But Colin would miss listening to the two of them, teacher and student, as they went over the words again and again. Not to mention that without the teacher in his house, he wouldn't keep learning himself, and he didn't want to stop learning to read. Silly though it might be, he was proud of the progress he'd made. Almost as proud as he was of Charity.

But then, he supposed pride was part of his problem. He'd always been ashamed, felt stupid, because he couldn't read. And so, out of pride, he'd kept it to himself, finding every way he could to hide the truth from others. There was no sin in not being able to read. Plenty of folks who lived in and around Frenchman's Bluff had had to leave school when they were youngsters, just like he'd been, so they could work on the farms or in the businesses run by their parents. He wasn't the only adult who couldn't read much beyond his name.

But this wasn't about him. It was about Felicia and guarding her reputation, and if that meant he couldn't go on learning to read, then so be it. He had no right to endanger her position in the town because he was too selfish to do what was right and proper.

"You're right, Randall. That would solve everything." He pushed off from the wagon. "I'd best get back to town. Charity and I'll be eating something cold from the icebox as it is."

"Thanks for delivering that new anvil for me. I was plannin' to come to town tomorrow to pick it up. You saved me the trip."

"Glad to do it." Colin stepped on the hub of the wheel and then sat on the wagon seat.

"I reckon we'll see you tomorrow night at the Dowds'."

"Reckon you will." He slapped the reins against the team's backsides. "Giddup there." With a rattle of harness and a creak of wood, the wagon pulled out of the barnyard and headed for town.

TWENTY-SIX

Felicia stood in front of the mirror, turned sideways, and assessed her reflection.

The dark blue grosgrain silk skirt had a full four-and-a-half-yard sweep, which emphasized the narrowness of her waist. The large scroll design on the fabric gave the skirt a stylish appearance, and the fine taffeta lining caused it to rustle softly when she moved. Her new shirtwaist was made from a solid light blue French lawn fabric. It had puff-top sleeves — the latest fashion — and an Alastor choker collar. And in her hair she wore a spray of silk flowers that had once belonged to her mother.

She reached up and fingered the delicate violets, remembering when they were given to her, remembering her mother's fingers running over her hair and the gentle smile on her mother's lips. Oh, the love that had been in her mother's touch.

"I want you to have these, my darling. They were my mother's. She gave them to me when I married. Now they are yours." Elethea Brennan had leaned over and kissed Felicia's forehead. *"Think of me whenever you wear them."*

"I will, Mum. I promise."

But in all the years since then, she'd never had occasion to put flowers in her hair. Tonight she did. She would go to the barn dance and talk with the parents of her students and drink punch with new friends and watch dancers swirling their partners around the floor. She would laugh and be gay and remember her mother.

I will, Mum. I promise.

The image in the mirror wavered beyond her tears.

"Mercy," she whispered, dabbing beneath her eyes with a handkerchief. Afterward, she tucked the kerchief into her reticule, took up her wrap, for the ride home would be decidedly cool, and hurried out of the house.

Charity was seated in the rear of the buggy while Colin, standing near the horse's head, adjusted something on the harness.

"I hope you haven't been waiting long," Felicia said as she drew near.

Colin looked up. She wasn't sure what the expression was that crossed his face. Not truly surprise, but something like it perhaps. But it was his slow smile that caused her breath to catch and her heart to pound.

"You look lovely, Miss Kristoffersen."

He thought her lovely.

Ba-bum ... Ba-bum ... Ba-bum.

She felt quite strange.

Ba-bum ... Ba-bum ... Ba-bum.

She could have returned the compliment, could have told him how handsome he looked in his black suit and derby. Different from the shopkeeper and father who had pulled her from the river, but every bit as strong and ... and virile.

Ba-bum ... Ba-bum.

He came to the side of the buggy and offered his hand. "Charity tells me you made that dress yourself."

"Yes." She took his hand.

Ba-bum.

Would she have the courage to dance if he were to ask her?

Ba-bum.

She shouldn't think such things.

Ba-bum ... Ba-bum.

Charity leaned forward, whispering, "I told you he likes it when you wear blue."

"Shhh."

The girl giggled as she leaned back again.

The buggy shifted toward the opposite side as Colin got in. He cast another smile in Felicia's direction as he took up the reins. "Ready?"

"Yes!" Charity answered.

"All right. Let's go." He slapped the reins and clucked to the buggy horse.

Colin had planned on telling Felicia tonight that future tutoring sessions would need to take place in her house rather than his. He'd intended to throw out the decision as if it weren't of any real importance, simply a matter of convenience. With Charity present in the buggy, he'd hoped it would keep Felicia from inquiring as to his reasons for this change. He didn't want to repeat Helen's accusations if he didn't have to.

But something about those deep bluish-purple flowers in her honey-brown hair and the way the shade of that dress brought out the hint of violet in her blue eyes chased all other thoughts from his head. How could a man think of anything else when such a vision of beauty was seated beside him?

Maybe Helen was right, after all. Maybe it *was* inappropriate for Felicia to be in his house in the evenings, even with his daughter present. And if not inappropriate, dangerous. Tempting. Precarious. Because right now, all he wanted to do was take her into his arms and kiss her until they were both left breathless and panting. He'd like to pull the pins from her hair and watch it cascade about her shoulders. He'd like to —

His mouth went dry, and he swallowed hard.

"Papa, Suzanne and Phoebe are right behind us."

The Summerville girls. That meant their grandmother was also right behind them. Terrific. At least the Summerville carriage hadn't pulled up beside them, with him looking guilty as sin.

He clucked to the horse, urging a faster trot from the big gelding.

Fifteen minutes later, they arrived at the Dowd farm. The barn doors were thrown open to the pleasant night air, and abundant lamplight spilled onto the hard, bare earth of the yard. The number of saddle horses, buggies, and wagons in the barnyard told Colin the party was well underway.

He hopped down from the buggy and went around to the opposite side to help Felicia disembark. Charity jumped out on her own and ran to meet the Summerville carriage.

"Miss Kristoffersen." He offered his elbow to her.

After a slight hesitation, she slipped her hand into the crook of his arm, and the two of them walked toward the barn. Just before they reached it, guitar and fiddle, flute and banjo, drums and tambourine began to play a lively melody. Very soon, couples swirled by the open doorway, the women's colorful skirts soaring out behind them.

Colin dared to look at Felicia again and was rewarded with an enormous smile.

"It's wonderful," she said, loud enough to be heard above the music. "I've never seen anything like it."

"Your first barn dance?"

She nodded.

"Would you like to dance?"

The smile vanished, and she shook her head.

It surprised him how much he wanted to change her mind. "Are you sure?"

Color infused her cheeks. "I don't know how to dance, Mr. Murphy."

"Tell you what." He leaned closer so he didn't have to raise his voice. "We'll wait until they play something a bit slower. Then I'll teach you. Okay?"

For a heartbeat, he feared she would still refuse. But then she nodded, and pleasure flowed through him.

Mrs. Summerville be hanged.

❧

Felicia felt as if she'd already been whirled around the dance floor in the center of this vast barn, and all because of the way Colin looked at her now.

"Miss Kristoffersen." Ellen Franklin hurried toward them. "I'm so glad you came. My cousin arrived this morning for a visit. She's a teacher too. From Oregon. I want you two to meet. I'm sure you have a lot in common. Colin, I'm going to steal Miss Kristoffersen for a while." She took hold of Felicia's free arm and gently guided her away from the entrance—and away from Colin.

The band of musicians had taken up their place in the loft in the latter third of the barn. On the ground floor, refreshment tables had been set up in the rear of the building, near another set of open doors. Bales of hay and straw had been placed in front of stalls on the north side of the building, providing places for people to sit. Dozens of lanterns hung from nails, pouring a golden glow over the festivities.

Ellen led Felicia all the way to the tables at the back before stopping in front of her husband and another woman who bore a striking resemblance to Ellen. "Grace, this is Miss Felicia Kristof-fersen, our new schoolmarm. Miss Kristoffersen, my cousin, Miss Mary Grace Todd. But everyone calls her Grace."

"A pleasure to meet you, Miss Todd," Felicia said.

"Likewise. But please, do call me Grace."

"And you both must call me Felicia." She looked first at Ellen, then at Grace. "I take it your school isn't in session yet."

"Actually, I'm not teaching at present. I stepped down from my last position to care for my ailing mother. She passed in the spring, but I haven't had the heart to apply for a new post as yet. So I accepted Ellen's kind invitation to come for a visit. I hope she won't regret having me underfoot."

"Oh, Grace." Ellen put an arm around her cousin and gave her a squeeze. "How silly you are. You could never be underfoot. You're family."

"Even family can get underfoot, Ellen. Especially a spinster schoolteacher without employment."

How fortunate, Felicia thought, that Grace had family who loved her and were willing to take her in. Felicia had been without anyone to turn to when she was in a similar circumstance.

No one? a voice whispered in her heart.

True. God had been with her. She had turned to Him in her despair, and He had brought her to Frenchman's Bluff. He had provided her with work and with a home to live in and with new friends and with children to care for and nurture and educate.

She looked over her shoulder, and her eyes found Colin almost at once, standing with some other men. As if he sensed her gaze, he looked in her direction. Her heart hiccupped as she returned her attention to Ellen Franklin.

Grace said, "Ellen tells me her boys are doing well in school."

"Yes. Very well. All three of them." This seemed the perfect opportunity to plant a few seeds in Ellen's mind regarding the possibility of higher education for R. J. But before she could speak, the other woman's expression changed, her eyes looking over Felicia's right shoulder. And somehow Felicia knew Colin was approaching. She turned around.

"I believe this is our dance, Miss Kristoffersen." He bowed slightly at the waist.

"I told you, Mr. Murphy, I don't know how."

"Lucky for us, I do." He held out his arms.

It wasn't wise. There were a hundred reasons why she shouldn't dance with him. A week or two ago, she could have listed them all. But just now, she couldn't recall a single one. She hadn't thought clearly since the night he almost kissed her. Since the night she would have *let* him kiss her.

She moved into his embrace as if they'd waltzed together countless times before.

He grasped her right hand with his left, and with his right hand on the small of her back, they began to move around the barn in time to the music. Around them, other couples turned and twirled — she saw them in her peripheral vision — yet it seemed to Felicia that they were alone, just the two of them.

Ba-bum ... Ba-bum.

What was it the Bible said? "Behold also the ships, which though they be so great, and are driven of fierce winds, yet are they turned about with a very small helm." That's how it felt with his hand on her back. It was a light touch, a small thing, and yet that hand steered her wherever Colin willed.

Ba-bum ... Ba-bum.

Oh, this wasn't a good thing. She shouldn't have come with

him to the barn dance. She should have accepted one of the invitations to ride here with other families. Just because Colin was her landlord and lived next door wasn't reason enough to arrive with him, and it certainly wasn't reason enough to dance with him.

When had this happened? It was one thing to discover he'd changed his mind about hiring an untried teacher who might marry and leave her position in short order, one thing to discover she was exactly the right teacher for his daughter. It was another matter entirely to find he'd opened his heart to the woman he held in his arms. Her large blue eyes looked up at him, filled with trust and … and something more. What was it he saw in their depths? Had a woman ever looked at him quite like that before?

No. Not even his wife. Was it possible she could have changed her mind about what she wanted? A life beyond being a schoolteacher?

The music ended, and the dancers around them came to a halt. Colin was forced to do the same, reluctantly withdrawing his hand from the small of Felicia's back and releasing his grip on her right hand. He immediately wanted to draw her back into his embrace. He thought again of kissing her. But that wasn't something he could do here and now, no matter how much he wanted to.

Hoping to force his thoughts elsewhere, he said, "And you didn't miss a single step."

Her cheeks reddened. "You made it easy to follow."

"Would you like to go back to the refreshment table?" He offered his arm.

"If you don't mind, I think I'll step outside for a breath of air." She fanned herself with her right hand. "It's rather warm in here."

Outside. In the dark. Away from watching eyes. "Of course. Whatever you wish. I'll go with you."

"No. That's not necessary. I ... I'll go alone. Look. There's Kathleen. I'm certain she'd like to dance with you next." She hurried away from him without a backward glance.

Smart girl.

TWENTY-SEVEN

Hugging the side of the barn, Felicia moved away from the light spilling through the doors. In the time they'd been inside, night had arrived in earnest, bringing with it the blessing of darkness, one the first-quarter moon couldn't contend with. She stopped and leaned her back against the barn, drawing in several deep breaths to try to quell the uneven beating of her heart.

Help me, Father! I don't know what to do with these feelings.

"You surprise me, Miss Kristoffersen."

Felicia's eyes flew open and she gasped in surprise.

"Have you no shame whatsoever?"

"Mrs. Summerville—"

"Is it your wish to hurt Kathleen by your behavior?" The woman spoke in a hushed but harsh tone. "She thinks of you as her friend."

Felicia pushed away from the barn, wishing she could see Helen's face. "I would never knowingly hurt her."

"And yet you take advantage of Mr. Murphy's kindnesses again and again. You risk his reputation and yours by blatantly running after him."

"I have never—"

"Frenchman's Bluff is a small town, Miss Kristoffersen. Do you think others won't notice your actions? Do you think they aren't inside whispering even as we speak?"

Felicia pressed her lips together, thinking it better to say nothing at this point. Inside she was shaking, partly in dread of what the woman might say next, partly in anger over what she'd said already.

"I plan to bring up this matter to the members of the school board next week. We cannot allow a woman such as you to mold the minds of our young people. I intend to ask for your resignation."

"My resignation? Mrs. Summerville, I—"

"Shameless hussy." With a *whish* of skirts, Helen turned and strode away.

Felicia fell back against the wall of the barn a second time, as stunned as if the woman had slapped her.

"Shameless hussy."

Memories flooded her mind, from the first time she'd met Colin Murphy to minutes before, when she'd waltzed in his arms. Did she care for him more than she should? Yes, she couldn't deny that she did. But had she acted inappropriately with him or toward him? Had she been indiscreet, shameless? No. No, she didn't believe she had been.

"Shameless hussy."

Merciful heavens! Whatever would she do if she were dismissed? She would be even worse off than she'd been when she came here. Who would employ her without a reference?

She closed her eyes a second time. *I'll fight. I'll fight for my job. I won't let her take it from me when I've done nothing to be ashamed of. Oh, God, don't let her take it from me.*

She drew another shaky breath, let it out, then straightened and walked toward the open doors, determined not to let anyone see her fear. She half expected to find the townsfolk gathered in small groups, looking at her as she entered the barn, whispering amongst themselves. Instead, the party continued. No one seemed to notice her appearance in the least. Perhaps Mrs. Summerville had advised them to ignore her when she returned. Perhaps the "shameless hussy" was to be shunned.

The thought had barely formed when Charity appeared at her side.

"Miss K! They've got the best cherry pie you ever tasted over there. You gotta have some. Mrs. Franklin made it. You remember how good her apple pie was? This is even better." The girl grasped Felicia's hand and led her quickly toward the refreshment tables. "I already had two pieces, but don't tell Papa."

It was difficult to remain grim when she was with this vivacious child. Mrs. Summerville's threats couldn't hold a candle to Charity's enthusiasm.

At the far end of the barn, she found Kathleen at one of the tables, filling glasses with punch, while Ellen sliced pieces of chocolate cake and put them on plates.

"Do you need help?" Felicia asked.

If Helen Summerville had issued orders to shun the schoolteacher, the word hadn't reached Ellen or Kathleen, for they greeted her with friendly, welcoming smiles.

"We'd love some help." Ellen held up a knife for her to take.

Before Felicia could round the nearest table, Charity said, "But first she needs to try some of your cherry pie, Mrs. Franklin. She needs to try it before it's all gone."

Ellen laughed. "Before you eat it all, you mean?"

"I wouldn't eat it *all*."

"Hmm." Ellen slid a plate toward Felicia. "I saved it for you. Charity said I had to."

"Thank you." Under the girl's watchful eye, Felicia took a bite. It was equally sweet and tart, with a crust that melted in her mouth.

"Oh my. Charity's right. It is even better than the apple pie you made for—" She stopped abruptly, afraid she'd revealed too much. Would Kathleen be upset to know Colin had shared the dessert with her?

"Randall says my pies are why he married me," Ellen said into the silence.

Is Colin the type of man who could be won by a delicious recipe? Is that how Kathleen won him? Oh, how traitorous were her thoughts! How unwelcome their direction! It couldn't matter to her what had won Colin's affections. It *mustn't* matter. It *didn't* matter.

Kathleen's response didn't sound as if she was upset. "I've tried countless times to get Ellen to tell me how she makes her piecrusts so light. To no avail, I might add."

Ellen laughed again. "I have few enough talents. I'd best keep this one to myself."

The truth struck Felicia like a blow. She would lose so much more than a job if Mrs. Summerville succeeded in having her dismissed. She would also lose these new but already precious friendships.

But I wouldn't lose Colin because he isn't mine to lose. I must remember that. Please, God, help me remember that.

Kathleen would always recall the exact moment when Oscar strode toward the back of the barn. His hair was slicked back, freshly washed, and he wore a fancy blue shirt and clean pair of jeans.

"I was hopin' we might have that dance now, Miz Summerville."

She didn't hesitate. She'd wasted enough time hesitating, worrying about what her mother-in-law might think, doing what her mother-in-law wanted her to do. No more. Not tonight. She stepped from behind the table and placed her fingers into the palm of his outstretched hand. He grinned, and she smiled in return.

Oscar wasn't a large man, but the way he held her as they danced made her feel small and fragile and oh-so feminine.

"You're the prettiest gal in the place," he said near her ear.

"It's kind of you to say so."

"Not kind. Just speakin' the truth."

Enjoying the compliment, she felt her cheeks grow warm.

"I reckon you know what it is I'd like to say, Kathleen."

The use of her given name drew her gaze to his.

"I'd like to be more than a friend to you. I reckon you know my meanin'."

Her heart hiccupped. She tried to ignore the feeling. "How old are you, Mr. Jacobson?"

He grinned that lopsided grin that she found so adorable. "Old enough to know what I want."

"How old?"

"I'll turn twenty-five come December."

"I'm thirty."

"Yes'm. I figured as much."

"I'm the mother of two."

"Yes'm. Fine girls too. They know their manners. Always polite to their elders. I've noticed that about them."

"Surely you can see—"

"All I can see right now is that I'm dancin' with the prettiest gal in the place. Like I said before."

There was no point protesting any further there on the dance floor. She could tell that he wasn't going to listen to reason. And truly, she would rather enjoy this carefree feeling. She could be sensible later.

They danced three dances in a row, never even pretending to leave the floor before the next melody started. But at the end of the third, a lively square dance, Kathleen found herself gasping for air even as she laughed.

"I'm afraid I must rest, Mr. Jacobson."

He offered his arm. "How about some fresh air?"

"Please. For a few minutes." She slipped her fingers into the crook of his arm. "But I should get back soon to the refreshment table so others can have their turn to enjoy the evening."

He nodded, then guided her toward the barn doors.

The cool evening air felt good on her skin. "It's been a long time since I've danced so much."

"I'd dance with you every night if I could." There was no note of teasing in his voice.

"That might be a bit much." She motioned toward the interior of the barn. "Wherever would we find music like this?"

He stepped closer. His voice lowered. "We wouldn't need music if we were married."

Her breath caught in her chest.

"Will you marry me, Kathleen?"

"Mr. Jacobson—"

"Call me Oscar."

"I'm older than you. I have children."

"Five years isn't that much, and I'd love your girls as if they were my own."

"Where would we live? You're a cowboy on the Double G. There's no place for a family there."

"I've got land of my own, a small but solid house on it, and the start of a good herd of cattle. You wouldn't do without, nor would your girls."

He owned land and cattle? He had a house?

"It's not all that far from town. You'd be able to see your friends when you wanted. Suzanne and Phoebe could see their grandparents regular like."

"Oscar, you hardly know me."

"You're wrong there. I know you enough to love you."

He loved her? Her mind tried to continue to argue. How could he know that for sure? And they'd lived such different lives up to now. And yet ... and yet her heart believed him. Believed he loved her. Believed he knew her. Believed she loved him too.

"Will you marry me, Kathleen?"

Her mother-in-law would tell her she was crazy, downright insane. Mother Summerville would never approve. She would say Oscar was a nobody, a cowpoke, a man without proper breeding or upbringing, unsuitable to be a stepfather to her granddaughters. Helen wouldn't care that he made Kathleen happy whenever she was with him. But Kathleen cared.

"Will you?"

"Yes," she answered, feeling breathless.

That crooked, wonderful grin of his appeared. "When?"

"When? Well, I don't know. We'll need to make plans. And Mother Summerville—" She felt a sinking sensation.

"Let's go into Boise City tomorrow. Just you and me. We'll get married and tell everybody after."

"Elope? Oh, Oscar. Do you think we should?"

"Yeah, I think we should."

It really was quite crazy. But if this was insanity, then she planned to enjoy every moment of it. "Let's do it."

Colin stood with a number of area farmers. Their discussions had roamed from this year's harvest to the mild temperatures and lack of lightning storms in August and September to the Klondike gold rush. But when the topic switched to politics and President McKinley, Colin excused himself and walked toward the refreshment tables.

As he skirted the dancers, he saw Kathleen reentering the barn on the arm of one of the men who worked for Glen Gilchrist. She looked as if she was enjoying herself. He was glad. He'd hurt her feelings a week ago, and that hadn't set well with him, even if all he'd done was speak the truth.

Arriving at the refreshment tables, he found Ellen standing behind one of them, visiting with Martha Daughtry, while Felicia stood behind the other, cutting slices of a white-frosted cake. A number of children of varying ages sat on nearby bales of straw, enjoying cake and punch.

"I think I'd like a piece of that cake," he said as he stopped opposite Felicia.

Her cheeks pinkened, and he liked thinking he was the reason. She lifted a plate and held it toward him, at the same time lifting her gaze to meet his. She was without a doubt the prettiest woman at the festivities. A man could drown in those eyes, and he was willing to be the one to do so.

"Would you care to dance again, Felicia?"

The color in her cheeks deepened. "You can't dance with cake in your hand, Mr. Murphy."

"I'll eat it later." He set the plate back on the table. "Do you think you could call me Colin?"

She looked beyond him, her gaze sweeping the barn, and he wondered what—or rather *who*—she wanted to find. Maybe there was a different reason for her blush. Maybe she wished it was someone else who'd asked her to dance.

Now there was an emotion he couldn't recall feeling before: jealousy. Foreign it might be to him, but he recognized it all the same.

He held his hand toward her. "May I have this dance, Miss Kristoffersen?" He saw "No" in her eyes, but before she could refuse him, she was interrupted.

"Go on, Felicia." Ellen gave Felicia's shoulder a slight push. "Go dance and enjoy yourself. I can manage here without you."

"But I—"

"Go on. I'd be doing the same if I wasn't married to a man with two left feet."

Colin chuckled. "It's true. Randall can't dance a lick." He took hold of Felicia's hand and drew her out from behind the table.

"But I can't dance either, Mr. Murphy. Not really. You know that."

"Call me Colin."

"We've already danced once. It wouldn't be—"

"Please." He took her into his arms, and they began to turn in time to the music.

A sea of emotions swirled in her eyes, eyes that remained locked with his. What was it he saw in them? Confusion? Hope? Fear? Trust? Dread?

Could he hope for something more?

Something lasting?

TWENTY-EIGHT

Why did I dance with Colin a second time? Knowing what Mrs. Summerville thinks of me, why did I do it? Once was bad enough. Such a foolish thing to do it a second time. Foolish, foolish, foolish.

Clutching her Bible and pocketbook close to her chest, Felicia walked hurriedly toward the church the morning after the barn dance. She'd slept little the previous night, and she was certain it showed in the circles beneath her eyes. And now, on top of everything else, she was going to be late to Sunday service.

Why did I listen to Ellen? I should have said no. Why was I so weak? It should have been Kathleen dancing with him.

But Kathleen had been nowhere in sight. And besides, Felicia had enjoyed those brief minutes in his arms with the music playing. They had been magical ... mostly. But confusing too. Utterly confusing.

Even if he was a free man—which he wasn't—she wouldn't be interested in more than friendship. She wanted to teach. She wanted to be the mistress of her own future. She wasn't willing to set her hopes and dreams aside. Not for any reason. Certainly not for any man.

But Colin wasn't just "any" man, was he?

A groan escaped her lips.

Arriving at the church, she dashed up the steps and into the narthex. It was empty, the congregation already seated in the sanctuary. Trying to calm her breathing, she moved into the larger room and took the first empty seat, next to the Carpenter family. She purposefully kept her gaze directed toward the pulpit and Reverend Hightower. She didn't want to risk making eye contact with Colin or Kathleen or Helen or anyone else. Not until she felt composed and under control of her confused emotions.

The organist played the opening chords, and the congregation rose to its feet to sing "Nearer, My God, to Thee". Felicia closed her eyes and let the lyrics rise from her heart, knowing that as she let go of her earthly cares, she would hear the Lord's voice with more clarity. And she wanted to hear His voice this morning. She needed Him to make sense of things. Things that, in the limitations of her human mind, made no sense to her at all.

By the time the congregation settled back onto the wooden pews, Felicia felt calmer. Calm enough that she could listen to the reading of the Scripture and take comfort in God's Holy Word. Calm enough that she could listen to Reverend Hightower's sermon and glean wisdom from it. Calm enough that when the service ended, she could rise and turn and face whatever came next.

Colin was about to stand when Walter Swanson slid into the pew beside him. "We need to talk."

Colin lifted his eyebrows in question.

Lowering his voice, Walter said, "Mrs. Summerville's got a bee in her bonnet over somethin'. Says there's a matter of grave importance for the school board to take up. Wants a meeting tonight. Just the board. You know, a closed meeting. She won't be put off. Lord knows I tried."

Colin felt like swearing. He didn't have to guess what this was about. He already knew. Helen Summerville was following through on her promise to call for Felicia's dismissal. As he should have expected. She wasn't the sort to make idle threats. Still, he'd thought he had a little time to make some changes that might satisfy the woman. Apparently, he'd thought wrong.

"Can you be at the schoolhouse tonight at seven?"

"I'll be there."

"Good." Walter slapped him on the back, his expression brightening, as if sharing the news with Colin had lifted the burden from his shoulders. "Great night at the Dowds', wasn't it?"

"Yes. Great night." He swept his gaze over the dispersing churchgoers, looking for Felicia, wondering if anyone had told her the news about the meeting yet.

He would put a stop to this. He *had* to put a stop to it. He wasn't about to let Helen Summerville ruin Felicia's life. Especially if he was the cause of it. He thought back over Helen's visit to him at the mercantile. If he'd kept his temper, maybe it wouldn't have come to this.

Silently, he said a quick prayer for God to help him. Then he stood and moved out of the pew, flowing with the last members of the congregation through the double doors and down the steps into the crisp October morning air. That's when he saw Felicia, talking to Jane and Lewis Carpenter. She didn't look upset. She must not know. He wished he could leave it that way, but he couldn't. She glanced in his direction. He drew a breath and moved to join her.

He exchanged a few pleasantries with the Carpenters, but as soon as they walked away, there was no excuse not to come straight out with it. "Mrs. Summerville's called a school board meeting for tonight."

Felicia's face paled. "She's going to demand my resignation, isn't she?"

"This is my fault, Felicia."

"It isn't your fault. I ... I shouldn't have danced with you."

He felt a sinking sensation in his stomach. "Is that what you think this is about?" He shook his head. "It isn't. It's about the evenings you've spent at my place."

"The evenings? Do you mean when I've been tutoring Charity? There was nothing improper about that."

"We were seen together. Last week. The night I walked you to your door." He drew a slow breath. "You remember."

"Oh." The word came out on a breath of air. "That night."

"It's my fault," he said again.

"No." She took a step back from him, straightened her shoulders, tilted her chin. "No, it's not your fault. I'm a grown woman. I must take responsibility for my actions."

"But—"

"What time is the meeting?"

"Seven. But Walter said it was a closed meeting. Only the board members will be there."

Her eyes widened. "I'm not to have an opportunity to defend myself?"

"Not tonight."

"But that's unfair."

"I know." He wanted to draw her into his arms and hold her close, but this wasn't the time or place for that. Not if he wanted to stop the rumors Helen was determined to start. "I'll do everything I can."

"Thank you." Her voice broke. "Please excuse me, Mr. Murphy." Then she turned and hurried away.

Kathleen stopped the buggy in front of the restaurant in Boise.

Am I doing this? Am I really getting married? What if—

Oscar stepped through the doors of the restaurant. He wore a dark suit, and for an instant, she wondered if it was him. He looked so businesslike, so confident—not to mention so handsome. She'd never seen him in anything but Levi's and long-sleeved shirts. But then he grinned, and she had her answer. It was him. He was here. And they were going to get married today.

He tied the horse to the hitching rail, then came to the side of the buggy and offered a hand to help her to the ground. "You look mighty pretty, Kathleen."

"And you look quite handsome."

"What did you tell Miz Summerville?"

"That I'm meeting a friend in Boise and will return on Tuesday afternoon."

"A friend, eh?"

"It isn't a lie."

He lifted the back of her hand to his lips and kissed it. "No, I reckon it isn't a lie, but it's not quite the truth neither."

"I know. But Mother Summerville has been in a foul temper for the last few days, and I didn't want to argue with her or have her forbid me to use the buggy. When we return on Tuesday, I'll tell her everything."

"And your girls?"

"I couldn't tell them either. They might have let something slip. But they're going to love you, Oscar, just as I do." She felt almost giddy with joy when she said those words.

"I'll be a good pa to them, Kathleen. I promise."

"I know you will." She wasn't certain how she knew it was true. She simply knew.

He motioned with his head toward the restaurant. "Let's go inside and get something to eat. I've arranged for us to meet the minister at the church at two o'clock. We've got ourselves a bit of a wait."

The time couldn't possibly pass fast enough to suit Kathleen.

TWENTY-NINE

At 6:40 on Sunday evening, Colin rapped his knuckles on the doorjamb of the cottage. A few moments later, the door opened to reveal Felicia. She wore a gray dress that made her look wan. Or perhaps she would have looked that way regardless of the color of her gown.

"Miss Kristoffersen," he said, "I was hoping you wouldn't mind doing some reading with Charity, even though it's the Lord's Day. And I reckon it would be better for her to come to you from now on."

Understanding in her eyes, she nodded. "Come on in, Charity." She held open the screen door.

"Papa's got a meeting at the school," his daughter informed her teacher.

"Yes, I know." Felicia looked at Colin again.

It had been a long, tense day for him. He could only imagine what it had been like for her.

"I suppose you'll bring word to me of what's decided," she said.

"Yes. Of course."

"Charity can stay with me until the meeting is over."

"Appreciate it." He longed to say something more, something that would encourage her and remove the sadness in her eyes and the tension around her mouth. But he didn't know what words would do that.

"Thank you, Mr. Murphy, for whatever you can do."

Whatever he could do.

Maybe if he'd thought about that beforehand, she wouldn't be in this predicament. If he'd never wanted to kiss her. If he'd tried to smooth things over with Mrs. Summerville when she'd come to see him at the mercantile on Friday. If he'd immediately spoken with Felicia about the location of the tutoring sessions. If he hadn't wanted to dance with her last night. Her and only her.

He nodded, turned, and headed off in the direction of the school.

Despite being a good ten minutes early, he wasn't the first board member to arrive. Helen and Walter were there before him.

"Evenin', Colin," Walter greeted him.

Helen didn't bother to turn to look in his direction. If she had, he suspected she would have sniffed, as if something didn't smell right in the room.

He knew the feeling.

Walter checked his pocket watch. "The rest of 'em should be along soon."

"I reckon." Colin sat in a desk midway up the first row.

No doubt picking up on the tension between Helen and Colin, Walter began pacing the length of the raised platform at the front of the classroom. He breathed an audible sigh of relief when more voices announced the arrival of the remainder of the board.

Daisi Benoit was the first to enter, followed by Miranda Reynolds, Benjamin Hightower, Yancy Dowd, and Gary Peters.

"Good. Good." Walter wiped away a sheen of perspiration on his forehead with a handkerchief. "You're all here. We can start then."

The two other women took seats near Helen at the front of the classroom. The men sat in desks closer to Colin.

Yancy said, "Why don't you tell us what this is about, Walter?"

The school board president looked at Helen. "Mrs. Summerville?"

She stood and faced the others, her eyes avoiding Colin. "I'm afraid something quite disturbing has come to my attention. It involves our new schoolmarm."

A murmur of concern was heard from Daisi and Miranda. The men were silent.

"Miss Kristoffersen has been seen frequently coming and going in the evenings from the home of ... Mr. Murphy."

All eyes turned on him. He pressed his lips together, determined to quell his rising anger.

"And they were seen embracing in the dark outside of her home just last week by a friend of mine who happened by. Naturally, my friend told me, and I took my concerns to Mr. Murphy at once. His response, I'm sorry to say, was unsatisfactory. As anyone with eyes could see on Saturday night, Mr. Murphy and Miss Kristoffersen have developed a certain ... affection for one another. An affection that has led to inappropriate behavior and—"

Heat rising up his neck, Colin stood. "Affection between two people isn't against the law, the last I heard."

At last, she looked at him. "You disappoint me, Mr. Murphy. I always believed you to be a moral and upright man."

"I like to think I am, ma'am."

"If you were, you would understand my concern."

"Look. Miss Kristoffersen has been helping Charity with her reading lessons. My daughter's struggled with reading ever since she started school. Nobody's been able to make it easier for her until now. But Miss Kristoffersen thought some individual tutoring would help her catch up with other children her age. That's why she's been coming to my place in the evenings. It's working too."

"Late at night? In your home without a chaperone?" Amazing how Helen could make tutoring sessions sound dirty and disgraceful.

"It wasn't late. Miss Kristoffersen and Charity study at the kitchen table from seven o'clock until about seven-thirty. Never later than eight. And while they study, I'm in the living room or working in my office in the store. How is that *improper*? How can that disturb anyone?"

"It's disturbing to any good citizen of Frenchman's Bluff. Who's to know you're telling the truth? Who's to know what's going on in your home or hers?"

He couldn't keep his anger in check any longer. "*I'm* to know!" He slapped his chest with his right hand. "Charity's to know. And by heavens, Miss Kristoffersen's to know." He pointed at Helen. "But no matter whatever else is true, it's true that it's none of *your* affair."

She gasped and her chin raised several notches in the air. "I will *not* allow my granddaughters to receive instruction from a woman of questionable morals. I expect their teacher to be a good Christian."

Walter's hands moved up and down, as if he were trying to press the anger in the room toward the floor. "Please, Mrs. Summerville."

Colin was having none of it. "She's a better Christian than you'll ever be. She's got more goodness in her little finger than you've got in your whole body."

Helen gasped her outrage.

"You gossip and call it public concern," Colin continued. "What hogwash."

"Mr. Murphy, please." Again Walter motioned with his hands.

Colin wanted to slam his way out of the building, but somehow he forced himself to sit down at the desk again.

"Mrs. Summerville," Walter said, "what is it, exactly, that you wish us to do?"

"I want her fired, of course. I want her to be sent away as soon as possible."

"Fired?" Walter looked from Helen to each board member in the room. "I hardly think we have suitable grounds for her to be fired."

Well, at least somebody's got a lick of sense.

The president of the board continued, "Besides, school is in session, and we can't be without a teacher. Not again. We went through that after Miss Lucas left."

That's not the right reason.

"We wouldn't have to be without a teacher." Helen's look was triumphant. "We just so happen to have a qualified schoolteacher living a few miles out of town."

"A teacher? Just who—"

"Ellen Franklin's cousin, a Miss Todd, has come to stay at the Franklin farm. Surely most of you met her at the barn dance last night or at church this morning. Miss Todd's most recent teaching position was in Oregon. She is highly qualified and has many years of experience." Again the lifting of her nose. "Unlike Miss Kristoffersen."

Daisi Benoit raised her hand, as if she were a student and Walter the teacher. "Mr. Swanson?"

"Yes, Mrs. Benoit."

"I don't wish to sound critical of Mr. Murphy, but if Mrs. Summerville feels this much concern, how can we ignore it? Appearances do matter. Surely Mrs. Summerville has the well-being of all of the children at heart."

I doubt that.

"Perhaps," Daisi continued, "we could put Miss Kristoffersen on suspension and hire Miss Todd as a temporary teacher while we determine the best course of action."

"Is that a motion?" Helen asked. "If so, I second it."

Colin looked around the room. "This is wrong, and you all know it." He rose to his feet a second time. "Maybe you haven't known Miss Kristoffersen very long, but you've known me for years. You've bought your goods in the mercantile, and you helped me when my wife died, and your kids have played with my daughter since she was only knee-high. You know me well enough that you shouldn't believe this kind of accusation. And because of that, you definitely shouldn't take this action against Miss Kristoffersen."

Yancy Dowd said, "It's just a temporary solution, Murphy."

Colin wanted to punch something. He wanted to shout. Instead, he shook his head and walked out into the night.

While Charity read aloud from her McGuffey's Reader — slowly but with few mistakes — Felicia's gaze returned to the kitchen window.

"Run, run, thou tiny rill; / Run, and turn the village mill; / Run, and fill / the deep, clear pool ..."

The meeting must have started by now. What was being said? Shouldn't she be there to look into the eyes of her accuser?

"In the woodland's shade so cool, / Where the sheep love best to stray / In the sultry summer day ..."

Why hadn't she thought of holding the tutoring sessions here in her little home right from the start?

"Where the wild birds bathe and drink, / And the wild flowers fringe the brink ..."

If she and Charity had met here in the cottage these past weeks, there wouldn't have been any talk nor any hint of impropriety.

"Run, run, thou tiny rill, / Round the rocks, and down the hill; Sing to every child like me ..."

But perhaps that wouldn't have made any difference to Mrs. Summerville. She was upset because she believed Colin had become interested in Felicia, when he was engaged to Kathleen.

Her heart skipped a beat as she recalled the way it had felt to dance with him, the warmth of his hand as it pressed against her back, guiding her expertly around the floor, the look in his eyes as he stared down at her. Once again he'd wanted to kiss her, and once again, she'd wanted it too. Perhaps Mrs. Summerville wasn't far wrong.

"The birds will join you, full of glee: / And we will listen to the song / You sing, your rippling course along."

Perhaps it was better that Felicia leave Frenchman's Bluff. But not this way. Not to be fired. Not to be let go without reference.

No job. No reference. No family. She would be homeless and penniless and forsaken.

Forsaken?

No. That wasn't true. She would never be forsaken. God had promised that He would be with her always. Still ...

"Miss K?"

She blinked, forcing her attention back to Charity. "Yes."

"I asked how I did."

"You've made wonderful progress." Not that she'd paid close enough attention to their session this evening. "Why don't we stop now? I made some oatmeal cookies this afternoon. Would you like one?"

"Would I!"

Oh, God, what will I do if I can't teach? This is what I've wanted

*to do for so long. It's what I waited to do all the time I was taking care
of the Kristoffersens. You know this, Lord. Will You allow Mrs. Summerville to ruin all of that?*

She rose and went to the counter, where she took two cookies
from a large white jar. When she turned around, she found Charity
standing next to her, an eager smile in place.

"I suppose you would like two of them."

Charity nodded.

"There you go." Felicia placed the cookies in the girl's waiting
hands. "And a glass of milk?"

"Please."

Felicia went to the icebox, pausing long enough to look out the
window. All she saw was her own reflection in the glass.

How long would the meeting last? Would the other board
members listen to Helen or would they listen to Colin? Of course,
he was accused of the same inappropriate behavior as Felicia. Only
he was a man. Men were judged differently than women were.
People would continue to buy their supplies from Colin's mercantile, no matter what was decided inside the schoolhouse tonight.

It's not fair.

She took the bottle of milk from the icebox and poured the
white liquid into a glass. "Here you go," she said as she set the beverage on the table in front of Charity.

A knock sounded at the door, and she jumped in surprise.

"What's the matter, Miss K? It's only Papa."

Her heart raced like a captured bird's as she moved to open the
door. One look at his face, and she knew the worst. "Charity, I'm
going to talk to your father for a moment. Stay right there and eat
your cookies."

"Okay."

She grabbed a shawl off the hook near the door before stepping outside onto the porch. "What happened?" The door clicked closed behind her.

"It looked like they were going to vote to suspend you and hire another teacher on a temporary basis. Ellen's cousin, Miss Todd. At least until they make up their minds what to do about ... about the appearance of wrongdoing. I can't say for sure about the vote. I was so angry, I walked out."

Tears stung her eyes, but she was determined not to let Colin see them. She walked to the corner of the porch and put her right arm around the post while looking down First Street toward the schoolhouse.

"This is my fault, Felicia." He didn't move from his place near the door. "I'm the one who put your reputation and your job at risk. I wasn't thinking straight, I guess. I should have realized how it could look to others, you coming to my house every night."

"But you knew nothing was amiss. You're a decent man."

"I'm glad you think so."

For the Lord seeth not as man seeth; for man looketh on the outward appearance, but the Lord looketh on the heart.

Yes, he was a decent man with a good heart, and she believed the Lord thought so too. Even if he shouldn't have wanted to kiss her.

Right now, she wished he had kissed her.

"Whatever the board decides, this cottage is yours to stay in, Felicia. For as long as it takes to make things right."

For as long as it takes to make things right. Would anything ever be right again?

"Did you hear me, Felicia?"

"Yes ... Colin. I heard you."

"I ... I guess I'd best get Charity on home."

"Yes, I suppose you should."

"I'm sorry about all of this."

"I know."

"Felicia, I—"

"Good night, Colin."

"Okay. Good night. We ... we'll talk again tomorrow."

THIRTY

By a vote of four to three, the board voted to temporarily suspend Felicia's teaching contract until further review. Walter Swanson, hat in hand, delivered the news to her on Sunday evening, half an hour after Colin took Charity home.

Felicia spent a sleepless, tearful night asking God why this was happening, what His plan was now, how she was to proceed. But if He answered, she couldn't hear, perhaps because of the waves of fear that crashed over her again and again throughout the torturous hours before dawn.

Early on Monday morning, she rose, washed herself, dressed, and walked to the schoolhouse well before any of the children would arrive. She collected her few personal items from the teacher's desk, then looked around the classroom while trying to swallow the lump in her throat.

In her mind, she pictured different children cleaning the blackboards at the end of the school day. She heard the youngest students reading from their primers, stumbling over words, grinning widely when they got things right. She saw R. J. Franklin, tall, handsome, so ready to break out of school and start living as an adult. She thought of the two orphan brothers from New York who had found parents to love them but who still needed help in adjusting to this very different world.

I had such hopes for them all.

She brushed away a tear.

She had a little money now, enough perhaps to get a room at a boardinghouse in Boise. But what work would she do once she got there? Become a maid? Find some sort of office work?

All I wanted to do was teach. It's what I've wanted for so very long.

The sound of throat clearing broke into her thoughts, and she turned to find Walter Swanson and Mary Grace Todd standing in the entrance. Her heart plummeted. Her replacement had arrived.

Walter cleared his throat again. "Didn't expect to find you here, Miss Kristoffersen."

"It's all right. I'm leaving." She stepped off the platform and walked toward them.

Grace's eyes were filled with pity.

Felicia stopped. "Miss Todd, you'll find the lesson book on the desk and notations about each of the children. They should ... they should help you get acquainted with the different needs of the students."

"Thank you. I'll do my best by them. I promise."

"I'm sure you will." Eyes now downcast, she hurried past them. Once outside, she stopped on the landing and dragged a deep breath of crisp air into her lungs.

But she couldn't linger. The children would begin arriving soon, and she couldn't bear to face them. Not while her feelings were so raw and tender.

She all but ran the short distance to her cottage.

❦

Colin was halfway between the barn and the back door of his house when he saw Felicia's mad dash up the street. He wanted nothing more than to go to her, to hold her, to comfort her, to promise that everything would be all right.

But what did "all right" mean?

Could he promise she would get her job back? No.

Could he promise that some folks in the community wouldn't judge her harshly because of what Helen Summerville said? No.

So what could he promise her?

His hands felt empty, as did his heart.

He continued on into his house. Charity was at the table, finishing the last few bites of her breakfast.

"Ready for school?"

"Uh-huh."

He drew a deep breath and released it. "There's something you should know, pumpkin."

"What?"

"Miss K won't be teaching today."

Charity stood. "Why not, Papa? Is she sick?"

"No, she isn't sick." *Except at heart.* "And I hope she'll be back soon."

The look in his daughter's eyes told him she knew he'd evaded her question on purpose. But how did one explain something like this to a nine-year-old? Especially when he hardly understood it himself.

Two months ago, he'd still been opposed to hiring an untried, inexperienced teacher from Wyoming. Six weeks ago, he'd wanted to keep his daughter from becoming too attached to the new schoolmarm because he hadn't expected her to stay in Frenchman's Bluff for long.

But somewhere along the way, Felicia had come to mean something more to him, something that was hard for him to define, even in his own mind, something unlike anything he'd felt before. All he knew for certain was that the thought of her leaving Frenchman's Bluff caused a weight to press on his chest. If she left, there would be an emptiness inside of him that no one else could fill.

"Papa?"

He shook his head. "I can't tell you anything more, Charity. We'll just have to be patient."

Crestfallen, she nodded.

"I'll take care of your dishes. You get your things and go on to school. Don't want you to be late."

"All right, Papa."

He watched her leave the kitchen, shoulders slouched. He felt the way she looked.

How do I make things right?

He picked up the dishes and put them in the washbasin.

God, if You're listening, I could use some guidance here.

✦

Although she knew it wasn't the same, Felicia felt a little like Hester Prynne in *The Scarlet Letter*. Not that Felicia had committed adultery. Not that she'd sinned in any way she could perceive. Still, she felt marked by Helen's accusations of impropriety. Everything in her wanted to remain locked inside her cozy cottage, away from others.

Yet as the day progressed, hour by agonizing hour, she felt the walls close in on her until she could bear it no more. She had to go out, walk, breathe some fresh air, do anything that might take her mind off the children who were receiving instruction from Miss Todd rather than from her.

She put on a hat, wrapped a shawl about her shoulders, and headed out, not caring where her feet carried her. Perhaps she would buy a new bonnet. Or if not buy one—she couldn't afford to be foolish with her money, after all—at least try on a few. That might raise her spirits. Not to mention a few eyebrows if she were seen doing so. That last thought almost made her laugh.

Almost, but not quite.

The trees that lined the east side of Idaho Street sported cloaks of red and gold, and leaves that had fallen onto the walkway crunched beneath her shoes. Autumn, her favorite season, was full upon them now. Beautifully so. Winter wouldn't be far behind. Where would she be when the first snow fell? In Frenchman's Bluff? In Boise City? Or somewhere far from Idaho?

It hurt to consider the different possibilities. She didn't want to think about living anywhere else. The town and its children had taken hold of her heart in the short time she'd been here.

Especially Charity . . .

And her father.

No. She mustn't think such things. They weren't true. She had no favorite students, and Colin Murphy was no more or less to her than any other father in town. He was just Charity's father. Only that wasn't true. He was also a member of the school board . . . and her landlord . . .

And Kathleen's fiancé.

She reached the millinery shop only to be met with disappointment. It was closed. A note in the window said Jane would return on Tuesday morning. For the best, Felicia supposed. Better not to be tempted. Only she wasn't sure where to go next. Perhaps she would simply walk out on the bluff, walk as far as she could go before nightfall threatened.

She'd reached the corner of Shoshone and Main when she heard a familiar—and dreaded—voice. Helen Summerville was talking to Walter Swanson on the sidewalk outside his drugstore.

Not wanting to risk being seen, Felicia spun around and went into the post office, remembering only once she was inside that the wife of the postmaster was a member of the school board as well. And when Joe Reynolds's gaze met hers, she was certain he knew everything that had been said in the meeting the previous night. Even more than she knew.

She wished she could leave, but it was too late for that.

"Afternoon, Miss Kristoffersen."

"Good afternoon, Mr. Reynolds."

"Glad you stopped by. Got a letter for you." He withdrew an envelope from a cubbyhole. "Here you go. From Chicago, I see."

Chicago? Could it be news of her siblings? Perhaps that was God's answer to the dilemma in which she found herself. "Thank you, Mr. Reynolds." She took the envelope and pressed it to her chest as she turned to leave.

"Miss Kristoffersen. Wait."

She stopped and looked back.

"Want you to know how very sorry my wife and I are. About what's happened. Miranda ... my wife ... we both think it's wrong, what the board's done."

Tears sprang to her eyes. "Thank you," she replied softly.

"Just remember. It's temporary. It'll get sorted out. You can be sure of that."

She nodded, unable to say anything more, afraid to hope for a better end.

Although she was eager to read the letter from Dr. Cray's home, she made herself wait until she was back on the porch of her cottage before she tore open the envelope and removed the sheet of paper from inside.

Dr. Cray's Asylum for Little Wanderers
Chicago, Illinois
September 30, 1897
Miss Felicia Brennan Kristoffersen
Frenchman's Bluff, Idaho

Dear Miss Kristoffersen,

I have your letter at hand and have tried to verify the information you requested.

According to our records, your brother Hugh Brennan was placed out in the fall of 1881 with a family who lived near Omaha, Nebraska. However, upon further review, it appears that he left that family in the spring of 1882 at the age of 14. I am afraid the reason for his departure and the circumstances under which it took place were not recorded. I can only assume that he was not content with his placement and struck out on his own. Unfortunately, boys of his age sometimes choose to do that rather than request reassignment through our office.

As for your sister, Diana Brennan, she was placed with a prominent couple by the name of Dixon in Cheyenne, Wyoming, in the fall of 1881. The Dixons moved to southwest Montana in 1890. Mr. Dixon appears to have been affiliated with the railroad. Our records show no specific town of residence and no further follow-up after 1890. It does appear that Mr. and Mrs. Dixon inquired regarding the adoption of your sister while they were in Wyoming, but there is no record in our files that said adoption took place.

I hope this information is of some help to you.

Most sincerely,
Adam St. Charles
Secretary

Felicia read the letter two more times before folding it and sliding it back into its envelope. Hugh's whereabouts unknown for fifteen years, and Diana with a prominent family somewhere in Montana, at least as far back as seven years ago. No help at all with finding her brother, and perhaps no help with Diana either, although she knew a little more now than she had before. But to think, she and her little sister had lived for nine years within fifty miles or so of each other and never knew it. Oh, if only ...

The sound of shouts and laughter carried to her, and she looked in the direction of the schoolhouse, watching as the children spilled forth like milk from a toppled bottle and spread out like tributaries on their way home. Before she could rise and go inside, she heard one voice above the others.

"Miss K!" Charity ran down the street as fast as her legs would carry her. "Miss K!"

Her heart broke a little more. How she treasured that sound.

Breathing hard, Charity arrived on the porch. "Why weren't you at school?"

"Weren't you told?"

The girl shrugged. "All Miss Todd said was she's gonna be our teacher for a while. But Suzanne says her grandmother doesn't like you, and that's why you're not teachin' today."

Felicia winced, and the desire to say she didn't like Helen Summerville either warred with the desire to do and say what was right. Thankfully, the latter won. "That may be true, Charity, but it's just speculation on your friend's part and shouldn't be repeated. Do you know what *speculation* means?"

Charity shook her head.

"To have an opinion or a theory about a subject without firm evidence or facts. It's better not to speculate, Charity." That was, after all, what had brought about her suspension. Mere speculation. "It's most often the same as gossip, and you know what the Bible says about gossip."

Another shake of the head.

"It can separate the best of friends. You don't want to say bad things about Mrs. Summerville because it's unkind and it might cause you and Suzanne and Phoebe to no longer be friends."

"Well ... okay. But I still don't like having Miss Todd for a teacher instead of you. Nobody does."

Felicia couldn't hold back a sad smile as she ran her hand over Charity's hair. "Thank you. It's kind of you to say that. But I'm sure Miss Todd is very nice and a good teacher. You need to give her the same chance you gave me." Her throat began to tighten, making it hard to speak. "Now, you'd best get on home to your father. He'll be wondering what's kept you."

"Okay," the girl said again, adding as she descended the porch steps, "but you're still gonna help me with my reading, right?"

She wanted to say yes, but she couldn't. She knew so little about what the next days would be like. "That's something you must ask your father."

"I'm gonna go ask him right now." And with that, Charity disappeared around the corner of the house.

After a second sleepless night, Felicia made up her mind. She would leave Frenchman's Bluff of her own accord. She wouldn't wait to see if Mrs. Summerville won in the end. It wouldn't be right for Felicia to stay, not feeling the way she did about Colin. She cared for him too much. Even more than she'd realized.

She loved him—and she couldn't have him.

What if he had kissed her that night outside her cottage? What might have happened next between them? Would she want to hurt a woman who had befriended her from the start? No, better she leave and begin again somewhere else.

She turned up the oil lamp beside the bed and reached for the letter from Dr. Cray's. A couple named Dixon. The husband worked for the railroad. Moved to southwest Montana.

It wasn't much to go on, but it was a start. How many small

towns were there near the railroad tracks of Montana? And even if she didn't find Diana, how much worse off would she be there than she was here? In fact, she might be better off. There would be no whiff of scandal to follow her to Montana. Not yet anyway.

She tossed aside the covers on her bed and sat up, lowering her feet to the floor and sliding them into her slippers. Her bedroom had grown cold during the night, and after putting on a robe, she went to add more wood to the stove. Then she began packing her things in the same trunk she'd brought with her from Wyoming, all the while tears rolling down her cheeks.

THIRTY-ONE

Ellen Franklin reached across the counter and touched the back of Colin's hand. "I'll get straight to work organizing the parents. You can count on me. We'll stop this injustice." She took a step back. "And Colin, I think there's another reason you can't afford to let Miss Kristoffersen lose her position." She pointed at him — as if he should know what she meant — then turned and left the mercantile.

What *did* she mean? He wanted to let the children of the town keep a wonderful teacher. He wanted Felicia's reputation protected. Even his own reputation protected. He wanted right to be done and Mrs. Summerville to be stopped.

But he didn't think Ellen meant any of that.

Without a word to Jimmy, he walked out of the store into his living quarters, closing the connecting door behind him. He went first to the window that looked out on Main Street. A man on horseback was headed out of town. A team hitched to a wagon was tied to the post in front of the bank. Farther down the street, three men stood on the boardwalk in front of the feed store, one of them gesturing, the other two seeming to listen to him.

An ordinary kind of day in Frenchman's Bluff. But it didn't feel ordinary.

He wanted to check on Felicia. He wanted to see if she was all right. But he didn't think he could. What if he was seen on her porch? What if it created even more gossip, making things worse? He didn't care for himself, but he cared for her. He'd promised he would make things right. He had to keep his distance for now.

"There's another reason you can't afford to let Miss Kristoffersen lose her position."

He turned and sat in his favorite chair. His gaze fell on the Bible resting on the table beside him. He opened it and withdrew the letter Margaret had written to him. His gaze moved over the words on the page, pleased that the letters were less jumbled than they'd been before, thanks to the practice words he'd been going over for weeks. It didn't all make sense to him yet, but one particular word stood out on the page today: *Love*.

"There's another reason you can't afford to let Miss Kristoffersen lose her position."

Love.

"There's another reason you can't afford to let Miss Kristoffersen lose her position."

Love.

He straightened as glimpses of Felicia flashed through his memory — lying on a boulder, talking to God; sitting in the schoolhouse at one of the desks, so excited about maps on the wall; riding bareback astride Walter's wagon horse; gripping that tree limb, going under in the river as the water tossed her about like a rag doll; beautiful in a blue gown, dancing in his arms, her eyes turned up to him.

"I love her." He spoke the words with wonder.

How could he not have realized it before now? He didn't just want to kiss her every now and again. He didn't just want to hold her in his arms while they danced. He didn't just care about her or feel a fondness for her or want to be her friend. And his feelings had nothing to do with wanting a woman's influence for Charity.

"I *love* her."

He slipped Margaret's letter back into the Bible, then let his fingers linger on the leather cover.

And we know that all things work together for good to them that love God, to them who are the called according to his purpose.

As the words of the familiar verse replayed in his head, he felt like laughing for joy. Either that or falling on his face in praise. How could it be that he'd doubted the truth of that Scripture for so long, only to see now that it was completely and faithfully true?

God had done so much more than bring a schoolteacher to Frenchman's Bluff.

Kathleen drew a deep breath as she opened the front door of the Summerville home, her new husband at her side. For forty-eight wonderful hours, there had been nothing in her world but Oscar. Certainly she'd given no thought to what Mother Summerville's reaction would be when they returned to Frenchman's Bluff.

But she was thinking of nothing besides Mother Summerville now. Her stomach was in turmoil, and her palms felt damp from trepidation.

"It's gonna be all right, Kathleen."

She looked at Oscar. It surprised her how well he understood her feelings and read her thoughts. Even better than Harold had after many years of marriage.

Her husband nodded, and she drew another quick breath before calling out, "Hello. Is anyone home?"

A *swish* of taffeta alerted her to Mother Summerville's approach a second before she appeared in the hallway. "Kathleen, I—" She broke off when she saw Oscar. "I didn't know we had a guest."

Oscar doffed his hat and gave a slight bow at the waist. "Miz Summerville. A pleasure to see you again."

Mother Summerville's response was an almost imperceptible nod.

"I ... we—" Kathleen began.

"I'm glad you're home," Mother Summerville interrupted. "Now you can see to your children yourself. I have been busy with this school board business. We've suspended Miss Kristoffersen's contract. Very nasty affair. And to think I wanted you to marry that man. You should have heard how Mr. Murphy spoke to me."

Kathleen turned to look at Oscar, confused and uncertain. Suspended Felicia? School board business? What had happened in just two days?

Oscar gave her a confident glance before addressing Mother Summerville. "Ma'am, I'm not sure what you're talkin' about since I haven't been to town in a few days, but we've got a bit of news of our own. Kathleen and I got married."

"*What?*" Mother Summerville reached for the wall to steady herself. "Married?"

"Yes." Kathleen forced a smile. "On Sunday afternoon. In Boise."

"But you couldn't ... you didn't ... Who *is* he?"

Kathleen slipped her arm through Oscar's. "He's my husband. And I'm Mrs. Jacobson."

"Where will you live? You don't think you're bringing this stranger into—"

"I have a place of my own, Miz Summerville." There was a firm edge in Oscar's voice now. "And as soon as the girls get out of school today, I mean to take my family there."

Something about the way Oscar spoke renewed Kathleen's courage. "What was it you said about Felicia?"

"We've suspended her. She's going to be fired. If it weren't for her interference, you and Mr. Murphy . . . Well . . . Not that I would approve of him now, but all the same—"

Kathleen turned toward Oscar. "I must see her."

"I'll take you."

"Yes."

In unison, they turned their backs on Mother Summerville and departed from the house.

Felicia sat beside Walter Swanson on the wagon seat, her arms hugging her satchel against her chest, her eyes turned toward the foothills along the Boise Front. So far, her posture had succeeded in discouraging Mr. Swanson from trying to carry on a conversation with her.

Odd, wasn't it? She hadn't been in Idaho all that long—only long enough for the season to change from summer to autumn—yet her surroundings felt more like home than Wyoming had after sixteen years. She would miss those brown foothills and the tree-topped mountain peaks beyond them. She would miss the Boise River and the small town of Frenchman's Bluff. She would miss Kathleen and the Franklins and the Carpenters and the pretty white schoolhouse and the children who filled it. Especially Charity.

She would miss Colin. How was it she had learned to love him and not been aware of it?

Tears blurred her vision, and she was forced to take out her handkerchief and blow her nose.

"Are you sure this is what you want to do, miss?" Walter asked.

"Yes." The word came out a whisper.

"If you'd just give us a little more time."

She shook her head. "Time would make no difference."

"Miss Kristoffersen, I don't believe you and Mr. Murphy did anything improper. I don't think other folks'll believe it either."

"It doesn't matter."

"But it does! If you'd—"

"Please, Mr. Swanson. Just take me to the rail station. I'll be obliged."

After the third knock on the door without an answer, Colin opened it.

"Felicia?"

He took a step inside. The air was cool, the fire in the stove burned down to coals.

"Felicia?"

He took another couple of steps. Still no answer. Not a sound. Where was she?

"Felicia, I'm coming in."

He moved into the parlor. Something seemed different to him, though he couldn't put his finger on what that was. He turned and found the bedroom door open. The bed was made, the room neat as a pin.

He turned around, letting his eyes roam the small room again. That's when he saw it. An envelope braced against the base of the oil lamp on the bedside table. With a sick feeling in his gut, he stepped toward the table and picked up the envelope. His name was on it, written in Felicia's distinctive hand. Distinctive because of the lists of words she'd written for Charity to learn. Lists that he'd used too.

"Felicia?"

He spun about to find Kathleen in the open doorway.

"Colin?"

"I think she's gone." He held the envelope toward her. "I just found this."

She approached him slowly.

"Read it, please. I ... I'm not sure I can."

Kathleen took it and withdrew the slip of paper. Her eyes perused it, widened, and returned to him. "Oh, Colin. She still believes you and I are to be married. She ... she wished us great happiness. That's why she left. Not because she lost her teaching position."

Colin rubbed a hand over his face. "I don't understand. Where would she—"

"I think I know," Kathleen answered darkly. Then she touched his wrist, saying with urgency, "But that doesn't matter now. Go after her. She can't have gone far. We just arrived back from Boise a short while ago, and we didn't see her on the road."

A man stepped into the kitchen. That cowboy who worked for Gilchrist. Jacobson. He'd seen him dancing with Kathleen on Saturday night. "You can take the buggy tied up outside," he said.

"Don't worry about how long it takes," Kathleen added. "I'll look after Charity when she gets home from school."

Colin didn't hesitate any longer. He strode toward the door.

"And Colin?"

He stopped and looked behind him.

"Tell her that Oscar and I are married, will you?" Kathleen moved to stand beside her new husband. "Tell her we're happy."

He felt a moment of stunned surprise, then he laughed. "I'll be sure to tell her."

He ran outside, jumped into the vehicle, took up the reins, and drove the Summerville horse and buggy out of town.

There had to be a touch of irony in that.

The rail station could be seen in the distance, and seeing it seemed to make Felicia's heart break all over again. She didn't want to leave, even though she knew she must. For everyone's sake, she must.

"What's that ruckus?" Walter said, drawing in on the reins.

Only then did she hear something. Galloping hooves and a man's shouts.

Walter twisted on the wagon seat. "We're being hailed."

"Wait up, Walter!"

She recognized Colin's voice. Her stomach sank and her pulse raced.

"Wait!"

Go on, Mr. Swanson. Go on. Don't wait.

The thunder of hooves came closer.

She squeezed her eyes closed. She heard the buggy stop, heard Colin's boots hit the ground, knew that he strode toward her side of the wagon.

"Felicia, where do you think you're going?"

"Away," she whispered.

Strong hands closed around her waist, and suddenly she was airborne, lifted off the wagon seat and then set gently on the ground. Her eyes flew open.

"You're not going anywhere, Miss Kristoffersen. Not until I've done this."

His lips claimed hers in the kiss she'd longed for, even when she hadn't known it. The kiss was gentle, yet it sent her senses reeling. She felt turned upside down and wrong side out. His arms gathered her closer, and she felt their hearts beating as one. Oh, if they could only stay like this forever. If they didn't have to face the world.

His lips parted from hers but moved only an inch or two away. "Kathleen sends her best."

She opened her eyes, wondering how he could say such a thing.

He watched her closely. "She said to tell you that she and Oscar got married and are very happy."

"Oscar? Married?" She frowned, confused. "But she ... and you ..."

"We were never engaged, Felicia. Not ever."

"Truly? It wasn't just a secret?"

"Truly."

Kathleen had tried to tell her but she hadn't believed her. She'd believed ... Mrs. Summerville.

"But there are still her accusations," she said. "Mrs. Summerville's. People still might think—"

"The parents are rallying. You'll be teaching again in no time. No one believes her."

Hope blossomed in her heart, yet it still seemed too good to be true. "It would be better if I go. There wouldn't be any more gossip. And I've had a letter. It's possible I might be able to find my sister."

"Don't go. If you want to find your sister, I'll help you. We can look for her together."

"Together?"

Once again he drew her close. Once again he captured her mouth with his. How could she have lived to be twenty-six years old without knowing how wonderful a kiss could be? It stole her breath and turned her mind to mush. And it drained the very last of her weak resistance.

He must have felt it go, for he lifted his head a few inches and said, "Come back, Felicia. Don't leave Frenchman's Bluff. Don't leave the children." He brushed his lips against hers, and his voice lowered. "Don't leave me. You've taught me so much already, but I have so much more to learn."

She smiled a little. "What have I taught you, Mr. Murphy?"

"More than you could imagine, my love. But it'll take me a lifetime to find the words to tell you."

EPILOGUE

A cold wind buffeted Felicia's back as she locked the door to the schoolhouse. When she went down the steps, she had to hold on to her hat to keep it from blowing away.

"Mrs. Murphy!"

She smiled as she stopped and turned. She never tired of hearing someone call her that. Sometimes, even after three months as Colin's wife, she needed to pinch herself, just to make sure she wasn't dreaming.

"Glad I caught you, Mrs. Murphy." Joe Reynolds hurried toward her. "Got a letter for you. I figured you'd want to see it right away." He waved the envelope in the air. "It's from that orphanage place in Chicago. Dr. Cray's."

Her heart skipped a beat, and a flutter of excitement erupted in her stomach.

"Maybe they've got news about your brother or sister," he finished.

It was difficult to keep much private in this town, Felicia had come to know. Especially when the townsfolk considered her one of their own. "Thank you, Mr. Reynolds." She took the letter from the postmaster. "It was kind of you to deliver it."

"Don't mind a bit. Knew you'd want it right away, and your husband was already by for the mail today." He grinned. "Well, best not keep you out here jawin' in this wind. You take care now."

She thanked him again and hurried on her way home, grateful that she didn't have far to go.

When she entered the kitchen of the Murphy living quarters, warm air greeted her along with the delicious smells of dinner cooking in the oven. Colin liked to spoil her this way, dear man.

She set her books and papers on the table, the envelope from Dr. Cray's on top of her lesson plan.

It wasn't often that a married woman was allowed to teach school. Society said a wife belonged in the home, caring for her family. But Colin had been prepared to battle the school board for her right to continue teaching, calling the common requirement by school districts for female teachers to resign upon marriage archaic and anachronistic.

Remembering that made her smile. As Colin's ability to read had improved, so had his vocabulary. He delighted in using new words whenever he could, and she delighted in hearing him use them.

But he hadn't needed to use those particular two words to convince the board. To Felicia's great surprise, they'd voted unanimously to let her continue teaching after their wedding. Of course, it wouldn't have been unanimous if Mrs. Summerville had remained on the board, but she'd resigned in a huff a year ago, soon after Felicia was reinstated.

Poor Mrs. Summerville.

But Felicia had learned circumstances rarely stayed the same for long. Life was about change. A time to sow, a time to reap, a time to laugh, a time to cry. And if she wasn't mistaken, her life was about to change again. God willing, another Murphy would be born in this house in another six or seven months.

Colin appeared in the doorway. "Hey there. You're home." Three strides carried him across the room, where he drew her close and kissed her, slow and deep.

Her favorite place to be — in his arms.

"I started dinner," he said when the kiss ended.

"I know. It smells wonderful."

"Charity's doing her homework. I was helping her."

Felicia loved the way he said those words.

"Want to join us?'

She shook her head. "Not yet." Stepping back from Colin, she picked up the letter Mr. Reynolds had delivered to her. "It's from Dr. Cray's. They must have learned some new information since their last letter." There was that flutter of excitement in her stomach again.

"Go on. Open it. See what it says."

She held the envelope toward him. "I'm too nervous. Will you open it, please?"

His gaze was tender as he leaned close to kiss her forehead. Then he took the envelope and broke the seal. Seconds later, he was reading the letter. A frown furrowed his brow.

Felicia clenched her hands, waiting, wondering, anxious, hoping.

Colin looked up. "It seems that when your brother left Nebraska, he returned to Chicago to live with your father."

"With my father?" She shook her head. "He . . . Dad was gone. He left before Mum died."

"Apparently he came back." Colin looked at the letter again. "It says they may know Hugh's last place of residence and will advise you upon confirmation."

God's goodness and lovingkindness overwhelmed her, and tears of joy filled her eyes. Fifteen months ago, she'd had no one in her life who loved her and no one for her to love. She'd been alone and had thought she would remain alone. But the Lord had other plans for her. Today she had a beloved husband, a cherished daughter, a wide circle of good friends—and now the possibility of a brother restored.

Once her life had seemed bitter but now it was sweet, and thanksgiving welled in her soul.

Thou hast turned for me my mourning into dancing: thou hast put off my sackcloth, and girded me with gladness; to the end that my glory may sing praise to thee, and not be silent. O Lord my God, I will give thanks unto thee for ever.

Smiling through her tears, she stepped back into her husband's embrace.

A Vote of Confidence

Robin Lee Hatcher,
Bestselling Author of
When Love Blooms

In *A Vote of Confidence*, the stage is set for some intriguing insight into what it was like during 1915 to be a woman in a "man's world."

Guinevere Arlington is a beautiful young woman determined to remain in charge of her own life. For seven years, Gwen has carved out a full life in the bustling town of Bethlehem Springs, Idaho, where she teaches piano and writes for the local newspaper. Her passion for the town, its people, and the surrounding land prompt Gwen to run for mayor. After all, who says a woman can't do a man's job?

But stepping outside the boundaries of convention can get messy. A shady lawyer backs Gwen, believing he can control her once she's in office. A wealthy newcomer throws his hat into the ring in an effort to overcome opposition to the health resort he's building north of town. When the opponents fall in love, everything changes, forcing Gwen to face what she may have to lose in order to win.

Available in stores and online!

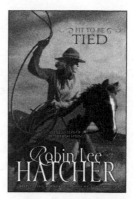

The Sisters of Bethlehem Springs

Fit to Be Tied

Robin Lee Hatcher,
Bestselling Author of
A Vote of Confidence

It's 1916, and Idaho rancher Cleo Arlington knows everything about horses but nothing about men. So when charged with transforming English aristocrat Sherwood Statham from playboy to cowboy, she's totally disconcerted. So is Statham, who's never encountered a woman succeeding in a "man's world." Their bumpy trot into romance is frustrating, exhilarating, and ultimately heartwarming.

Available in stores and online!

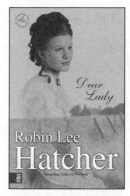

Patterns of Love

Robin Lee Hatcher,
Bestselling Author of Firstborn

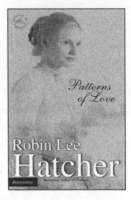

In rural Iowa, life is both the planter and uprooter of dreams. As love, long delayed, springs to life in the heart of a young Swedish immigrant, one man struggles with his withered ambitions—and new blessings that could take their place if he would but allow them room.

Patterns of Love is book two in the Coming to America series about women who come to America to start new lives. Set in the late 1800s and early 1900s, these novels by bestselling author Robin Lee Hatcher craft intense chemistry and conflict between the characters, lit by a glowing faith and humanity that will win your heart. Look for other books in the series at your favorite Christian bookstore.

Available in stores and online!

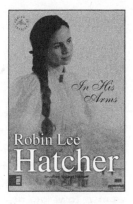

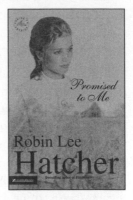

Wagered Heart

Robin Lee Hatcher,
Author of Return to Me

When Bethany Silverton left the gen-
teel life of Miss Henderson's School for
Young Ladies back in Philadelphia for
the raw frontier town of Sweetwater,
Montana, she had no idea how much
she would enjoy the freedom and danger of this wild country.

A conservative preacher's daughter, Bethany can't resist the
challenge of charming the most attractive cowboy in town into
attending her father's new church. She never dreamed that the
cowboy would charm the lady.

But Hawk Chandler isn't the only man vying for Bethany's
affections. Ruthlessly ambitious Vince Richards thinks Bethany
is perfect for him: attractive, gracious, just the woman to help
him become governor. And he is determined to get what he
wants at any cost.

Drawn to one man, an obsession of another, Bethany's quiet
life is thrown into turmoil. She wagered her heart on love. Now
she has gotten more than she bargained for — and the stakes
are about to become life and death.

When Love Blooms

Robin Lee Hatcher,
Author of Wagered Heart

From the moment Gavin Blake set eyes
on Emily Harris he knew she would
never make it in the rugged high country where backbreaking work and constant hardship were commonplace.
She would wilt there like a rose with-
out water. He'd be sending her back to Boise before the first
snows. He'd be willing to bet on it.

She could say what she wanted. Emily Harris didn't belong
in the hard life of the Blakes. Beautiful and refined, she was
accustomed to the best life had to offer. Heaven only knew
why she wanted to leave Boise to teach two young girls on a
ranch miles from nowhere. He'd wager it had to do with a man.
It always did when a beautiful woman was involved.

Emily wanted to make some sort of mark on the world before marriage. She wanted to be more than just a society wife.
Though she had plenty of opportunities back East, she had
come to the Idaho high country looking to make a difference.
Gavin's resistance to her presence made her even more determined to prove herself. Perhaps changing the heart of one man
might make the greatest difference of all.

Share Your Thoughts

With the Author: Your comments will be forwarded to the author when you send them to *zauthor@zondervan.com*.

With Zondervan: Submit your review of this book by writing to *zreview@zondervan.com*.

Free Online Resources at
www.zondervan.com

Zondervan AuthorTracker: Be notified whenever your favorite authors publish new books, go on tour, or post an update about what's happening in their lives at www.zondervan.com/authortracker.

Daily Bible Verses and Devotions: Enrich your life with daily Bible verses or devotions that help you start every morning focused on God. Visit www.zondervan.com/newsletters.

Free Email Publications: Sign up for newsletters on Christian living, academic resources, church ministry, fiction, children's resources, and more. Visit www.zondervan.com/newsletters.

Zondervan Bible Search: Find and compare Bible passages in a variety of translations at www.zondervanbiblesearch.com.

Other Benefits: Register to receive online benefits like coupons and special offers, or to participate in research.

ZONDERVAN.com/
AUTHORTRACKER
follow your favorite authors